# The Whole of Life

Other Works in Dalkey Archive Press's
Swiss Literature Series

*The Shadow of Memory*
Bernard Comment

*The Ring*
Elisabeth Horem

*Modern and Contemporary Swiss Poetry: An Anthology*
Luzius Keller, ed.

*Isle of the Dead*
Gerhard Meier

*My Year of Love*
Paul Nizon

*Walaschek's Dream*
Giovanni Orelli

*With the Animals*
Noëlle Revaz

*Why the Child is Cooking in the Polenta*
Aglaja Veteranyi

*Zündel's Exit*
Markus Werner

# The Whole of Life

Jürg Laederach

*Translated by*
Geoffrey C. Howes

DALKEY ARCHIVE PRESS
CHAMPAIGN / LONDON / DUBLIN

Originally published in German as *Das ganze Leben* by Suhrkamp Verlag, Frankfurt, 1978



First edition, 2013


Library of Congress Cataloging-in-Publication Data

Laederach, Jürg, 1945-
[Ganze Leben. English]
The Whole of Life / Jürg Laederach ; translated by Geoffrey C. Howes. --
First edition.
pages cm. -- (Swiss Literature Series)
ISBN 978-1-56478-907-5 (acid-free paper)
I. Howes, Geoffrey, translator. II. Title.
PT2672.A32G313 2013
833'.914--dc23
2013038385

Partially funded by grants from the Illinois Arts Council, a state agency, and the Swiss Arts Council Pro Helvetia

swiss arts council
prohelvetia

The publication of this work has been supported by the Max Geilinger-Stiftung, founded in 1962 in Zurich, Switzerland, to promote the literary and cultural relations between Switzerland and the English-speaking world

Max Geilinger-Stiftung

www.dalkeyarchive.com

Cover: design and composition by Tim Peters

Printed on permanent/durable acid-free paper

CONTENTS

## Translator's Preface

*"I can assure you that no movie will ever achieve the speed of prose. Human beings just haven't realized that yet."*
—Jürg Laederach

Jürg Laederach (born 1945) is a writer, translator, and saxophonist who lives in Basel, Switzerland. He studied mathematics and physics before he switched to Romance languages, English, and musicology. Once regarded as an enfant terrible of Swiss literature, he has published more than twenty-five books of fiction and essays and won a number of literary prizes, most notably the Austrian State Prize for European Literature in 1997 and the Italo Svevo Award in 2005. Among the writers he has translated into German are William H. Gass, Walter Abish, Thomas Pynchon, Maurice Blanchot, and Gertrude Stein. This may provide an idea of where this jazz musician's literary predilections lie. He writes what is often, but not terribly accurately, called "experimental" literature, because it "experiments" with the ability of language to refer to reality. Actually, all literature must do this, but some literature, like Laederach's, is more up-front about how language creates its own reality. The logic of literary verisimilitude is based on conventions of reference to time, space, and objects. In particular, we rely on language to impose philosophical and psychological order on the mishmash of image, logic, and expression produced by our minds when they confront the world "out there." Laederach knows that language is only as reliable and stable as the minds that use it; in other words, it is unreliable and unstable. It *pretends* to mean things while going on its merry way. Laederach follows it on this merry way, trying to catch up with it once he's let it loose on its path of trickery and misbehavior.

*The Whole of Life*? Three hundred pages cannot contain the whole of anything, except perhaps all of the words in a three-hundred-page book. So even the title entitles us to skepticism when taking on Jürg Laederach's prose. Skepticism like Montaigne's famous question: "What do I know?" One of the two august dedicatees of the book, Ludwig Wittgenstein, answers Montaigne thus: "What you know is what you can say," to paraphrase the *Tractatus* 5.6: "The limits of my language are the limits of my world." The other dedicatee is Gottfried Wilhelm Leibniz, he of the *Theodicy* and the theory of monadism, with its concept of sufficient reason: No fact can be real and no statement can be true unless there is a sufficient reason for that reality or that truth, "although these reasons usually cannot be known by us" (*Monadology,* section 32). Both Leibniz and Wittgenstein go for *the whole thing*, even if this means pointing out that the part of the whole that complements our partial part and thus makes it into a whole consists of that which we cannot know. For Leibniz, this is God (who famously moves in mysterious ways); for Wittgenstein, it is the Unutterable (godlike for present purposes). For Laederach, language and the knowledge it provides move in mysterious ways and can barely stake out *anything*, much less the Eternal Cause or the edge of the expressible, and so here the threshold of the unknowable is much lower than for his predecessors. Laederach's language breaks up and breaks down, it repeats itself like music does, and it teases us into the idea that if language is to account for human perception, thought, and emotion, it has to leave behind the received realm of conventional facts and how they are made.

Thus the limits of the whole of life in *The Whole of Life* are the limits of its language, and the life and language in question are those of Robert "Bob" Hecht, a twentieth-century Swiss (the book appeared in 1978), who, like many other men, has a name, a work life, and a sex life. In this way Hecht is a sort of Everyman. Not only the content of his life is representative; so is its function within "the system," which is to say its dysfunctionality. His is a story as assembled within a mind, that is, Bob's mind, for which neither space nor time nor logic nor grammar (nor even psychoanalysis!) is an effective organizing principle. And so we cannot take the notion that Bob is an Everyman too far. Bob Hecht is normal by virtue of the fact that he is abnormal, but that is the limit of his representativeness. To join the sport of wittily paraphrasing that first line from *Anna Karenina*: "Normal people are all alike; every neurotic person is neurotic in his (or her) own way."

Among the dysfunctions of Bob's life is its relationship with time. This is not the story of Bob Hecht on a timeline, that tool that pretends the past has an existence outside of minds. Rather than following before-and-after logic ("Youth," "Adolescence," "Midlife"), the novel follows a logic of rough categories of life. Part one is "Job." Part two is "Wife." And part three is "Totems and Taboos," which brings us to the next great intellectual precursor after Leibniz and Wittgenstein: Freud. He proposed in *Totem and Taboo* that primitive societies collectively go through what he had identified as the individual stages of psychological development in civilized societies. Here he committed the error of assuming that civilization is not fundamentally primitive. The whole of "civilized" (twentieth-century, Western) life seems to be based on those things that we well-developed primitives must worship (totems) or not mention (taboos) because they are *too sacred* for mere mortals like Bob and us. The totems include sex and work and their symbols (beds, bedsheets and typewriter sheets, typewriters, a house and its rooms), and the taboos include parts of the past, notably Bob's "depth psychology" and the Shoah, and parts of the present, notably a bordello for women and the economic secret that the best-quality flesh is produced by cannibalism.

While "Job" does acquaint us with some of Bob's jobs—cemetery and highway gardener, lounge pianist, job seeker, and government bureaucrat—and "Wife" conveys in excruciating detail the temptation of an impotent man to commit adultery (if only he could) in the firewood-based economy of a ménage à trois, "Totems and Taboos" combines work life and home life in Bob's "writing business," his attempt to merge being entrepreneurial and being creative in the form of a cottage industry (where the cottage is a suburban tract house). The result of this dream job is nightmarish. The chief marker of time passing (besides the progress of writing the text itself, once by Bob and once again by his subaltern Peyer) is the mysterious appearance of additional desks, those totems of the writer's work whose German name seems somehow primitive: *Schreibtisch*, "writing table," a sacred altar that associates the scene of the very concrete act of eating with the scene of the very abstract act of writing (and which for Bob and his wife Ann also becomes the scene of the very sacred act of trying to have sex).

Bob Hecht's identity is divided and subdivided by the sections of the "trilogy" and their subsections, but also by linguistic reference. He is first identified as "my Bob," and soon we suspect that it is Bob himself who considers himself "*my* Bob." "Job" and "Wife" are written (mostly) in the third person, and "Totems and Taboos" is (mostly) in the first person. And so Bob Hecht is variously referred to as he, I, my Bob Hecht, Bob Hecht, Robert Hecht, R. Hecht, Hecht, Hecht Bob, Robert, and Bob. Each of these pronouns and names points in the direction of someone, but none of them alone, and not even all taken together, does a sufficient job of it. Referring meaningfully to the whole of "Bob Hecht" is the job of *The Whole of Life*, but it quickly becomes apparent that the only way to put Bob together is to take him apart. (Synthesis requires analysis. The path to the infinite is through the infinitesimal. The only way to produce an excellent chicken is to feed it on chicken—see the end of "Totem and Taboo.")

With all this linguistic slippage (at one point Bob actually slips on a postmodern banana peel), the tragedy of Bob feeds on the comedy of Bob, and vice versa. I invite the reader to have a good laugh and a good cry, if possible at the same time.

. . .

Translating this book in which language is a moving target has been a great challenge, but a very satisfying one. Trying to decide what is sociolect, what is dialect, what is idiolect, and what is *bonne chance, cher lecteur!* is not easy. I had much valuable help via email from Jürg Laederach himself, and I thank him for his good humor, precise explanations, and encouragement. My wife Christen Giblin got an earful over the months of translating, and I'm grateful for her patience and advice, and for pointing out that part one, chapter 22, is intriguingly Kafkaesque (take a look and see what you think). Thanks to my colleagues at Bowling Green for making possible the leave that made this work possible. Earl Britt, Anita Britt, Jess Simmons, Vassiliki Leontis, Neocles Leontis, and Vince Corrigan all listened to passages of the translation and gave valuable advice. Any outright errors are my own doing.

# The Whole of Life

*For Gottfried Wilhelm Leibniz*
*and Ludwig Wittgenstein*

# JOB

# 1

My Bob Hecht once again found himself on a shoulder of the highway; the broad road served Lake Biel by draining it beneath itself, hardening the dried-up swamp into concrete, and sinking thick long heavy piles into the dry mass.

Bob Hecht had come from the teachers' residence, had felt his body heat gradually fading away through a wide panoramic window, and had cooled off without its getting any warmer outside; the energy economy of the miniature Hechtian universe seemed eternally to incorporate the titanic debit of little old Bob into the inconceivably more titanic assets of his surroundings.

Bob's face: directed toward the dividing line between the highway lanes.

Bob's suit: an unpicturesque black vest with a similarly black pair of pants, clean, presumably thoroughly brushed.

Bob's inner ear: twisting and turning along with the songs of the Widow Wattenwyl, a siren enthralling with *brestes rounde and hye.*

Hecht collected himself, for he was quite scattered, looked around for the last steel-blue strip of the familiar body of water at the edge of his field of vision, and recorded a small image until he was doing nothing more than looking ahead and marching along while ceaselessly saying to himself "my name is Bob"; perhaps marching and speaking softly was an installment payment on the debt of his titanic original sin, or at least a down payment toward the burdensome reckoning that could be considered fortunate if Bob were going through a dry spell; if he had been walking across the saltless water, the young kitten would have been drowned to death, weighed down by stones, in a whirlpool.

Bob was marching and breathing when a pot of exhaust fumes as big as his head overtook him; after 130 kilometers Hecht shuffled along a row of houses and entered a dairy shop. There was no one inside, no one was selling anything, and a member of the National Council from the north of Switzerland popped up from behind an empty tub and drew a wire loop around Hecht's ankle, pulling the loop tight, at first gently, and then tighter, and then so tight that . . .

Hecht ran in pain back into the storeroom; a greater pain followed, because pains travel in clouds and because the flying carpet on which pain rides from Gibraltar to Gibraltar is no thoughtless or made-up figure of speech, but does in fact exist; Bob yanked open the door in the middle wall of the dairy shop and stood in one of the secret, undisclosed, and delusionally attack-proof deliberation chambers of the domestic cabinet, which was just voting on a crisis bill after supporters and supporters had secretly paired off.

Behind Bob the man in question raised his hand, whispered at the ceiling, snapped his index finger out of his blazing fist, coughed up a shot of fantasy lead, a deadly piece of brain shrapnel, and with a click opened three more fingers with which he formed the rifle bolt, and thus the man from the north could be understood to be a man of peace who was careful about whom he associated with and had possibly even gotten an inside look at the widow in an exhausting moment of merger.

"He wrapped that loop around me three times. I'm exhausted!" cried Hecht, rolling a black pant leg up to his knee. They had to read his wound and apologize for it without delay and accept it even more quickly in lieu of payment; he was going to cover the loan he had overdrawn with the blood that those in question were about to shed.

The whisper inhaled, speaking inward into a mouth, and two fingers were clicked back while two were pointed forward like a sawed-off double-barreled shotgun; the disgusting revolting nauseating man was performing his sign games with his slow hands; Bob Hecht's vulnerable back was included in the message, and a breath that had been held was gradually drawn further in, and a mouth that had been wide with satisfaction at Bob's fear of it now pouted into a red ring that was closeable with muscles and let a lot in, and the sound that Bob was hearing was a fine whistling that desired graveyard peace and the interment of all cemetery gardeners to boot.

The ankle Hecht displayed appeared unscathed; he was facing grim retribution for taking up the time of the entire parliament; those in question bared their teeth when someone bared his body, the skin of which bespoke teeth that had impressed themselves upon it. Between knee and foot, indeterminable, a blue ring ran around Hecht's leg, as if it were to be detached at the dotted line; but the leg left those in question cold. The blue ring made those assembled feel Hecht's secret rage, which was not known even to Bob himself: a rage that his whole life long had remained a mere seedling, of which its scrawny shoots gave evidence: one of these was Bob's mindless servility, which wrote eager concessive clauses where others broke their necks.

"Hecht!" Bob cried once again and repeated his chapter and verse about the wire loop.

"He drew it tight three times, your enemy did! I am no less shocked than I am outraged! I bid you . . ." cried the Chairman, whose hometown, including his mother, his grandmother, his auntie, and the lady who sold him herbs and spices, was falling victim during just this debate to a conflagration that incinerated everything, which would cause him to bend over in grief, but which later made him, as he persisted in this bent condition, greater and considerably more influential.

Bob's inner ear: *Zmitts i mine Chleidli bin i, I'm all inside my clothies*, vocalized the widow Annie Wattenwyl from the highest branching bough of the tallest artificial tree in the deep dark bear's den.

Bob's suit: the vest had hung itself over his arm because it was disgusted by Bob's sweaty body.

Bob's face: eyes squinting cross-eyed, because there was no longer anything to see in front of him, and behind him nothing could be seen.

To Hecht, that ingenious fellow, it seemed proven that what concerned him was taking place behind his back; the man in question croaked out one more shot and dropped his hand and opened it anew and pushed it, palm outstretched up to the knuckles, behind a broad cummerbund of ruby-red nappa, behind which fat-repressor the Villiger cigar was keeping warm; Hecht was convulsed and embellished by a thought of himself that had been sung at the cradle in order someday to become a trilogy.

"Just how did you find us fellers, us law passers? I would imagine by high treason, no doubt!" the Chairman asked.

It was nice for Hecht to hear the other man immediately append an answer to the question, and graciously request of him, Hecht, that he take no notice of the uncertain man's answering himself.

"With our convertibles we speedy lawmakers take two hours to get here on the autobahn, and you come barging in here as if our House was just open to the public, like . . ."

Bob nodded and felt relieved in the face of the face in front of him that there was nothing going on behind his back anymore; what was happening was finally clear again.

Hardly anything else did happen; she, Annie Wattenwyl, gathered up her pleats and squatted in the fork of the tree like a winged toad; the man in question let himself drop, crossed his arms behind his back, came onto the floor of the hall and crawled toward the front row of parliamentarians' seats, toward a shoe that protruded before him like a pneumonic tower of soft leather, into a heaven of woolen stockings. The National Councilor who belonged to it, too much squeezed into his bench to draw back for Bob, extended the leather tower in such a way that its sole slid into Hecht's face, from forehead to chin. In a fog of dust, the quality of brushedness of his own suit was lost to this sole in one fell swoop.

"Cross-examination: how did you find us here?" the Chairman fired off.

"Let me work!" Hecht piped.

"I'll get you something to drink," the man in question offered.

"Milk," said the Chairman.

When my Bob raised his head again, the Chairman placed the white glass on his lower lip and forgot it there. Then from his bench the leather tower kicked out very roughly. Hecht, as he collected himself for a moment and leaned like a woolly bear in quiet torment belly-first against the family tree of the widow Annie Wattenwyl, felt himself to be so unhappy that he had to remain lying down awhile with the kick in the head before they pulled him out of the first and only arena of his life. The exhaustion took the no longer expressible rage, unknown to him, along into sleep, and Hecht, absentminded, had become even poorer and more forlorn, but also less harried, insofar as the first harrying had now already taken place.

Now he had put the shoulder of the lake highway behind him and with his writing was even more in hock to those in question, who behaved more or less as creditors and understood retribution only as revenge for the attack on the cemetery that had never taken place; Bob Hecht marched along calmly, owing to a lamentable inner certainty, his ear to the widowhood, and he sent the man who was operating behind his back into the running, surprised by the fact that this man was so destroyed, but somehow it was therefore he who was destroyed, somehow pure and white and tired and fine.

## 2

At the time Robert Hecht bore up well under a round face, an oblong body, and short extremities—his arms were somewhat longer than his legs, and his serious, all-too-serious shoulder injury pursued him for about three years without being noticed by him, though sometimes it was painful enough to bother him. At the time of his first employment search he recovered from it bit by bit and was once again capable of swinging his beloved and urgently needed arms and to offer himself a limited helping hand. One evening his nearly inaudible cry rang out: "Help!"

Hecht was a slave to his own simplistic thinking, which in certain circumstances led to anxiety states and blocked itself like steel on steel. In these mental blocks all of Robert's memories of Bob Hecht as he had been before the great crisis disappeared and turned up again at best in his dreams, as if disfigured by an acid; at least that's what his dreams looked like. They were, as soon as they faded to black, only character-based, and not plot-based thrillers after all. "My branched nature only shows up in the first few seconds, and then there's nothing but trees."

Hecht screamed. Rather often. He chanted away empty afternoons with bird-throated exclamations, and sometimes he sensed something, but it never assumed an outline: unfortunately or fortunately it remained ungraspable.

Like all old lounge musicians who have fallen out of demand, Hecht, when everyone was looking back at his piano, opened a radio and television business, thus adding to the number of those big stores that punctuated the streets like transformer housings and cast a scanty light on the sidewalk, if there was even a sidewalk going past them and horsebean stalks or barberry bushes hadn't overgrown the display windows until the store was smothered in a stranglehold of plants, until the wood paneling was so warped that Hecht was standing in an antechamber that had assumed a spherical shape through natural processes or else had been pressed into a spherical shape.

Robert's display windows required especially solid glazing because the passersby clung to his display windows and, as soon as the World Cup mania had softened them up for "going down and staying down" they would have smashed the glass to smithereens. They would have all pushed the splintered glass into Hecht's shop, crushed it all underfoot and poured through the window opening that was still edged with splinters along the wooden frame, into the radio and television shop, while Hecht would still be busy fastening bolts and rolling out extension cords, so that they could steal or disable as many television sets as possible in the event that Hecht hadn't made them the gift of an appliance after the defeat of the home team.

In a case like that it would have done no good for the lounge musician Hecht, who was aging rapidly after his playing time, to stand up to the crowd and yell: "Please leave me my appliances! In return I will play and type something for you on my piano."

At times Robert could also have surmised something whose outlines he could have described, but he didn't interpret even outlines as surmises; they were already too distinct, more or less certainties, and the fact that when Bob Hecht was standing in his shop, Hecht surmised something like "Bob Hecht is standing in his shop" was probably insufficient for something as nebulous as a surmise, with which even a Hecht had to gild his trivialities. "I surmise that I am standing in this store, and at the same time I see myself standing in this store. Additionally, a third person is also imagining exactly how I would be standing in this store: with that, the foundation would be laid on which I might in fact be standing in my own store."

He had, Hecht thought, come into this world without further ado and he stood his ground in it.

Subsequently there arose irregular sexual encounters with a dark girl who, due to a deficiency disease that was attributable to undernourishment three times a day, suffered from scurvy; Robert feared the consequences of a case of unpredictable co-habitation tuberculosis that would have banished him for years to a sanatorium high in the Alps and there, within that isolated locality, into an even more isolated, more limited place within a room with bare walls and brief, taut, well-tended nights with girls only in memory, if memory remained. "I would have wished for myself and for all others a greater beauty, but I am basically modest."

Along with a first shovel, fastened to a short, stout handle, the realization came to Hecht that he would have to use the shovel for burying all of the appliances, constructing an earthen wall over the appliances, and doing no more than boring the pointed round wood of his hands into the soil.

The work at the highway nursery was cunningly underpaid, but for the planting and repotting accomplishments required of Hecht it was still too highly remunerated. While sticking in the signs bearing plant names, which were composed in Latin with ballpoint pen, Hecht toyed with the idea of kidnapping himself in order to squeeze out a ransom from the head gardener with fictitious notes to the nursery. The amount demanded would provide information about the emotions that were accorded to Hecht. To force, as the blackmailer R. Hecht, the blackmailee R. Hecht to compose a ransom note, to sneak, as the blackmailer's emissary R. Hecht, the ransom note into an editorial office at night, to observe, as the observer R. Hecht, the naked rage or the stone-throwing old-man's rancor of the head gardener emerging from behind the nasturtiums, to slip and slide around, as the blackmailer's bag man R. Hecht, while standing on damp black-and-red leaves in the forest late at night while morning approached, waiting for the nursery to deposit the packet of money with the millions that R. Hecht was demanding for his return to the workplace—and which, as he knew, he was definitely worth—in the inevitable telephone booth out on the edge of the suburbs, in order to give the blackmailer's bag man the mousetrap possibility of coming into the ten-digit sum shaken loose by his disappearance in the shadow of the commissioner's hefty magnum. "You cannot demand of me that I go through that, all of that, I believe."

Hecht was not a bad financial theoretician. Rather, he wasn't one at all. Ann, that is to say Annie, whom he hardly approached, or if he did, only up the spiral staircase of her gracious instincts, bathed Bob in her solicitorial, slightly stubborn countenance, became a preservative, artificially sweetened, and rubbed him down with increasing diffidence using her green and pointed little mouth, which resembled two pencils. Owing to the fact that a woman can possess a mouth that looked like hers, she was released from the bottomless inclination to chew up number 4 pencils in reality, as if she were going to construct a beaver dam out of the pencil leads.

Hecht emitted desperate signals. "She propped her outstretched hands right above her knees. Sometimes she looked at me. I believe she was sitting down the whole time."

The signals did not arrive, and Bob Hecht received some that were just as desperate but simply sent them back until Ann received his desperation in spite of her desperation. Ann seemed to have resorted to working over Robert, who was always seeking her out but was never sought out by her, with a shock therapy that alternated between love and the withholding of love—how little was required for him to say "this is love," and how little she then had to withhold from him for him to cry out, "it's all over!"—to the extent that over time he had to grow weak and in the worst case even melancholy.

Robert, once again incapable of working thanks to his relationship with that woman who was still inviting, but more and more obscure . . .

If once the head gardener, when a light was shining in the greenhouse and a wind was battering the azaleas through the transparent louver, did not feel like lounge piano, and if the head gardener once again was making Hecht, who had disappeared in an abandoned corner of the greenhouse and was shoveling and making a mess with what he was digging up, tear around in circles on the motorized piano swivel stool until Robert Hecht's shirt was the hardest thing about Robert Hecht, then Bob Hecht gave free rein to the feeling that he immediately had to do a favor for the head gardener, even if the boss was only harassing him halfway brutally, by way of thanks; and hardly had the seedmaster stopped talking when Hecht proffered to him a bouquet of flowers, wrapped in tissue paper and massaged into a club; a bouquet picked at his place of work; for the most part it consisted of chicory that a squadron of active flea beetles had infested down to the roots; pilfering chicory cleaned up the medians of the highways that the nursery lived off of by planting them on public contracts in the most favorable way, since for each bouquet that Hecht held out toward the face of his boss, two drivers blinding each other in the night collided on the median and shaved off some plant matter there as well.

Thus the weeks passed into the gauze, and Bob Hecht increased his experience velocity, as a reagent to the delayering and the dark-flake crumbling of the manure dumps to be shoveled. The experience-tachometer often displayed 130 per hour and more, nothing but work techniques that stupefied him and others, and which culminated in efficiency jokes. "If I run over the extension of the main faucet with the wheelbarrow, I save three quarters of a step from the begonia bulbs to the Neocide sprayer. That makes 75 thigh reps per step for every hundred bulbs that have to be sprayed. The kneecap lasts 5,000 kilometers longer."

Robert, before he got thrown out of there too, definitely had to pay a visit to Ann, who gave up a little desire for a secure situation at his side on the second floor of the boutique, and thereby risk some carnation money. The visit could not be put off. The visit would last longer than a carnation, it would definitely go beyond the money he'd brought along, that much seemed to him to be guaranteed.

Even though the dark woman was far and farther away from calling Robert what he loved to be called, that is, a lovable man, an attentive man in inessential trivialities, and a man gifted with an evil, attacking eye, nonetheless through the monotony of a quiet and steadily sinking—but then again hardly sinking—relationship, she had gotten into a paralysis; so much so that she, as far as experiencing her surroundings went, always ended up with him who reflected this paralysis back at her, and thus everything seemed good and worth continuing in the same way. "Unless one of the two of us can't stand it anymore or wants to keep going."

The yearning for eternity and spaces that are white, endless, blissful, shrunken to a childhood format—or else expanded to a childhood format—Robert could no longer imagine this, considering the type of activation that he planned, carried out, and peculiarly enough planned again right away with Ann; it was only vague now; it did not remain a yearning, but he clung to the memory of the yearning as if to an old object on the mantelpiece. They would both have been active in the field of myth creation, as soon as the lounge musician R. Hecht was back standing in the nursery, or else up front in the greenhouse on the swiveling piano stool; with the metal spirals under the rear end of the man who was typing away at the keyboard and strewing lots of peat across the black keys; the pedals in use were already squashing fresh onions, and the black wooden music box was filled with wild rose cuttings. "Whenever the gondolier on the canal begins singing his barcarole, the flounders of the city of lagoons lie down on their backs." At first they would have tried, like all bit-part actors, to get mean one more time before they die and knock down the filled-up barns. "I've wanted her nature for a long time." Somehow a piece of furniture will then have gotten between them. Ann could have claimed it was his injured and hanging beloved arm, and he would have replied how could she mix up his total accumulated and untouched essentialness with his arm, even if everything that existed could be mixed up? Well-versed in his customary woolgathering, she always created rooms for him in which he seemed to be a normal person and did not let any of his bizarre behavior show, the way he usually did . . .

The head gardener, and Bob didn't hold this against him, was not quite so delicate when he . . .

Who to complain to about what the head gardener undertook against Hecht? . . .

Robert Hecht had obligated himself to the nursery, and as part of the bargain he had to accept the rights that others had over him. To the extent that Hecht strained his memory, which had packed its bags and was sitting, ready to move out, in a corner of his head that wasn't even bloody anymore ("afterward I won't have to think back on anything anymore"), this memory showed him—with the big train station hand signal that it also liked to use to immediately wave him off in disgust—a nearly quadratic human phenomenon, without a harelip or a skin graft, which is to say a duty-obsessed Anglican lack of attractiveness; this was Ann, the obscure woman who was incomprehensible to him, the woman who was interested in nothing because she was interested only in fields outside of Bobby's, and who therefore did not receive her man and also did not show him any affection anymore, but only an entitlement reduced to the missionary concept; if Robert did not convert immediately, it cost him his breakfast; this lack would have been more bearable if the techniques that led to its creation had been somewhat more diversified.

Thus they made do, he humming, she staring, in an anxious clench that was easier for both sides because it was insincere, and in a depression that was almost not dispiriting, with the rapid passing of not such a great distance on a spiral track whose mid-point, as was clear to both of them, they would never reach, or if they did, then as changed people.

Changing was something that Hecht no longer wanted to take the effort to do. He left Ann behind in the boutique, where she tried on medium-length things and, hardly was she rid of him, determinedly pursued a precipitous career, a phenomenon at the side of his purchaser: could there have been any reason for the head gardener to be on the second floor more and more often, other than to draw her to him and to push himself on top of her? For what reason, if not someday to grab her with his earthy paws, to drill into her and fondle her while stirring up dirty dust, did this very Lord and Master of the Soil feel the garishly colored summer rags on the racks that she administered and had neatly arranged according to the sophisticated aesthetics of straight lines and right angles, with the sense of taste for easily intelligible orderliness that the boss of all grubs imposed upon the nature that he cultivated; median strips planted in rectangles; no plant without its four corners; clean edges, marked off with dead-straight-bladed spades by the checkered Hecht. "I staggered away, I staggered away."

In the coming and going months the greenhouse had finally become Hecht's constant whereabouts; a warm thermos bottle around noon was a break from the hand shoveling or the rotating ragtime playing. In Robert Hecht's memory—it could not be gotten out of his head, not even with blows to the head and by smashing the crown of the skull—the frequently repeated quadratic, possibly human apparitions caused every face that had anything to do with Hecht to gain in breadth. When Hecht asked aloud why these rather hated countenances were growing so broad, everyone pulled a long face; "Question asked in the wrong environment!" The faces spoke: "You are abnormal, old timer, you'd be better off expressing yourself only in pits that you've already dug yourself and then cover back over like a tomcat covers his leavings."

So much for the wise faces. Bob Hecht moved between them, mediating, as a stupendous virtuoso at the piecemeal revelation of his own inabilities.

Now, his instrument was not hard to identify as a concert grand, by its enormously hard wood block, by the astounding coldness of tone, by the gypsifying strings which were fatter than a female jurisprudent, fatter than a woman with a law degree; one who could have let loose on him a gluttonous maelstrom from her hand; Hecht was of the opinion that a female jurisprudent, as soon as she had found out about his workplace, would have in no way been able to let loose a maelstrom on him that scared him; but if the female jurisprudent did not know of his workplace, then Hecht was as good as swallowed up by the maelstrom; and until a maelstrom had been located, Hecht was also scraped up somewhere between his skin and his gardener's apron; in the evening Hecht shook sandy skin and the sound of a maelstrom horn from inside the back of his cotton shirt. "That's how mixed-up that seems," the faces drove home to R. Hecht.

"I wear an overcoat. The wool is threadbare at the creases, I lay it out flat, the creases remain, I crawl in to be together with myself, then I have a checkered pattern on my chest, that's no child's play."

Bob H. was permitted to congratulate himself on the fact that in the time of his rapid decline there was no female jurisprudent in his vicinity, because all female jurisprudents had just sent off all the flowers that they would ever send, at one fell swoop, and because never again in his lifetime would one single female jurisprudent ever avail herself of a nursery.

Whenever Hecht thought about how, even back then, without having completed a new training course for this new occupation, he was able, while lying in bed and in the dark, reaching across the lonesome edge of the bed across the lonesome brink, to insert as if automatically the miniature cassettes that were always able to play back to him his dusty jeremiads over and over again—each tape was a ready-to-play whiner—then Hecht had to admit that he had undergone a learning process. Not only had the gadget allowed itself to be paid for by him, it went right ahead and put him through his drills as well. This drilling by gadget had been included in the price of the gadget; maybe that's why it had been so high. It was a sort of coming to terms with the past that was typical for Bob Hecht's memory in that it gave three cheers for the past. "When I've made tape insertion into my occupation, then the highway can spit up my right pant leg."

Hecht's work output, as further months flitted past, passed by the highway nursery while leaving hardly a trace; and they left hardly a trace on Hecht himself. He drew the consequences from the whereabouts of his memory and drove it out of himself. If Hecht coughed, then he was clearing his throat of slug exterminator, with which he powdered himself using small watering cans; then he knew that soil on one's hands causes an inflammation of the tendons of the thumb; as a reaction to this presumption there was such a frighteningly frequent hand washing at the hose that Hecht's hands themselves became as pale as soap and peeled off in specks and flakes while being scrubbed clean.

And so for a long time Robert's hands remained reddish, somewhat irritated, and they hung on his severely withered arms into the upper third of his short oblong body, which grew breadthwise with every flower bulb that he afforded himself, so that Hecht eventually had to completely give up the midrange on the piano, because from the end points of the keyboard, where his shoulders were located, twitching, and where his body shot forward panting into the tunnels, not a single truncated finger could elicit a tone from the middle anymore; not even picking at the key that stayed down every time it was pressed and had to be lifted back up with a potting spade for every new note, before the short arm with the too-short finger pounded it back down almost to the pedal.

"The ball of my thumb doesn't fit into the pit of my eye beneath my cheekbone anymore; so how am I supposed to get my eyes out?" With this, the revenge of the world of objects on Hecht's failed condition seemed imminent; in mid-September R. Hecht dug both hands deep into a flowerbed and, bending over and using a low wall as a lever, broke both his wrists, then dug his wrists into the ground and broke his forearms, disjointing himself piecemeal and refusing offers of help to the median strip of the highway: he would not go to "the squares" without musical accompaniment; at nine in the evening of the same day, in order to move his decisions along, he consumed a little weak tea and a paste derived from chaff, spackled out of a mortar. Press it lightly, and it became restorative, a slight pressure on this suture, and his memory blushed and screamed; a pebble splashed into a fire pond, a heavy animal with sharp claws ran across the wise faces lying horizontally and took tasty tidbits out of them with their teeth.

The head gardener, who thanks to the process of Hecht's gaze had turned into a repulsive person with a gangrenous body that basically should have been totally amputated at his head, and with hands that were seriously defleshed and had perforations as big as the head of a pin from the prongs, rubbed himself with drawing salve every night without hesitating while rubbing or receiving a cry of "you deviant!" from an eaten-away face; this head gardener was ultimately as outrageous as Hecht needed him to be, and he got one of Hecht's hand gestures that bore a ingenious, significant, and work-shirking character delivered to the rod-wrapping room, and he slit Bob's hand open and laughed. For Robert, this was a discouraging form of fun: "My birth was easy and quick."

The projected cemetery grounds were located, relative to the entire subdivision's area, very centrally and with their park-like design they offered a welcome relief from the adjacent residential zones.

After Hecht, armed with nothing but a piano stool, had beaten a hydrangea senseless in the basement of the nursery, Novemberish-Decemberish, he ran with a dangling club by the shop that the barberry bushes had overgrown and had the management, which the head gardener was also subordinate to, send his final pay envelope, and stuck it in the kangaroo pouch of his green apron. Standing in front of the main spigot, he clicked the golden chain closure into an eyelet and, with the spade fork that he retrieved from the rack, he hacked into a few upper, particularly thin panes in the greenhouse and wriggled out into the cold. In addition to that he laid a spade-fork tine onto an edge splinter, dropped to his knees and bent over for a piece of man that had fallen off of him. Hecht's light descent made a couple of shrubs shudder, and the head gardener smothered a laugh to death in order to pull the heavy, metal neck ring out of the drawer with the thick, clumsy gloves. Bob Hecht rather valued not having to see or have any memory of that anymore, and he did not let it be a lesson to him for later, because no Later came that was in any way different.

## 3

After my experiences at the autobahn nursery I ran very quickly on the shoulder of the highway out into the beloved country. There lay a field that with its extensiveness challenged me to step onto it. I would have been better off not doing that, for it led to a new peculiar kind of experience.

On the field that I stepped onto without thinking about it, Bob saw a farmer with a citril finch fluttering over him. No sooner had he put a rake into my hand than we entered into a close relationship. The events themselves worked in our favor. No sooner had I left the city than the wild adventure began. The next morning we scattered barley—the citril finch had disappeared—for the chickens, milked the cow, and got into mischief with the butter. At least the chickens were pecking; they knew enough to appreciate their meal tickets. Later they scattered. The duration of our association was a relative one. Once again, for the last time, as it was to turn out and as was already foreseeable then, we ate a slice of hard bread together, where the sun was shining and external influences remained excluded. He or I divided it—the slice—down the middle or from corner to corner. With so much good fellowship, the miracle that he started to confess did not fail to happen, at least not for long. After the butter had run out the day before, it burst out of him: "My cow." He was raising her, he said, in order to get better milk, better milk all the time, with more fat content. Significantly, he said, the fat content of the milk was not dependent on the fat content of the cow. His cow's body and the consistency of her milk had nothing to do with each other. On the contrary, they really could exist alongside each other without any mutual influence. The speech of the farmer was the kind where the speaker grew teeth over the words, teeth that he sank into the obvious as his prey. It could be the case, said the farmer, that his cow produced hundreds of liters of milk with a single milking stream, but her body was no longer up to that kind of production. Then, as is to be expected with so much cajoling, the cow herself will turn into milk, adding even the flesh of her body to the reports of the dairy industry's success. On the other hand, if she were to suffer from a hunger that in certain years cannot be eliminated even with straw, dandelions, or rye kernels, then her appearance would likewise waste away, and the few drops that his knuckles could then squeeze out of her would be unfit for human consumption because of the udder, chafed bloody, which his accustomed hands treated with the necessary care. That was too much for me. Cowering against the stove, folded into the stovecraft, I fell asleep until the daylight woke me. I had the feeling that this day was the decisive one and was dawning for my sake; it was encouraging to be in the midpoint of time for once.

I was sitting in my one-bedroom apartment with the telephone apparatus in front of me. I picked up the receiver and tried to be so telephonic that the sound would have to reach all the way to him. A breakdown in our agreement still seemed premature to me. The farmer himself, when he heard my shrilling, answered. "I'm on my farmstead, they're pecking and mooing again, and who are you?" he asked. Out of disappointment I pulled the telephony out of the wall the same way I would have pulled a small icebox out of the wall, if there had been a wall there. Everywhere I perceived walls with no effort. It was possible they were supporting the house in which I lived together with other people I didn't know, considering how well that was going; it was not going well; it's just that at the spot where due to my despondency I would have liked to pull the telephony out of the wall, there was no wall. The builder must have forgotten it: it seemed to me that when it came to telephony, people didn't immediately think of a wall or supportive structure. It's possible that this was because the distance that already existed, and was steadfastly expanding, had to do with numbers that supported themselves in and of themselves. I had been unburdened by such thoughts during my time in the country, and I also hadn't needed a set of scales to prove to myself that it was easier for me, that I seemed easier to me. A few days and weeks slipped away into the countryside, which shrank so much that I could cross it in five steps. What had suddenly died and was lying on its back and keeping its water to itself was my old citril finch, to which I would have given another year, including the needed birdseed. From his death I could see that what he should have been pecking had somehow consumed him and that, as he lay on the packing paper under the perch, there was not much left of him. This minor domestic collapse demanded a brief accounting, for perhaps it had actually happened for my sake. If, however, I stood in the midst of dying, and if the dying was happening in my favor, then I was better off passing on my discontent before it was too late for any transferral. On my way to his farmstead I stepped onto the field, as before, without thinking about it, and tripped, without watching out for myself, over a bundle of alfalfa that had been left lying there or was growing there. It had attained an amazing density that we would never have dared dream of in the springtime. When I had put days of fruitless searching behind me, my calendar, ironically a farmer's almanac, ordered me to put an end to the search and erase the brief happy time with the farmer.

"Ten days in a row,
then let the search go,
don't complain anymo'"

More falling than walking, in any case moving downward, I came across his farmstead, which, in the haste of departure, he must have left where it lay. It could hardly be assumed that he had been permitted to pack up his farm and barn. I turned over the hay, and he wasn't lying underneath it. With much prudishness

I approached her udder; he wasn't sitting behind it, but his one-legged stool was leaning on a lonesome rung. Whatever grew went upward; whatever was not up on top had stopped growing; whatever wasn't there had not managed an appearance; whatever I came across twice suffered from redundancy; whatever was shining glowed brightly and dipped the green growth into its bath; whatever was wet was nourishing wherever it could be and wherever it had tongues; whatever he had produced could no longer be gotten rid of; whatever, like him, had hung its existence on a nail, would never come forth again so that I could have grasped it. There wasn't much going on anyway, as far as grasping was concerned; for the most part I kept my eyes closed and wanted my skin to feel whatever was radiating warmth here and now. The vegetable patch expressed itself stably and untragically whenever, in the time that followed—which overpowered me with the feeling that I had missed something and could never get it back again—I concentrated on telephony; once again I attempted to roar at him and did not fear the humorousness of my lung blasts. No one answered; but a glowing stove seemed to be burning beneath me. I jumped up so fast, sat down, and ran into the next room, only to jump back into the first one. That was the effect of one burning coal or a ton of burning kindling. Who had put them under steam, I did not know.

I never did see the farmer again, who had surreptitiously escaped while I was roaming around within the city walls; even though the wish that I might get the chance to see him grew cold very slowly; strictly speaking: my further plans were over and done with when Bob turned his back on the field whose stalks, sharply pointed at me, challenged me to step onto it, and later, later, ate my feed himself without emitting a sound or a kernel, because my lips were closed and sun and quiet and cheerfulness had entered into his restlessnesses.

## 4

After the development of a few of his secret virtues in the company of the farmer, Robert H. had returned to the city. This fair city was full of architectural successes. For a short time, Robert had made it. Robert had become an upper-level bureaucrat, a civil servant. He inclined to great conscientiousness. The management had a use for him. He was not urgently needed, but on the other hand he was assured that he was better than no one. Somehow, Hecht believed this. As a child he had chased his companions now and then, but he was not one of the ones who caught them. Robert had a hard time getting over disappointments, and even now he remembered that one well. Mostly he looked energy-charged into the future, and he was being propelled into the future that he feared when he thought he too would take place in that future. Then he was more or less located in the future, and in the future he came off even bigger. Robert's moods were stable—he toppled over only every few semesters. He was unfortunately one of those people who often fell into a rage, and he made up for that by repressing other things. His feelings had become impervious, because when he put them on track, they ran all the way to the depot. These coupling services with that which could be expected of Hecht were appreciated in the real estate office. In those days Robert once again had red spots on his face and throat. Sometimes he doubted whether the poor tenants who sought him out and complained about the wind that was blowing from the government—all of the real estate managed by Robert belonged to the iron fist of the state—even listened to his considerations. Even when they were intentionally unfolded in a clear voice. All who sought out his office were to have access to him; their long complaints were answered by his own, which were even longer. No sooner had someone turned his door handle than Hecht Bob suddenly became the public realm, but luckily he didn't spread himself around very well. The tenants still showed a growing interest in the government, in the landlord government, even though this government did not place any advertisements for itself in the newspapers; the apartments that it owned were a form of propaganda that was mixed in the most skillful manner with the threat of eviction at any time. The patience of the tenants was incomprehensible, for Robert signed whatever was pushed in front of him. Unfortunately he could not stand everybody who came to him. Robert's hands were more restless than his feet, but they were needed less. Without his hands, the official stamps stayed inside the desks, and the desks stayed shut in the morning; and in the evening too, after Robert had locked their drawers with a key and hung the key next to the door, and locked the door with the next key. At worst, Robert did not go home after work, because he had lost the capability of the way home. His impression that he was expendable was intense and found support in the fact that during Hecht's illness the work of the real-estate office continued as it had during the illness in which Hecht had stayed in the office. Thus they let him play along, but he wasn't playing a role. Almost every week there came a complaining tenant that Hecht couldn't stand . . .

. . . so that Robert did not think that his likes and dislikes, which seemed to him like a colorful play of his soul, could have anything to do with the relationship of the tenant to the government. Admittedly, this government blew its tenants out of the apartments, and still the apartments were dusty, there were matted pillows of dust on the door handles, and nails were driven into the walls for the sole purpose of nailing the wallpaper to the plaster. Never any pictures. For every hundred apartments, one book, one set of instructions, one cooking pamphlet. It seemed to Robert that when he was making his rounds his thoughts were also making rounds. Am I bringing them back? No, rounds.

Robert's office was better furnished than the apartments; one day no one entered it at all. As pleasant as it was to be left in peace, still Robert was afraid that he had gotten closer to his sense of dread. Now they thought he was sick even when he was present, even though he sang softly and was even able to sing much louder. In the next room there was a bell clanking like a teaspoon hanging by a thread against the bottom of a frying pan suspended vertically. If Hecht thus called to mind all of the suffering on earth, out there, farther away, wherever he took his mind, floating approximately, then he expected that, more or less as a reward for a righteously lived life, his own birth would once again be rescinded. It would be best if that happened shortly before his promotion. A catastrophe right in the middle of a joy could not be foreseen. And the catastrophe remained a welcome end to that joy, as long as Hecht did not survive it and then have to think back on it as its casualty. The moisture-dispensing machine in the government hallway gave one more cup of de-creamed coffee for the same coin, and Robert quickly shoved the second one . . .

. . . unless he had lifted his glasses and now decisively turned down so many complaints after all. Managing the apartments, which provided some flow and variety, actually wasn't so bad. The bell sounding seemed to rip apart the heavy main door. Robert gave no further thought to court orders once they were carried out, because the bailiffs passed the assignments on to the marshals, and they never followed the instructions for the evictions as precisely as they reported it later. Under them, an immediate moveout became a two-hour moveout. The tenants were allowed to take a full two hours to clear out, and in the report it remained immediate. Erwin was an unshaven epileptic, Martin was an old furniture mover who jammed the armoires under their—the evictees'—arms as if they were matchboxes. Tore them down the stairs so that the friction could have set the house on fire. This was not without its dangers for Hecht's work situation, which was not that far away from those localities. At first there were always the complaints. It started with simple complaints where the plaintiff realized too late that it was the government he was bringing a claim against. To be nearby and yet remote, to find the path to oneself and yet discover only a worn-out wreck: if that wasn't worth mountaineering on the pay scale! As a beginner it was fun for Hecht if the finance department or the architecture office got beat up by the administration or the city council. The corridor screams were shrill and drowned out the teaspoon in the frying pan and drove small waves into his office. Through this screaming the not-yet-humiliated complainers came, still unused-up in their coats. Then, from the temple-crushing hats that they took off to him, they poured out a scream that even got to Hecht a little bit. Bare heads hatched from under the brims, shining, and descended into a visitor's chair. Then it was Robert who executed general-staff work on them and then dished himself out to them too. He used them overwhelmingly to find a home for what he couldn't be bothered with. And strangely enough: no complaint ever found its way to the government, which watched over Hecht as well. The tenants were too humiliated, for Hecht could only attain certainty that they would put up with his transgressions by knocking them flat and letting a lot of air out of them until they almost couldn't inhale any more. Those complaining and inconsolable Indios studied Hecht's hardwood floor while they, without noticing it in their distress, were already in his strategic sandbox, where he shoved them back and forth until everything they knew had unexpectedly become the substance of their complaint. On this foundation they could then be shaken down and worked over. Hecht did not like silence, and so he just started talking, to the rage of the tenant, who could not bear this disturbance of the proper order of business. First the tenant had his endless right to complain, and only then was Hecht allowed to air his own discontent. Lately some unpleasant people had also come into the enjoyment of his skills. He was capable of quickly putting some life into a rather boring appointment, but sometimes he just let the embarrassed silence drag on and tormented both parties by remaining mute for a long time and rummaging in old fire records, which had a frightening outward effect. There was hardly anyone who did not confess upon interrogation that he had also committed arson and should be taken into custody. If he sat through the whole day, Robert could not quite do whatever he wanted. On top of that he began to suffer from indigestion in a rather undramatic way; it may even have all been in his head, and Robert did not make a tragedy out of it. His feet, which were invisible to him, seemed to have gone missing. Out of pure conscientiousness, Robert would have to scoot back on his chair to get another look at them. On the two armrests sat Martin and Erwin. When Hecht sensed what they were up to, he pulled himself together and threw an imploring smile their way that said something in 3,000 words that meant "I." "In the name of the state, you are fired," Hecht said articulately to the evictors. "Fired?" asked the furniture mover, pulling moveable Erwin toward himself and raising Robert's desk with an outstretched arm over Robert's head. A threat, most likely, for desks held up in the air have a threatening effect, and there was no doubt that the man who was holding it up in the air was indeed someone who was capable if needed of letting go of it in thin air or dropping it out of a clear blue sky. "Fired?" asked Martin. The desk was trembling. Robert swallowed coquettishly and attempted to move the ailing Erwin to have some sympathy with a person in an inferior position. "Without delay, if you please," said Erwin, who at that moment was healthy. "Get out," warned Martin, who was so moved by Erwin's loyalty that Robert inherited something of that emotion . . .

. . . because Hecht had it made for a long time. He had finally been what he had become and again became what others had remained. Much more gently—to the last, Martin commanded a gentleness that could be awakened with gratuities and Erwin-strokes—much more gently than in the case of the parliamentarians, Hecht effected a surreptitious . . .

. . . weak finish . . .

. . . and undetected withdrawal from the sparsely furnished labyrinth of complaints, supplications, legal cases, and settlements.

# 5

After this thoroughly fabricated contact with the lovely government that didn't exist at all, the time had come for Robert to cast a stern eye on his own rooms in order to find out whether he shouldn't assume the blame for everything that he always palmed off on others. In Hecht's apartment an endlessly long and winding hallway, which a corkscrew must have bored through the walls, led to the room he was occupying.

In one of its corners lay a tattered cardboard box filled with death notices, all of them printed, the space for the name filled in, blackly bordered, bric-a-brackly beribboned: "Today after long, impatiently borne affliction, etc.," his name printed in the space right after the ominous "called home," which, taken simply as a phrase, made the all-powerful authority of the omnipotent Master of the Universe more or less hang as a layer of air in space; it was a layer of air like the one he sensed when he leafed through the death notices and dog-eared their corners, and so it was a warmed layer of air, which is to say that this was how mercy radiated.

A needle had pierced the cardboard, and in its eye it trailed a strand of cashmere yarn. Unfurled above the package was a spreading red-silk parasol weighing approximately twenty pounds, whose fabric hung down in shreds: the power of the sun's onslaught: perhaps light was more than mere radiation.

At its peripheral edge, the parasol was stuck to the stone slabs of the floor with huge drops of congealed isinglass, the stone slabs gray with thread-shaped inlays like tripe in aspic. Foodstuffs had been amply tossed about and had left indescribable traces behind. Whole piles of Bircher muesli and dried-out bread pudding were lying at the feet of the stove, which was disconnected from the gas line.

After he had detected in himself an inexplicable rage at women, he began to scream: "Snoopers, tormentors, movers, destructresses, rubbish, pick that up." He knew of no one who moved like that, who was everywhere at once and yet never assumed a shape, the way the female admirers who buzzed around him every day did or did not do; even if he was imagining it, it was still true.

Hecht's apartment, easily accessible to all these gossamer body snares in female form, riddled with windows and infinitely permeable—across the walls, slots, barriers, cracked, clogged, trickling, dribbling, and at their best velvet-mossy—was located in the middle of the city, on a busy street on which the whole of life was spawned urbanly and spermatically; it was a shameless boulevard where everything looked as if it were run by the public sector; on the other hand, parking cars and bicycles was permitted only for minutes at a time. The most striking thing about this street, the Fuhrweg, this artery and traffic-trough, was the slight wind that picked up fluff when he stuck his head out the window; if the window fell down, then the head was severed; but if he braced it with a wooden dowel, then it stayed up a while and hummed.

"If we enter a tunnel, then in the past there have already been many heads that were severed upon exiting," he said in a convoluted way, his mode of expression a spiral staircase leading to dusty museum rooms, whither his knowledge of all of the cultural assets of his epoch, on the whole extraordinarily pleasing, had wandered, at least his knowledge of those assets that this epoch would leave to the next epoch, which was to follow this epoch; his cough was getting worse, which is the way a case of consumption coalesces.

"O apples of my eye," he whispered, under the spell of his sense of this sacred moment, and pulled his head back in, betaking himself to the reception rooms. If a female visitor were shown into the reception rooms, then he would initiate her into the secrets of the house: that the rooms were constructed according to the principle of the pair of scales: each room that was not currently occupied and serving the purpose of habitation was located seven stories down below the ground and was summoned up at the push of a button (he simply placed his hand on the wallpaper) just before it was entered.

"The fairy eats bromine," he giggled. At that time he was constantly surrounded by the sisters (of the Catholic hospital), in the gentle custody—which left his flowery words untouched—of the servants of the order. It could happen shortly before nightfall that a doctor mingled with them who took him aside, who giggled hardly less than Hecht and found hardly less pleasure at his jokes than he did in constantly making them up. "The fairy scarfs down bromine," and pulled in his belly in the region of the breastbone so frighteningly far that his spinal column threatened to become visible from the front. The doctor, wearing a peculiar, absolutely bizarre cap, as if he was about to go on a mission with a flame-thrower, on his hands two surgical gloves three sizes too big, with their fingertips overlapping by several fingers' breadth, wrapped a cord around his chest and cut into him slightly by pulling the loop tight so that a thin, red stripe ran around him. Was that a scorched-skin policy or was it not? If it was not one, then everything stayed the same; but if it was one, then everything was different, at least with regard to his hands. They were no longer allowed to cross over the red line and take a trip to the knee, for if it were the case that it was such a policy, then his surface was now subdivided, and he broke down into two unequal parts, even long before they would actually cut him up; that is, they had come for the purpose of cutting up, as one could tell by their aprons and by the fact that the cars were parking on the boulevard for as long as they liked. In addition, a few dozen bicycles were leaning against the foundation walls of his house, waiting for the collapse.

He would have had to be a wiser man than he was to overlook these signs—explicit and clearly formulated threats. He would have had to be a much more sensitive man not to decipher the threats that the doctor had blurted out while subdividing his body. They indicated that he was supposed to take one of the cards out of the box under the parasol and send it to his mother.

"The fairy scarfs down Blomine," he giggled, for as chance would have it, one of the sisters, a powerful one with enormous, excessive, virtually philanthropic bread-baker-hands, was named Blomine. She laughed as she received the news that she was being consumed. The other Catholic women sat around on their stools in stoic silence, playing solitaire.

Whenever he expressed the wish to do so, they let him go to the window, let him hammer in his wooden dowel, the prop, with the little hammer or with his elbow, let him look out upon the scenes where they were going at it, where they were toiling away and busy with the heavy, fanned-out bullwhips; once a day he went into the kitchen in order to take a morsel of leftover food out of his mouth, which was unexpectedly populated by dumplings and sour, slightly resinous spheres; in time, they grew back faster than he could remove them because in his gums, in a pocket of skin, a manure bank must have formed which bore fruit—wet, expanding mouth fruits that were not lessened by piloting himself through his continued existence by being able to inhale broths through a straw; the kitchen, to which, after he had stuck his head in the oven on the solstice and turned on the baking and the broiling elements full blast, any supply of energy had to be cut off. Helpful screams wrapped him in the heavy parasol, and Sister Blomine dealt with him as if he were an unruly pound loaf of bread, and after he had run across the intersection that lay outside the propped-up window to catch a taxi, she laid him in the round bed that was skulking along the walls; it was there, there everywhere, of an immaculate presence and cushioned like a thick, steaming carpet that steadily endured the pressure of the feet and the corkscrew. In this flood of softness, resilience, and timidity, a silvery thermometer swerved toward the apple of his eye and cried out his temperature after a test bore. In case whatever was ailing him was a clean bodily fever, the fairy would make him well and tidy up his leftovers before supper; and so he lay, slightly sprained, seven stories below ground, running his hand in a cross-stitch over the patterned wallpaper, and in the corridor she made way for the finely sprayed plaster coating.

## 6

The village was built right next to the mountain. Stones protected the roofs from flying away in the wind. Maybe the wind would blow the stones away, but Robert felt no wind, even when he stuck his finger in the fountain and held it up as if he were in school and had to report a bolt of lightning. In the stones, moss was growing, or better, between the stones. There was also moss on the banks of the brook into which Robert never stuck his wind-finger. The brook took a turn next to the inn, which had only a minor influence on the meals in the inn. The banks were eaten away there, noticeably eaten away. A thicket of bristly shrubs and supple creepers covered them. Every evening the village pricks visited the inn and palavered geopolitics. The inn was peaceful, motionless, and suitable.

"You are pretty, Ann. I like to stroke your cheeks. You remind me of an earlier Ann," Robert said and thought he was bodacious.

"I used to climb trees," she said, "and that was at an age when I refused to acknowledge my gender. And even then the village fellas would gather around the tree to help me climb down."

"I like your hair, the way it drapes on your shoulders." Hecht was gradually convincing himself. "I also like your back, smooth back."

"It is as white as a fish. I don't like fish. You whack their necks on wood before you gut them."

"And I really like to run my hands over your hips," Hecht murmured. "You have the heavy scent of velvet and corduroy about you."

"I always feel hot in the pillows," she said. "I can't help it."

"Do I make it hot for you?" Hecht asked. Always with these quotations from pamphlets.

"No," she smiled, running her hand through his hair, preferably thinning hair.

"Your warmth," he whispered, licking her shoulder. Then they kissed, pressing against each other. Ann moaned under Robert's embrace.

"What was before that, even earlier," he asked.

"Even earlier I wore pants and rough shirts," she said. "I went fishing in the brook, I climbed trees, I chased away lousy lovers with stones, and I drank liquor like a man."

"I don't like men. They're so cruel. They're so limited. They have no idea of who they are."

"That's what attracted me," she said. "Do you mean Lulu the Earth Spirit? Men actually do know a thing or two. It's not worth being a man. I gave it up."

With her hand she drew his head to her mouth, which was speaking trivial texts.

"Back then all of them were friendly to me, and empathetic," she said.

"I don't mean Earth Spirit," he said. "I'm too unbearable in bed for that."

"All of them were extremely friendly to me," she said quickly. "I didn't have any breasts, I was all flat up front and I wore boys' pants with carpenters' pockets on the knees. My hands were all crusty when I pulled the silvery fish out of the water. I was cold and I shot cold glances all over the place. For hours I watched the fellas sleeping. I never got tired, even though I was totally exhausted."

This speech, Hecht thought, was an achievement. He was in no position not to measure up.

"And now," he asked, "are you happy with me?"

She turned toward the wall and rolled herself up in a ball. Robert's trembling lips sought the nape of her neck.

"No," she said.

Cautiously he pushed his hand between her arm and her body. How come she was thinking of these psychologically troubling news items in this village and not at home, where he could have countered them by looking up a saying from Father Sigmund? To cover his bases, Hecht bit her on the ear. She remained still, as if she were dead.

"I could write you," she said while departing, "but I'm not going to do it."

Robert stood wordlessly next to her, third car from the engine, and the last one in the train.

"Do I even have your address?" she asked. "Well, I'm not going to take anything into consideration, but I am disappointed. The whole thing was a waste of time."

She smiled at him through the windowpane. Hecht moved his mouth to say something undistorted to her, but he produced a white cloud of breath. She had immersed herself in a newspaper. Geopolitics was keeping with the decisions that had been made in the inn. The newspaper pages covered her up except for her fingertips. Robert knocked on the window. She touched it from the inside with a tongue as dry as sand.

"I was fantastic," he said shamelessly, "but when you leave, my imagination starts having flings on the side."

In the days that followed he did a lot of hiking. From the ridgeway he looked out over the village. He let himself get sprinkled on by the spraying waterfall and got out of the way of the trucks on the winding roads and climbed over low walls and wire fences. The village lay in the shadow of the cliff. The wind—it was simply not perceptible—had blown the stones from the roofs together into considerable piles. Moss was growing on the meadows, on the houses, by the brook, and even the inn conformed to that homogeneous green, which farther up had to do without the trees.

"What else do you expect from mountains," Hecht said to himself. This invective was smart-alecky, and a relief.

Three or four brawny lads carried him home. His mouth was pursed, frozen in the pose of suction. His hair was hanging over his forehead and being brushed away from it. His foul-mouthed manner of speech suggested that he was drunken and vomiting language. He constantly let out his own stuff and engaged in pertinent comparisons with that awful Stauffacher woman. "You really oughta shut your trap for once," said the double innkeeper, who stayed in the room until the following morning, spitting with a sigh into the washbasin and reading *Ich* by Karl May.

"I know, I know," Hecht howled over and over.

The peak period of landslides was past. "There's no mountainside that's going to calve and smash you," said a village prick one evening while they were having a beer. "It's sad, but you aren't leaving me," Robert sang in the evening whenever he reached out the window to tear some moss off of the roof. At night, when he was sleepless, the wood creaked in the hallway outside the door, and sometimes a serving tray clanged up the narrow steep stairway. Like the hero with his tongue torn out Hecht gibbered when he had put a fever thermometer under his tongue and ordered ice cream from the brewery. *Ullgh*, the sound when he swallowed spittle; and Robert's sole consolation was that the nocturnal creaking was still audible when he was asleep. Two heavy supporting beams twisted into each other there, joined each other in two recesses into which, before it was rolled to bits, Robert's new, upper head piece fit exactly, while his bulging eyes were served a railway-car window pane, licked clean, on the serving tray, which had sprouted knobby, scurrying legs, and behind the window Ann was carving away at a round, light-colored piece of gneiss.

# 7

Gradually Hecht grew quiet. Quiet was the only possibility for him anymore. As if he had to make up for a year of lost sleep. Hecht had to lay into a castrated coffee. It was the decastrated stuff that caused his disquiet. It had to be overcome so that he could get along better. Robert had to put cross-country runs through the forest behind him. Quickly stuff a forest into the closet in his office. He was so tired then, when he came back from the forest! The bed waited, throwing its blankets over him. One foot stayed outside as a thermometer. Then the bad things descended upon Hecht. Tuning in all the dream stations meant: knowing everything that he would experience in the next fifty years. The only possibility for defending himself against this was to get down to work on the spot. As soon as Hecht woke up, there was a compulsion to undo the work by starting to read books that he had already read and forgotten again. This time he deciphered them in order to forget the code they were written in even more thoroughly than before. In time he gained practice in skipping over things while reading, but skipping over things was nothing. It was a matter of not registering much of anything at all, but in that case forgetting was easy. Forgetting was harder if you had registered something. But nobody had to register even the smallest thing, and with the forgetting of even the smallest little thing, the smallest relevant notation had become superfluous. Reading things out of existence, a method that S., a judge, had taught him. He had used it to increase his weekly output of written opinions two hundred percent. Still too little by half. "Where would I be if I put everything that I write an opinion on in my head?" Reading made Robert lame to a high degree, at least that's how he felt after a few pages. Now he was also getting worn out by the pages where he only acted like he was reading. And he'd end up by getting tired in advance when it was time to sit down and act like he was reading. Ultimately he would destroy the thought that it was even possible to act like reading was happening, and not always forgetting; hopefully this thought could be destroyed. Hecht was having a hard time hitting it with his brain, because the thought would not hold still. Microstructures were Hecht's undoing, hardly had he gotten into them. That must have been his passive behavior, letting himself be swept along; he used to jerk his knees apart and cut himself in the ball of his thumb with a sharpened coat hook before the turn of each page, crying Seize me, o Shatterhand. On that workday Robert got so endlessly worked up, and should have been displaying behavior as calm as they wanted him to be, and he had to leave the house without delay. Hardly was he standing on the street when he noticed that the kitchen was no longer accessible. Immediately a wolf pack of hunger attacked him; with ragged bites small hungerlets laid waste to the warm blind passages of his empty innards, and big hungerlets were wolfing madly behind his navel, where the scissors had cut him off from his mother. There was nothing left for Robert but a painful poverty of nutrition. His nails could fall out, "and they will do it too"; his thinking, this time encompassing the Ultimate, was well on its way into the Ultimate when he started a new job, this time a job for life. It was a half-day job that paid about eight hundred. Not eight hundred each month, but eight hundred each time. Unfortunately payable only in two years' time, and thus much too late. By then he'd have starved to death a long time ago, now that he was thinking of hunger. Having arrived at the outermost end of a weak spell, but still not at the end of his thinking by a long shot, Hecht had no other choice than to skin a leg off of a grilled-chicken stand by preparing fifty packages of French-fried potatoes that had been fried in the grease of other French-fried potatoes that in turn were frited in their predecessors' grease, so that the grease was probably a secretion of the

French-fried potatoes in general, and these potatoes were stewing in their own grease, and the sign said "Fresh Fries." It seemed appropriate to Robert to demand a hundred-fifty per package. What needed to be thought over was where he could fritter them away again as quickly as possible. For example, earning hundreds of thousands with the Fresh Fries, rising to become the Fries Kaiser of downtown and investing the hundreds of thousands back into chicken, seemed moronic to Hecht. Letting the hundreds of thousands proliferate in ground beef stamped into meatballs was even more moronic. It was, however, ingenious to double the hundreds of thousands and multiply them in both meatballs and chicken. You could get hot and sticky thinking about it and your shirt collar could tighten up on you, when Robert thought of all the overflowing freezer chests where over and over again there was a frozen chicken leg jammed between the frame and the lid. Pounding millions of times on the lids of thousands of freezer chests and hoping that the chicken legs would finally be pinched off. Thinking went ahead, moving on; between its vandalisms, sometimes some essence gleamed through. With his right hand, during the first stage, Hecht offered for sale nothing but hot Bernese, on that white paper tray with the crimped edges. The sign said "Genuine Bern" and Hecht invented a binary system for himself by which any Bernese who wanted to buy a sausage was stabbed and put on the grill over the flames so that the second Bernese who wanted to buy Bernese sausage could get his wiener, no questions asked. In this way, fifty parts of his clientele were satisfactorily served, and the other fifty parts were offered in such a way that no further complaints ever crossed their minds. Every second customer held out his hand palm up and got a bit of mustard daubed on the base of his thumb. Experiences from the Confederate Army Service stood him in good stead: preparation of fifty packages at a time with minimal outlay and with the technique of offering an outward appearance while supplying the inferior ingredients on the inside of the offer. Robert rolled the skin-colored protective papers over the Fresh Fries. As soon as a second Bernese—the first one was still screaming as he died on the grill, not from pain, but from surprise that something so definite was happening to him in the middle of Bern—as soon as a second Bernese accepted the preheated snack from Robert's preheated hands, he became uncertain which of the two packages was the first wiener. Hecht was so good at turning the split French potatoes lengthwise that the whole thing resembled a tender little wurst; with the skin paper twisted to a peak at each end of the proffered body; stab the whole affair in the back with a toothpick and put two small black Fresh Fries in the Bernese's hamster cheek. Hecht's famine moved into the pulmonary region; every time his Majesty's emissary traveled in his airy coach across the snowbound bronchial plains of Robert's pulmonary steppes, the wolfy big and small hungerlets howled and leapt at the guest's mental legs. Within Hecht, handicaps nomadized. In no time he became rich. At the last wrapping up, just before the big cashing up, he became boundlessly calm in his certainty. The Bernese noticed this and, insulted, they stopped buying anything. The city-center ring was half empty, and the other half was eating behind packages. Definitively settled in his calmness, Hecht pounded a stake with a crossboard into the sidewalk soil, stuck his hands in the hot grease to wet his finger, and started counting, peeling bills off a big bankroll. Starting from the crossboard, a strap was slung around his lap; sitting calmly tethered, now only twiddling his toes. The toes were afflicting nothing, the toes were a piece of Hecht that knew nothing, not yet. Three years had passed in a flash. If only it had been three hours! The last skin paper was wrapped around a princely attorney's fee. All of it for Hecht, to take home, not to share with anybody, to be spent by him alone. And then he could also go looking for the two black Fresh Fries in his cheek pouches. "One paper cup is enough," Robert said when he refused the second cup of coffee in the hamburger bar. "I see the look on your face," said the server, who was just putting the payment for the first coffee in a cabinet behind bars. "Take back this paper cup and leave me nothin' but this coffee here," Robert screamed feebly. "The way you look, you've been thinking some pretty mean things," said the cashier, who tore off the outer lining of one of Robert's pockets in order to force his way through to the payment for the second coffee. Very quickly, Robert upended the paper cup in spite of and together with its contents and sent it sliding back across the counter like a high-heeled curling stone. The coffee did not run off in tongues, but seeped out between the paper cup and the counter. Robert had acted as fast as lightning. Without thinking about it very long he had taken this step and acted. The cashier got something for his assumptions, namely a confirmation. "There are customers who suddenly turn into boars, pigs," he said wiping up and chasing away coffee spatters with the dishrag across a white countertop. Now and again Hecht had to afford himself this chance. Or else where would I be? Where's the forest for the forest run? I must crawl back into bed. There I have to find a method by which I, without getting up, I can earn the sums I have to expend. And I must get more and more, stronger and stronger, higher and higher. I will attempt a modest escalation of Hechtness; after all, now I'm rather well off and now I'm permitted slowly, without false shame, to reward myself by crawling back inside. If only the ego could remain in there, forever.

## 8

Spherical bed. I'm lying on top of a ball, touching the mattress at only one point, turning over in my sleep like a compass needle laid on lubricating oil, trying to keep my balance as an apparatus artiste and still always falling down on the wrong side. I want to fall out of bed on the left side and I'm always falling on the right side or the foot of the bed, that is, when I curl up while lying down and start to slide, without being able to abandon the curled-up position, since everything is already long since cramped up forever. "Forever" means: until the next morning. During the day I get totally relaxed. "Totally" means: the cramping gets even worse; even in the spots of my soft flesh, for example in and around my cheek flesh, I get as hard as iron. I only have to bump against the wall once and I'll break through to my neighbor's place, and with a karate chop I immediately transport him one apartment farther. These atrocious vortices and round dances of my metal constitution create pure fallow fields around me, wastelands of ruined partitioning walls and bricks. I just blew the main chimney off the roof, from inside the iron lung, and it too struck a possible communication partner dead. The elements are giving me the silent treatment, and I'm never the first one to speak. But instead. Lying down and starting up the balance exercises. Curl up—stretch, and its opposite: stretch—curl up. As if shot from a bow. As if I had swallowed a ramrod that all at once turns into a spiral spring in my stomach. Participating in your own straining, causing changes yourself. At seven in the morning the radio makes me trim like it does anybody else; the radio hurled against the wall, and the six-year-old preschool girl of the banking executive next door is lying with my head wound in a certain room 453. If I hear her screaming, I find my equilibrium on the water bed, no, that's wrong: if I find my equilibrium on the waterbed, I hear her screaming. She's little, and she's gotten even littler in the meantime. I've lost my sleep. I was never that far off from losing it, and now I die on night watch, light death or heat death, great will be her sighing, her absolute anguish, her distress founded on injury, on top of a ball she will be. For my sake, the sake of the great artiste, who was, just as she was to herself, sensitive to her. Change of beds soon. Now the dream of the century . . .

## 9

Holds second hand out from the bed. Bawls. Pulls blanket over his head. Coughs, yells: "Mother!" Drums a strangled march on the pillow with his fist. A button on the pillowcase comes undone. Quietly button up, scratch clumsily at the buttonhole, turn buttoning right into therapy. Hits, when he notices its tonelessness, the bed frame. Stretches one arm farther and farther out. Lets his arm go. Lets himself get dragged out of the bed by his arm, which is now stretching farther by itself. Muffled thump. Puts, when he's lying on the floor, his arm on a leash. Pounds out a permissible radius. Coughs. Squirms. Inclined toward a private idyll. Yells: "Mother, that's her, that one there!"

## 10

His windows are covered with blue paper; if he stands in his room, he has the feeling of an occupant who is living under water, his bed is made of Novopan, a particle board that is supported by twenty-five tin cans; he doesn't sleep on the floor because of genuine or imaginary cold vapors that could penetrate into the small of his back; his bed is nothing but a mattress, hard as wood, with a soft woolen blanket pulled over him, and accordingly he suffers from ribs and shoulders broken on the wheel, and as a sleeper he becomes acquainted with his protrusions and edges and would rather be a mollusk (isn't he one already?); on the end table five slightly used matchbooks: the remaining matches standing rank and file have their sulfur heads precisely broken off; he eats them on sandwiches. Lamp with heavy base rocking ponderously, in danger of tipping, the falling lamp means certain death for the victim standing beneath it, the lightbulb with chrome plating above shines below, and across the way the train station stands noisily, its cupola robs him of the midday sun, instead a cost-free time reading on a gigantic clock face glowing inwardly every five min., to the right the post office with a built-in shipping room, a hundred yellow stinking cars in a row, at eight in the morning a hundred postal delivery drivers with wind-up keys in their backs mount the cars, tracing graceful curves on the parking lot, ten minutes later half of the cars are wedged together and turned to scrap metal because they never work out who's supposed to leave first on deliveries and who's supposed to go later, back to the surface of the end table under his blue aquarium window. Sometimes the enumeration of objects lying next to each other can in fact produce an ambience, often even a drama: a frozen, totally undeveloping one that characterizes existence. Paintbrush, box cutter, harmonica, a 2.50 deutschmark rubber monster with a revolting fake-skin paw, this is what he was inside out, ready-made mortal fear in the face of the eternal duration of his two-room-lodging existence, high old-style ceiling, posters advertising artificial fertilizers with the green lips of cabbage heads parting vagina-like, magnificent Cockaignish beasts from agrochemicals, and the cabbagey green lips observed folded over on each other permit an eye to penetrate through them, through five layers, yielding, making room, without the eye's ever making its way to the center of the cabbage head. Cigarette papers, rolling tube, tobacco can, flash bulb, deceased graph-paper pad (volume calculations scratched into the table top, meaningless with cases, crates, and perfect cubes, maybe backless stools), the walls sown full and paw-smeared with sketches, nothing but sketches, nothing thought through, monstrously fantasized makeshifts, the ends of lines suddenly jutting up like broken threads out of insane spirals. The end of the line can be fastened to a cylinder, turn the crank, and the spiral gets spooled onto the cylinder. Short bookshelf Arno Schmidt through Stan Joyce, supports are molded metal spheres stained bluish, disconnected telephone, alarm clock with bent hour hand with its tip stabbing into the clock face at twelve o'clock, unbuckled power belt on the floor by the bed (no doubt robustly absorbing the so-called "ground vapors"!), on the sill a camera tripod, never a camera, maybe used for land surveying. Nearly buried in the midst of this detritus of objects: himself in the flesh, drift toward the Maghrebian swamp soul, chewing sweet loukoums, give me one, I'll stick that crud in the middle of the green cabbage. When he thinks about how many possibilities he still had just a few years ago, he can—considering the prospects that are still left to him—only feel deprived. The cabinetmaker in the rear courtyard was a Nazi and funnily enough still is.

# 11

Hardly had the tea party gathered with the biscuits when the scrawny woman came up to the table and cried out:

"You are my sweetie pie!"

The scrawny woman with the transparent veil on her hat indicated a glutton with a coral-red face who had come so far that his double chin held his napkin.

"You! Especially you! Yessir!"

In the scrawny woman's voice there was such an undertone of sincere outrage that the group interrupted its chewing for a moment, put down the crepes, and stopped plucking the green stems from the strawberries.

"Your manner besmirches and exhilarates me, yes, both of these more and more!"

The glutton who was being addressed with decency by the tall, scrawny lady through her uniformly gray hat veil, a clean-shaven, round, and vividly rosy Hecht, began to weep from perplexity since no one was hurrying to his aid.

"You insatiable pig!"

On the contrary, everyone laughed and gave a round of something like applause with their knives while the scrawny whip hissed. Maybe he seemed comestible to them. Anyway, the way things stood, he was sprinkled with comedos, if those weren't just common and ordinary warts. They never lost their appetite—the meat lottery was rich with delectable winning bets. It was the scrawny, jittery lady who was the first to be moved, how cruel hadn't she been to him. Sobbing, she handed him her handkerchief so he could wipe off his tears, but at the same time she did not totally keep a secret of the fact that she would have been happy to see him rub the salty liquid onto his various items of clothing with his chubby hands. That is, hardly did he start to apply the hankie when the scrawny lady, who had taken a seat in his immediate vicinity for a later peck on the cheek, tore it away from him and stuffed it lovingly into her withered bosom, between her suntanned breasts.

Finally there turned up—so far he had been lacking—a burly gentleman, avowedly in the prime of life, behind the double-folding tea table. He declared that everyone was in their own shoes, and that great hunger dictated a tooth for a tooth. As far as the mass of the glutton and fatso was concerned, then he, the burly gentleman, was relying on the assumption that it was inseparably merged with the fatso. His merciful judgment followed the principles—to put it elaborately—of a French moralist of the waistline. He would place the napkin upon the face of the fatso in order to rescue the pastry. Beneath the napkin the fatso would be able to do whatever he wanted to; he would even be allowed to stick out his tongue. The greasy monster. For several more minutes the group heard his quiet sobbing, which accompanied her gorging and refused to let itself be integrated into the charts of humiliations, which in no way favored their abolition.

How they laid into the cookies and berries. Gargling tea into the bargain. Damaging the gold rims of the cups with fantastically chomping biting tools, teeth if possible. Throwing sugar cubes across the table. Condensing milk as well. Adding arbitrary amounts of baking goods. They grew red and sticky and had to rinse themselves off with lemon water. For this purpose, a tall shower was set up in the flowerbed with the Lent lilies. The lilies dying. Holy Saturday.

"The poor flowers!" they cried, distraught. They were full of feelings about the things around them. Roughly delineated, their affections obeyed the same laws as the seasons, alternating or rotating. As long as they did not love each other, or as soon as they did not love each other, the scrawny ladies and burly gentlemen had to love other things around them. The gentleman in the prime of life let his tremendously restrained voice be heard:

"I'd like to kiss that poor pork belly on the forehead!"

The others followed his example. The whole park leaned forward. It was a complete waste of time, that most regal of all emotions, during the enjoyment of which a fire broke out in the garden and destroyed at least double the amount of all dancing bears, hairy quadrupeds wearing hairnets and sievelike muzzles, for in the spring the slightest increase in temperature struck them a fatal blow. Where spoons served as levers, the wobbly Wedgwood tipped over. The scrawny lady rallied her cries around the concept of Quiet, and the others

"My, how pointless that is!"

"My, how charming he is!"

kissed the glutton so as not to leave empty-handed, for like many a sausage, this one was not missing its side of bacon. To his boar's rump, weeping like a trumpet, ten lanky bodies temporarily puttied themselves. They loved him, a word, very much. They bit Bob and sent him under the sunlamp. The color of the cakes and strawberries. They pawed him and applauded him. Delicate red, in all events with funny, stuck-on seeds, when the scrawny lady offered Bob her cheek and carved the whipped cream for him.

## 12

When Bob had turned approximately eighty years old and dried out, he naturally exhibited the desire to experience something. After countless experiences a new one, or the first one in twenty years. It concerned me only to the extent that a certain reassurance was associated with it for me, since at last, before night and stillness seized me, a blind evening could fall, the first quiet, sightless one since I started running dry. On the 15th of July of last year, which was not the last one for me by a long shot, I molested a thirteen-year-old boy in a public lavatory. As misfortune would have it, a few days after my birthday he felt a natural need, but one that deviated from my own; bewildering, my exact memory, the perfect calcium memory. With a handy square socket key, which was sexually, as it turned out, aroused, but found me in an absolutely certifiably sane condition, I opened the door to the lavatory where the boy was located. Memories of my previous, already covered-up arousals increased my current one to the point of an excess that appeared to me retrospectively as quite respectable, as long as I was looking back, which I, since I've been conceiving of my existence as totally future-oriented, considering the goal that is hanging over my head, no longer do. I succeeded in cornering my boy before I locked the door. I locked it from the inside, I presume, with the same square socket key, although I could have used the latch installed for this purpose; this remained the only failure in my otherwise unbroken and seamless course of action. That the locking of the door took place from the outside was unlikely because in a summer season that was marked by persistent drought hardly anyone felt the need that would have driven him to precisely this lavatory; such was the sweat-inducing power of the sun that it licked up every secretion from the skin, so that contrary to this not very palatable reference, it was a very appetizing summer, in which—this had not occurred for a long time now—it was especially the inner secretions that found a powerful voice, but unfortunately in protest. Where then was my brain, my poor, afflicted head, for which strontium, I mean calcium, is the final corset?

Because in a summer season that was marked by persistent drought hardly a resident ever felt a need without seizing the opportunity, rare opportunity, to hurry home to his wife, when I let that cross my mind, Bob ordered my boy to be quiet, or else. For the or-else sentence, which was threatening of course, I had thought up the most ridiculous of all contents, and given the extremely moronic impression I make, I had never assumed that it would make a strong impression on any person, much less a healthy, small, impudent boy who was certainly already playing with the thought of killing or maiming his father. Quiet, or else something's going to happen, Hecht said in the colloquial form that was customary in this quarter, which over many years I had acquired without any great effort, but under duress. Thereupon I undertook with my boy, who seemed used to such things, and with my reddish thing, those acts which had little similarity to coitus, and unfortunately did not even achieve the extent of that paragraph that made the accursed Criminal Code fall down on my old and therefore highly sensitive spot; it fell from a high vantage point. "It is a matter," I told myself, "of your final piece of evidence in the trial, you old famished swine, the trial in which the corpus delicti and the delinquency are identical, that is, you are identical with you, by committing yourself *and* an offense, having your corpus publicly confirmed; now give it, you wrinkly boar, your best." How else was I supposed to prove to the boy I was fifty years old, for as a fifty-year-old Bob had disclosed himself by means of interspersed reports on border watches served and enjoyed—to my precious boy, whose rather unfounded intimidation grew visibly deeper during the sounds that my lips, admittedly felty and cyanosed, were emitting? My lips were still better than my eyes, which never lost sight of his blue jacket, a rare specimen, especially the right eye, whose absolute directional independence from the left one had apparently been definitively established fifty or sixty years ago, years that had passed by without a trace. I ought to tell the story of my eyes. Not here. I don't like to be reminded of it.

My boy, while we were crouching in a dark corner, had to fulfill wishes for me that were the same as or similar to, perhaps greater than, the ones that Bob had fulfilled for him after he had restrained himself so conceivably little. Was I supposed to know whether he had the same desires, or whether they took form in him gradually, or whether they would keep growing with him? Unfortunately I was deficient at proposing hypotheses of all kinds, for the mere appearance of hypotheses was enough to provoke a powerful disgust in me. I had confronted them as an incompetent for so long, well, no longer than fifty years. All figures are rough estimates. Even though Bob subsequently fled, the nearby residents, who had probably sought out the neighborhood of the lavatory for this purpose, were able to catch . . . I could tell a repellent story about neighbors who . . . their most intimate circle; who never . . . beyond their most intimate circle; forget it. Neighbors who had lurked behind their front doors were immediately able to apprehend me, to bind my hands behind my back with my belt and to determine my age and sex. Hardly had I entered the gray-painted, extremely cozy, multistory building when I made a comprehensive, eighty-year-old confession, although I skillfully mixed up the actual explanation for my deed, not a monstrous one, oh come on, for my deed, so that eventually, while constantly chewing my calcium pastilles, which they had let me keep, I was able to plead calcified forgetting. I believe I did my best at the time to help the seed of irritation sprout most felicitously in my surroundings, which were whipped into an outraged incandescence by the usual mugginess. "How could I," I yelled as loud as my full mouth permitted, "when I forget myself, not also forget my needs, forget my girl?" Whereupon a comprehensive examination of the duly distressed boy, who had been dragged along as a witness, at least brought the true shape of my girl to light, and did this all the more convincingly when his parents too, who had not forgotten this fact about him, described him as a boy: "If he," screamed his tall mother, "wasn't a boy, then we'd have to make him into a boy if for no other reason than the way he behaves otherwise." "For this weather-beaten, toothless Wotan," his father turned, whispering to a man in uniform, "there is simply no explanation." In any case my harmless little joke had the most unexpected and dogged success, even if on the other hand the lever with which I intended to set the exoneration machinery into gear had slid out of my hands, which were now dangling free once again.

From then on the man in uniform felt pressured to take over my oral feeding. Neither to the statements nor to the pastilles that he shoved into my mouth did I say no, in fact, I suppressed a blackish jubilation. Up until then, my mouth said, I had never been sexually active in that way, and moreover: even if the existence of my gigantic family with its multiple members, available on demand, proved my long-standing and quite definite neglectfulness with regard to preventive substances, which I unfortunately tend to perforate before using, regardless of the time and space in which this use takes place, then this very family is nonetheless a powerful testimony to me, its chief ancestor and general manager, pastille. The man in uniform was painstaking with Bob. In a simple and very understandable matching-up, my mouth ascribed the deed, which it suddenly found itself forced to refer to as a misdeed, to my condition and my ceaseless activity as clan chieftain, pastille, before Bob, wanton yet content, pastille, let my voice echo through the building, pastille, pastille, I couldn't stop swallowing, I coughed and reared up before Bob, sinking back, not my final sinking by far, gulped the darkness around me, pastille, now blind and prepared, down within me.

## 13

What's coming is hard to put into words. It cannot be grasped. Has no outline. Hardly casts a shadow. Has nothing purposeful about it. Or maybe it does. It is not totally glassy. Nothing is known about its initial cost. It's completely watertight. It is clumsy and impractical. Somehow characteristic. Although its character never becomes visible. Even if Hecht looks at it for a long time. Of course it is exposed to view. But its innards are all the more mysterious. From the outside it just looks the way something like that looks. Looking at it and determining its approximate "appearance" misses the point of what it often is. If it is a matter of "appearance," then it is at best "the way it looks." Just the way something like that looks. Long, in fact, rather. Wide, somewhat less than long. Deep, for the most part deep. Precisely at the shallow spots it slides infinitely far down. It has no type of carrying handle. A drain out of which gushes speak. Perhaps it can be taken at its individual word before it's over. Loudspeakers should be installed. But those are rumors. Better than silence, anyway. Hecht doesn't give his word, but he often slips on it. The people behind him are diabolically true to nature: they've even installed slips of the tongue in him now. It's too approximate for a speech aperture. Luckily it's still able to communicate, even that way, with almost everybody. Its full steam is still coming, humming, softly closing, rolling, wounding. Hardly any hair growth. Self-organizing. Set up to give itself leaders and superiors, whom it obeys. Mauls them when it's being insubordinate. Which hardly ever happens, but it can, it is left open as a possibility, almost unseen. The people behind it even think of safety valves, though it hasn't felt even low pressure within itself for a long time. Who in the world thinks of safety valves, anyway? As if someone invented the piano before music. But behold, it has them. Safety valves. No pianos, at most an occasional untempestuous Bösendorfer as a flower shelf. It has been granted safety valves without a struggle. It is said to be very skilled at organizing. It weaves no net because it is the net. By no means can it do everything itself in the domain that consolidates. But rather. Hires somebody who does things it has no idea about. For example, it employs Hecht as a specialist. Pays him a wage and attention to him. That's more than you'll get other places. Other places you pay as much as a wage so that they'll pay attention to you.

It supplies Hecht with weapons. If he needs any. You can always use some. Unfortunately it prescribes how they're to be used, outwardly, outwardly. The way it's regulated. If you're not equipped, it is armed. And not that primitively. It isn't such a pile dwelling of that kind in the lake. It has practically no tanks, maybe sometimes a hardened plate to protect the heart, which beats. Otherwise unarmed. That means: with its profound lack of insight anything is possible. And anything goes. After a month it can throw you out. You'll make a soft landing. At this moment it takes everything away from you. Aha, a parable. But every parable knows what it means, and the Hechtian one knows a quarter of that. Hecht no longer has anything. In full view of the public. That's embarrassing, but it makes him famous. Fame always has positive aspects and is also displaced by them. It makes you somebody. You can continue as somebody if required. Just not for very long in the same place. That's a condition. Otherwise its behavior would make no sense. True, it often does make no sense, but this senselessness is part of its program and should not be confused with the loss of meaning that it expects of Hecht. He takes it at its word. It takes him at his existence. That's how coldly it goes for the whole shebang, which on the other hand is funny, that is, that's how coldly it goes for the funny bone; does the funny bone deserve such a thing? Hecht wonders. It has the freedom to answer or not. He has the freedom to exist or not. To see where the debit and credit are. Have a good time for the time being. It knows Hecht. The fine facts in his case. For him, he really is somebody. It's practically started paying attention to him. It seems to have distinguished. So much the better for you, or for it, I'm not sure. It likes the ones like that. The ones like Hecht. It almost doesn't know ones like that, which is to say, hardly, but marginally it does. It is not very analytical. But it is take-apartical, if that makes sense to you. Dismantling as a specialty. Solos in unscrewing. The screws are sucked in by its converter, and when they thunk against its floor they turn to gold. It will eat up some of Hecht's account. At the end of the month he'll have somewhat less there than at the beginning of the month. Not much. His consumption doesn't go *that* quickly. And nothing happens loudly either; in fact, glassy: you could talk and sleep on that. Let's not make it more difficult than it is, admit it, you know what I'm talking about. The wanted poster refers to a Bloody Joe, just one.

Let's look at it from a human point of view. This adjustment of our optics usually promises precision as well. Maybe, seen humanly, it simply won't speak to us. All it wants to do is to do something, to us, something with us. That's absolutely possible. Viewed anthropocentrically, that has rhyme and reason. And if you merely believe that it could be, then that's absolutely sufficient to make it so that this is the case. That this is thus the case is, however, necessary if Hecht is to believe that it could be. False. The sentence before the last one is false. Seen from the point of view of this sentence: the sentence before the sentence before the last sentence is false. Of course, True or False doesn't make any difference, for it depends on the assumption that there are other possibilities in its uncast shadow. A few of them will show it to you. Voluntarily. It's not every day that it has someone like you. It will enjoy you. That is understandable. Sympathy makes the eyes overflow with sympathy. You cannot take everything from it because it is not clear. After it has achieved so much! Even if the achievement doesn't look that way; which is to say that, among other things, it achieves nothing. And as if that weren't enough, it achieves even more nothing. Therefore nothing and once again nothing. Hard to believe, but who believes anyway? Not Hecht. This is how it's seemed for years now. So nobody can say that what it achieves is Zero. That's all we needed! But it sends the Zero into its converter and manufactures a ton of positivistic units. Then it takes revenge on the speaker. Its vengefulness cannot be proven as a rule of thumb, but there, here, it gets revenge, there its lightning strikes. It takes Hecht into service. It exploits him. It drives a coach with him. If Hecht is a tire, it punctures him and makes him hiss. If Hecht is solid rubber, he's abraded and erased. Under the pretext that he scribbled. It wipes off its own graffiti. Doing so, it grows somewhat smaller, but what does that matter? This could be in Hecht's future. You don't need to think about that. Avoid it. It's going to overtake you anyway, it'll catch up. If that's what it wants. If it turns out it wants to, you will have known where to look for the reason. Hecht does not complain when it torments him. Doesn't blame these conditions on anyone. It pushes him away leached out, into the lap of the lowest bidder, who doesn't know what to do with him there. Hecht would have to build up a second career some other way. At least not in the lap of an older, well-meaning gentleman. Seeing this, even it would laugh and die. It is not so uncaring that it wouldn't laugh at others' misfortune. It cannot be. That would violate the unwritten consensus. This is not a consensus, because it is not written down, but it is one precisely because it is not written down. It could not afford to violate this consensus. And so it does not afford itself that at all.

Once someone actually wanted a pension from it. To continue as a retiree. So as to not have to start over from the beginning going through the glassy shaft. Who was it? Certainly not the Palatine Prince von Birkenfeld. A joke? No joke. Ernst, Hecht,

Grünhorn, bloody Grünhorn! I beg of you: just go there. See for yourself. Spring for someone who'll examine it preventively. He will say the same thing, namely yes and no, or first yes and then no, but in any case not nothing, but nothing and more nothing. But never the total nihilation, it's far too lazy for that and baldness scares it. Cast some light on it sometime and take a look at the shadow that it retains. If you see a profile there, Hecht will take his shoes off. Just try to get over it when it gets one over on you. Come on, now. Not so shy, it's wearing a Tyrolean hat, that's what I said, a Tyrolean hat. On his alp there is some sin. It rises up in front of you. Come on, now. You almost mistook it for your neighbor. Or he mistook it for you. How many of you are there, anyway? Don't be so timid. It really can't help its blueprint. It's living it out. It's merging with the one that it presumes is within it. There's nothing unnatural about that. It's nothing, but in no way is it unnatural. Hecht is frozen. Hecht freezes. If they have words, I have words. Luckily I never have words. Nothing and more nothing. Now Hecht has gotten lost again. So close to the goal. Unheard-of. They should abolish these life goals. And that's not all, again it doesn't achieve anything again. Refusal? That would proceed from the assumption that at some point in time something could exist. But yes, it does. There is so much something. The abundance with which it bestows piles up in its chambers. Of course it sends its chambers into the converter. There they are modified. The chamber that it has bestowed full of something drops in at the top of the converter, and at the bottom of the converter the differently materialized chamber comes out. And as a logical consequence it itself does too. What now, just a moment ago, came, is hard to grasp. Weaponless? Just sometimes not long in the same old place. Oh, Hecht, it can do all those things. Close to the goal? Hecht, put on your shoes, you are not that timid!

## 14

It goes without saying that it is assumed here that people will box each other's ears, kick each other, stick each other's heads in a pail of lime, and in the long term people would like to smash and destroy and suck each other dry, drive each other to suicide, make each other change careers, suggest emigration to each other, denounce each other to someone on whom they both depend and thus cast light on oneself, bring everyone else to the point where they attack him, cause complications for the person who is not oneself and is in one's way, draw the straightforwardness of developments out and around corners; it goes without saying that this is assumed here.

The will to make a deal with each other disciplines even these impulses, and one bears the smoothing-out of the waves with composure, because gradually one gets to know oneself and knows that wanting to disarm and wanting to mutilate the opposing negotiating affiliate and the affiliated opposing negotiator and the negotiating affiliated opponent is part of the métier and has always been part of it, and will always be a part of it; everyone is relieved to palm the occasion for this naked murderous desire off onto the other guy, who is also already relieved by his palming-off, only innocent people, only innocent people, only unintentional people.

I count Hecht among the non-sensitive. That is punishment enough for him, with his rigid empathy face. JOSEPH HOLZER AND HIS WOODCHOPPERS PLAY IN A BEER GARDEN. Things have become so uncomfortable for Hecht that he flogs the hair at his temples with his twitching jaw muscle, sticks out his eloquent tongue, and while passing the company sign says BAH.

# 15

Something seems to have occurred, but once again I have not happened. Instead *it* has: the most lamentable thing that could happen to us before the award ceremony. That's all we needed. Why not that? He. He of all people. I have nominated him and now ruined everything for him. I bought him a watch.

With my income I can afford to get him a watch. It's never too late for a watch that will benefit both of us. For a while he played with it. Still does. When I watch him, the time does not pass too slowly. He listens to it, winds it up, straps it on, lifts up the crystal, takes out the upper sprocket, and fits it back in wrong. Maybe he's hoping that it will make the award ceremony start sooner. He will regret this hope up until the moment that inserted it into him.

A lot of beautiful rubies. Together they cost eighteen times as much as the whole watch. A lot of useful activities. They pass the time for him, practically put it to flight, they will kill it. He'll stick the winding stem into the wet snout of the corpse of time. Already he is almost feeling fondness for the object that displays a new dimension of his existence, and eventually becomes a substitute for existence. He now lives ticking. His acceptance speech will pulse like a metronome, five beats per second.

He will not arrive there punctually, but he will look punctually at his watch. Why he won't do that remains to be said. Hasn't it been said already: who is claiming that it hasn't been said, not yet? For an upbringing leading to punctuality with the devout exercises of appearing on the dot of the second in remote rooms of the house, he is intimidated enough, which, however, simply corresponds to the considerations with which I bought it for him; in fact, it exceeds them. It is not something that is unhappily seen by me if I am confirmed after the fact by the willingness of my victim. It's an almost sentimental value that prevails between the—if the expression is permitted—presentee and his flat watch, round as a fried egg. Except that it doesn't run. It has a little tic. Which was stated in the operating instructions. Which I wadded up a long time ago and stuffed into a parking meter. Its hands are the same length. Stuck together. They move only with each other. "I want to see ten o'clock," he says, on the assumption that ten o'clock has something to do with the jury. False assumption. The jury claims not to know anything about ten o'clock. I'm the only one who knows that. I wadded up a relevant written notice. Pretty soon the parking meter is going to jam. But that's nothing. In comparison. "I want to see twelve, and I mean right away," he says. And by that he doesn't mean "twelve clocks," which, given the five extremities of his that come into consideration as strapping-on points, would be inane; instead he means "twelve o'clock," not clear whether noon or midnight. Sun for all, shade for none. That is the theme of the laudatory speech. It is given without him. Mission accomplished. At an angle of one hundred twenty degrees its identical hands stick together.

He turns the winding button, moves the two hands forward, making the anticipation smaller, as small as the dwarf of his prospect of receiving the prize after all, due to prompt attendance on a carved-wood podium where something is awarded. If he were there in time, and an award were made, then because there is no one else there far and wide they would have to award it to him, and he, rolling up his sleeves and his eye on the face of my gift, would let himself be begged on bended knee, God knows.

A turn of the winding button moves the big hand and the big hand forward, which are stuck together in great harmony. When I purchased the watch, the hands were on "ten to six" and that configuration repeats itself all around the clock face. If he impatiently twists the big one forward, then the little one waddles along behind. If in mortal fear he stops the little one, the big one acts the quiet little man. And during this time in which real time passes, they are getting ready, in the anteroom of the auditorium; fat, never-again-skinny, incurably adipose, once wiry gentlemen twine a finger plant around the backs of the heads of thin ladies made slender by age.

He twists away at the winding button, the prizewinner does, and holds a dress rehearsal of his scandal by pretending to refuse the prize, and then finally he is surrounded by eight elders and six elderettes, all of them on their knees, beseeching presences bidding him to enter the field of the prize. He twists at the winding button, trying to retain the time of acceptance, twelve o'clock, hand on hand as if they were glued. He wants to have time as cheaply as possible, as effortlessly as possible. He is not dripping with sweat, simply because soon the hour of the lie will toll for him, when he shall trip over the threshold to his determination to hedge his way through, once again.

The current status of my nominated candidate, because he does not measure up and cannot be brought up to the expected high level within a useful time frame (the time frame of taking off a coat, time frame of catching one's breath, time frame of healing an eye injury), can be a hardship that is a signal blessing. And I misunderstand him while he twists at the watch hands, while his chubby-cheekedness in the wake of his motionless standing, which makes the bones between his joints seem to grow shorter while the joints shift closer to each other, his stature grows shorter, and he is eaten up by some glutton located in his belly, gradually and imperceptibly.

Now he's twisting the winding button. Now almost without a pause. At some point it eventually has to be twelve. The stroke of twelve and then go. It's only midnight once. And then he does not want to sleep. Or at least not alone. He wants to share it, his leftover sleep on his leftover bed, with at least one elder and one elderette. I apologized for not wanting to share it with him and smoothly talked my way out of the thing. In the end I extended my hand to him, the one I used to hold my nose. First he must be educated for the prize. And the first form of education, the results of which it is impossible to verify at any time, is punctuality. Punctuality, the courtesy of kings; heavens, how long has it been since reverence for chronometry needed this adornment in order to deny its educational character. I'll wager that the candidate feels like the tamer of his time, while irrespective of this it remains the grand *dompteuse*. He twists the winding button. In the back room, a white periwig shoves a stony set of dentures into its chin. Pulling down the zipper frees the laudatory speech from its tight fit between those little teeth.

He pulls out the winding button. Toy watch or no toy watch. He seems to think it's real just because it allows for certain mechanical manipulations. This pulling-out-the-winding-button is a temporally limited action, something minor, hardly visible from the back rows. What will remain visible is the inclination of his head, his grasping of his left arm, his general pulling together of all things that can be pulled together in a face. What will be visible is the hesitation at the decisive moment: white hands of death send a black velvet pillow floating toward him, upon it the award with an official seal, the diploma for correctly handled syntax in the proper interest.

I have educated him. He does not hesitate to accept it, the prize, but before he receives the velvet pillow he adjusts his watch. He wants to receive said object when the clock strikes twelve; this public mythology must coincide with a factor in his private one. He will accept the pillow and start into the first sentence of thanks, with the culminating thought, "whenever the clock strikes twelve and they award something for which I am the last remaining person, then for me this metaphorizes the night-watchman state that takes care of its burglars and puts them in a subsidized burglar villa where they . . . my god you are all so kind to me today I really did think . . . you already know all of it anyway . . ." He *would* doubtless behave this way and, fidgeting with his wrist, stop only briefly, if I *had* given him a real watch with which he could quickly produce twelve o'clock, with a leg up so to speak. I gave him a toy watch. Which refuses to be toyed with. Which will teach it to him, it.

If someone doesn't know that an action produces nothing, then he can repeat his action as often as he likes. Or have it repeated by a now dull-witted subordinate. Each time it happens futilely. A proposition: this action does not happen a touch more futilely every new time that it happens, but it does happen a degree more clearly every time. He too will realize this in due time. What again? For instance, what if the toy watch that I bought for him, if I remember correctly, at a second-hand stand outside the zoo can't be set to twelve? The hand is clenched with the hand at an obtuse angle. Sun for all, shade for none: this can no longer be the theme of the laudatory speech; the hesitation has gone on for too long; an artificially dentured foot-scuffling embarrassment-based throat clearing has, with bared, gleaming pivot teeth, built for him the last golden bridge leading to the Inevitable. Fascinated, he has participated in himself. The ancient, thousand-year-old presenter was not able to put up with this for very long. And he began to batter away at him with the lectern lamp.

The prize-refuser, who has taken it off and suddenly fit the sprocket back into it, the right way—even that was pointless, all in all, because it has no clockwork installed in it—the candidate, who is hesitating and letting his hesitation congeal, suddenly senses, if not the passage of time, then at least the breath of urgency, the pressure of haste. He is possibly fabricating internally, not visible externally because it is so small, a swooning shortness of breath, a strained deep breathing, stress on the innocent bleeding organs. The realms before his eyes grow gray, turning into true twilight, which he brightens up with his own lamp.

The most beautiful landscape is a whitish sailcloth. Above it is a dry buzzing and splashing. Trees and logs sharpened into stakes at the top stab into the firmament. The lake is dark blue and is starting to produce a tiny mean dangerous billow; it tilts back a reed stalk and brings a dead fish closer. The white slender diving bird forgets its calling and stays under after diving. Near the red buoy it is ejected. In the meantime the buzzard has suffocated and a child is standing on its chest in order to reach up to the jam cupboard. From the cubbyhole it removes a still-living dog-faced jay with mouse-remains in its flews. It stares slack and apparently hypnotized at the autobahn and alights on the head of the child. It wants to let itself get run over and takes a step forward and is dragged along by a large white mouse. The mouse is too big for the jay's horny claw. In the trunk of its car the landscape shows the man with the most rapidly inflicted critical injury of the weekend. He is lying between the seedlings that were emptied into the sag of a deck chair. Red and white stripes, in two hours the morning will be breaking, one more morning. For a long time now the morning has no longer been cost-free. In a wind that spreads the yew branches at their tips and makes two flat boats nod against each other, the sailcloth droops. The landscape is rolled around the mast, and the mast is thrust into the hysterically fluffed-up flank. He starts to bawl, not waiting for the reading lamp to be driven under his skin. He bawls away.

None of this is seen from the back rows, and all of this happens to the candidate who has failed this time as soon as I put in my vote for him. He can't help it that I've bought him a watch, at the second-hand stand where you can get them for a song. He can't help it if I've plunged him into motionlessness in which he puts up with the onslaught of the emotion-extinguishing jury; he is bent over his own arm, visible coloration of the face, and a vivid fur color shows on his cheeks: he has now shifted away from the wise man into the vicinity of the sturdily chewing Scotland sheep.

. . . and all of this because of that crummy watch with two identical, stuck-together hands that was bought for him by me at the second-hand stand at or outside the zoo. He, the candidate, has my support; I give it to him from the wicker chair. The wicker chair is caned, dividing my poor back into little meatballs, flesh gathered together into fingery bulges, flesh that pushes through the meshwork of the chair like mushy stuff at the butcher's. Get going with his prize! I shout. If I shout it long enough, I'll get it, because I'll be better known than he is, one day. Incidentally, it's just a matter of showing up at the podium on time . . .

He, my candidate, who is he? The foolhardy supposition that it's Hecht is hereby ventured. Wasn't too difficult either. Considering the personnel that one can get by without nowadays. Certainly it's Robert who's being talked about here, and by others besides me. That others come to mind and not just myself surprises me. There must be some malfunction. Of an intellectual sort. Most pleasant. No longer alone. No longer entirely.

Not entirely like that. That's not how things are supposed to work. Hecht twists his winding button. He is seized by rutting, rutting for the prize that he's supposed to get at midday today. Hecht wants to produce twelve o'clock quickly, so that he can pick it up sooner. Maybe: prize be on your way. Here I'm permitted to get sentimental. Adieu, prize, farewell and be on your way. He twists away at his winding button. Twenty to twelve? A quarter to one? Between them there's nothing. Sixty-five minutes have gone up in smoke. He cranks away at his winding button. It happens. In vain. Now the fourth boy has started bawling too. The infirm old-man candidate, shuffling with his alpenstock, jolts onto the platform of his insight that everything would be over soon, and he frees the laudatory speech from the zipper of the youngest lady in enraptured attendance. Her face spontaneously says: the script calls for me to smile here, but it also calls for you to see through it. Shaky and mumbling, desperately somehow weeping water, Hecht twists the winding button.

And it is by the frequency of the repetitions that occur before it pauses in discouragement that the learning ability of my victim is calculated. Dullards require twenty to fifty times. Before even they see clearly. Something happens. Something doesn't happen. Once again they jam the reading lamp into his side. That's how nice everything is for Robert. And why? I bought him a watch. Twelve o'clock? Shadow border? Courage, courage, this is only the fifteenth stroke.

## 16

The officer's mess of the 85th Dividend Division was on leave in France. Hecht along with it. He crossed the service bridge, scanned the strings of tracks, made a mental note of the placement of the semaphore signals, went home to the veranda, took a sun bath, then down the steps into the railway station itself, asked the stationmaster next to the slightly greasy second-class waiting room: "Where is he?"—He must have left on a train; the way things stood, there was nothing left to do but go away, and doubtless he had had trouble explaining his departure to them, so instead of long elucidations he had made short work of turning words into deeds. "No idea," said the stationmaster and disappeared into his rather soapy office. In front of a stand, H. ate an ice cream that melted out of the cone onto his fingers, then headed up the path between the bath houses, past the thatched roofs, past the green light into the Restaurant Central, schnitzel with rice, then continuing with his day's program, indoor pool and twenty reps with the leg scissors. He had to use a private railway schedule, none of the trains for the past week would have been possible for him; or he had sent for one to come for him, a wacko idea! Then across the shunting tracks into every little station building, investigation—a ridiculous one—of the switchpoint lights, later a question to the trackman: "Where is he? Did you see him leaving on a trip?"—"Dunno, nope, don't have anything and I seen even less than that," he answered and disappeared into the clapboard shed. The station was going off the tracks, and if he hadn't been looking for the other guy, he would have sat down, as long as the description remained so simple, in order to sketch a murderous image of the empty depots. Then he gradually got beside himself, damaged like an envelope that is not stitched back up after the contents have been removed, back to the veranda, where the warming beams made his discontentment with the times disappear. He had always been a big nervous bladder, and the other guy had too. His front door was very heavy, beveled at the edges, the doorbell didn't work anymore since a cable that went past the heater was singed, a fuse was blown, and the electrical system too was short-circuited, so that water damage was the only thing that would have increased the comfort to the level of a palace; the electricity, radio room, bedroom, shower, toilet, kitchen, corridor, closet, radio room chased each other in circles; it was possible that the radio was to blame for everything. Soup, he thought, and late in the afternoon he heard the exclamation, very clearly: "I've got him!"—before starting over again from the beginning. It had been, to put it wrong but quickly, funny in spite of the astounding degree of coldness in which they had spent and formed the night, a seamy night.

Edwin Hummel, the festival man, an un-Dionysian of nearly Blue-Crossian proportions, was presented with the ultimatum of either keeping up till he had to quit, or to quit if he couldn't stand it, instead of giving the merry attendees a hangover with the missionary zeal of his abstinences. Alfons Hadig dropped to his knees in his mind, but with devoted longing laid a boiling monologue to his velvet cat on that ice that even the assembled elephant herd, in spite of or because of its soul-trampling lock-trot, was not capable of breaking. Alex Wander, who a few days of his past ago had had his furnishings pawned by petition, assiduously acted the tormented lover, who in spite of an unfailing lack of backbone would not be granted the lot of pillow pasha to a yet unemancipated woman—he treated every woman too well, so that a growing luxuriance and rebelliousness were the consequence. "That is just like Buffon's needle problem," Hummel giggled, "If ell is less than ess, then how great can the probability be that they will intersect when dropped?" "In German," said

Margaret, "'to free oneself' when applied to a woman means 'to take off one's clothes,' and this is the German language's contribution to female emancipation, the language as the female correctional officer for all male pigs." Hadig, putting his monologue on a back burner that could not be far enough back for him, calmed her down with the flat of a hand that waggled gently in space and belied everything virile. Bruno-Theo Essen, de-coated and standing on a broad foot, streamed his staggering tartar into the palate of an immaculate pepsodentress, with the explanation that as an individual and herbal amateur he planted two spindle trees and hydrangea in his rooftop garden that were making a show of their new offshoots in the rain. Margaret held her pointed hands folded over the calvados in a smoking drinking-prayer, while the cushiony balls of Laura's thumbs hesitated their way up Edwin's lapel: a lurking monitor lizard in the tropical sun in the equinox. Hecht, shuddering at his own gumption, asked the plump woman, "Have you read one of the Tropics? It doesn't matter which one. In Cancer there is a passage that is a sheer verbal treasure trove." Hadig's shadow was outlined on the pale wall with an almost cozy mood of dreariness as Anacreontic Writing on the Wall, with the cylinder battery. Ann smiled in spite of the excitement that had been caused in her by the circumstance that an invitation had originally also been conveyed to Therese, the trackman's daughter, perhaps at night and from mouth to mouth; after all, the gentlemen studying at the university were on vacation and were not being so strict about it.

Atop the formally successful *réchaud à gaz* Hecht distilled his insidious one-hundred-and-twelve-proof liquor from five kinds of kind-hearted juniper before he—it was time for this—showed the cutely awkward humor that everyone was used to from him: he laughed in the direction of Ann, the peaceful producer of aura and grace, and offered her, as if to any given stenotypist, a proposal of marriage, deceptively friendly and maliciously cheerful, for he captured her with ingenuousness and changed his tune as soon as they had had a few, which was inevitable, and in the general wasteland they bit on the iridescent bait, which never flashed. Not without pleasure Margaret became the witness of how he, drink-mixing, exposed Ann to an ambivalent permanent blotchiness and she opined, in smart and rhythmically ripped-up fragments: "Yes, Robert, and don't go to so much effort with her, she wants and elsewise take!" It was the evening when Wander, if he had been able to, would have wound himself up into a proffered fist, until the bout was past; but who was supposed to proffer him a therapeutic fist? Bruno-Theo, maybe, that sniveling person? Ann, whose hand Hecht had once shaken, drummed a few dark techniques sprung from said hand into Bruno-Theo; Essen's palate, in its hollowed-out helplessness, extended its besieging, woe!, non-ingratiating atmospheric nimbus toward the female lecturer; teachresses intimidated him to the point of disappearing. On Essen's neck, two red, soon scraped spots, because Essen, as the result of a misunderstanding, had appeared at the celebration, for the sake of special merriment and smiling and floating, in a Carnival disguise. He was probably supposed to be a giant mouse, wearing a protruding stuck-on nose with drips and a choker that put his face in a vise so that every sideways glance was a torment; it was a sort of head-screw at neck height; in addition this blind man's bustard wore a magnificent tailored suit of white rat skins and two magnificent glued-on muttonchops, which, when he, full to the brim, dared the first contradictions, slipped over his jaws on a vertical path into his shirt, while Laura, expecting this disintegration for some time, swung at this man who was coming apart at the seams, her round-bellied glass three-quarters full of Hecht-brandy. Star of my flame, you burn me terribly in the shadowy place, Hecht declaimed, the He of the evening, slipping from the most childish allusions into urgent unambiguity, and he raised his ceaselessly distilling arms in a step-by-step unfolding up to his shoulders so that in Erlenmayer there was a hissing brewing and a nearly mental roaring, and he splayed the glass flask, grabbed by the neck, away from himself, to let the high-proof nova finish its fusion reaction; in addition, his circumspect ergasiophygophyte, famous for this initial reserve, needed the officious time for consideration; the She, Ann, on the other hand, kept her gaze focused strictly inward, on her implanted Gutenberg-Richter scale, the natural, velvet-draped seismograph that announced the quake to her, and at the same time she reveled as if she were deliberately holding back the ultimate, the subject matter, in Cameroon's skyscrapers, in which natives, sitting on their haunches, whittled their scarred, whittled-down cult figures; quite alone and without any accompaniment she had been there, she said, she had intruded on her own initiative and seen the mahogany chips falling; one especially dark man had asked her with a throaty voice, his whittling knife hanging from his arm, for a gratuity, which generously had not been given. The cult figure thus acquired, a slim one with nine probably overpowerful penoid features, she would bring along the next time she got an invitation. "Oh, I see," said Hecht dismissively, "you mean something like this; I'd like to know who the people in a cult like that choose as their minister of culture." At every giggle from then on, Ann hopped onto her fat feet in order to inspect, breathing heavily from the effort, the ongoing events at this stage of the festivities, and to sink back down onto her shamelessly checkered sofa seat and to spread out a bit of lip vermilion with the tip of her tongue, which made Therese stare rather unsympathetically but honestly spellbound at this obstinately unreserved and yet sealed mouth, which, still without Hecht, was already shedding color while lipping to itself, every inch a testimony of a rococo lonesomely thirsting for the appropriate signet. It had been terribly funny, and Hecht, after the last round of drinks, had plunged into the turrets.

You can never know, he thought, you will never be able to know, what drives her to do it. For me it was comical and ridiculous, but I can't figure out that foreplay, that's her job. The other man was lying in the room, his shirt next to him. "What have you done?" he asked him. Nudged, the other man rolled over flat on his stomach; he must have kept going until the wee hours and poisoned himself with his own booze. "What were you able to do with her?" he asked. The other man did not make a sound and stayed belly-down, with one arm angled under him. His hair was playing in the breeze coming through the window, and there was no reflection on his dilated eye. He turned him over and looked at him. So that's why. I didn't suspect that, but of course. He must have been lying outside on the garden chair, and that's where she found him and carried him inside. She, as the more rewarding object, should have been the one he was looking for, but she was sleeping upstairs next to Therese, who had now gotten the picture as well. I wouldn't have thought she was up to it. I always thought he'd lay her on the tracks and take off by train if anything like that ever happened to him. After he had pulled the window shut from the outside, he shuffled back to the palace in tennis shoes. Time to strap on the feedbag. The train to Angoulême was just speeding through.

## 17

Crisis everywhere. No acceptable job was open. There was nothing Hecht could apply for. Even at the fire insurance company he did not find that little position that was supposed to have kept him warm through the winter. He did not have the choice between several offers, e.g., in a ministry that had suddenly become depopulated and was looking for an un-used-up pioneer. All of his honest efforts stood under a bad sign. Robert could not remain the man he was, for if he were to become somebody, a change was required. Unlike his services. Unfortunately, on close inspection, Hecht could no longer very well become the assistant to the chief financial officer. Money had been abolished for several weeks, and the civil service of the City of Birth and Death, which was now in the red, was living on the barter system. One fish in exchange for half a woven basket. In the allotment gardens they went hunting for blackbirds, and whoever used to spend Sundays stitching tapestries in the bright warm alkaline air was now trying to dispose of his products in exchange for a good draft horse. Hecht's position in the network of these transactions would not serve his interests; in any case, he lacked the sound training that would have done him some good in this altered system. No single good old-fashioned ingenious idea would take the bearer of all incompetencies, namely Hecht, as high up as he, before he got ensnared, wished to go. He cast off the last of his personal initiative like so much body odor.

A large poster with a photograph of the rooms and victims of a typewriting school. The fact that they, the victims, are staring more or less in a state of bloodlust at the wall with the flashing demonstration keyboard provides them with their only possible relief. As accompaniment they are spicing things up by panting *pshaw*, *oof*, *howgh*, *aye*; things relinquished to the margins, deletions. Nightmares slink into the secretaries' finger pads, and the slick gentlemen sit with their weighty, unused brows, without propping themselves up on their elbows, because permission to do so is not given.

The prerequisites for successful productivity faded with every minute that he let pass by without a fundamental decision. Turn himself inside out like a vest? But was he less deformable than a vest? The body whose form he would have fit had not been found. The way it seemed to Hecht, success suddenly didn't mean so much to him anymore that he would want to throw himself into energetic sacrifices for its sake. He made inquiries with the new mid-level cadres. He endeavored to achieve choice forms of politeness, and soon the last chance had been forfeited. I tried to exchange Hecht's old but hardly used writer's chair for a still-edible flounder. They explained to him at the exchange center that they had already laid down the rules for material compensation: wood for wood, meat for meat, coal for coal, and if need be a well-built foxy man for a well-built foxy woman. As far as food went, if you didn't have any of your own to offer, now you couldn't get any more. Hecht asked the cadres at the exchange center on what basis a deal could be struck, whether on the basis of connections, or on the basis of bribery, or on the basis of an extremely abbreviated stint of service learning from scratch. They ordered him to cut a trial piece out of himself that was still edible or else looked like it was still edible.

Anatomical refinements trigger convulsions of the diaphragm, and the shameful defect produces cruel, microscopic comedies; if the hand that could spade up the garden as a shovel, lamenting loudly, slaps on the typewriter keys so that the little hammers get hung up on each other just before they hit paper, then the tender little spatula finger gets jammed in the keyboard and when twisted back out defaces every business letter; fortunately everything here remains an essay, even that which bears blurred handwriting; concentration is limned on the faces of the examinee who is brought up to tempo. A genuine period of concentration with a nine o'clock break.

When Robert realized what a mess he'd gotten himself into, he would have liked to call his future employer, the chief financial officer, in order to inform him about himself. No big surprise, the telephone was destroyed. The little iron hook on which he hung up the receiver moved from back to front instead of from top to bottom. The failure to establish contact left Robert a good part of his privacy. And what a privacy it was! Everything in it belonged to him like the contents of a pocket, and he felt that every one of his gestures meant "homeland." And elsewise: with contact: others were carrying out a plundering of familiar values on Hecht: because he was supposed to make them familiar with him, they were gradually, by baby steps and by cruelly humorous bunny hops, making him a stranger to himself. Hecht could not explain his future self to the chief financial officer.

The faces have nothing to do with—which can be disregarded in this context—with putting on faces. No put-on face is made into a game, if for no other reason than that the expression of feelings is an indescribable expression, which a few measly sorrow muscles cannot conjure up around a friendly mouth. The eyes are semi-totally wide open; after all, the eye is a sphere of which too much remains in the dark. The finger totalities hover, ready to type, suspended blades being threatened with the guillotine; hence the at worst bittersweet lightness in the stress of maximum speed: nooses laid out by the school principal are drowned out by the clatter of gallows humor. Hecht, the boss would like a word with you.

"Have you, Robert Hecht, participated in the typewriting course required by us?"

"I attended the commercial course at the Joyce Berlitz School."

"How did you hear about Berlitz?"

"I heard someone talking about his course in the sauna; I . . ."

"I trust you, that's fine, you heard me right, I don't want to see your certificates. Your confident demeanor is sufficient for me."

"I beg of you. I beg of you. Now my speech will go off on a tangent: I also took part in the Alpha Typing Course at the Alfred Poglmann School. My speech will return from the tangent: I will say: I beg of you."

"What do you beg of me?"

"I beg of you to be permitted to express to you my gratitude. Tangent: Is my statement both affirmative as well as grammatically topnotch?"

"But I beg of *you*. Expressing gratitude is permitted."

"My ankles are getting all fat from lack of formality, sir."

"No trouble at all, Hecht. In single file off to the sauna, belly to ass, ho, please, after you."

"Ho. Tangent: that is a good sound. Return tangent: Ho. Commentary: Har har!"

Hecht could not explain his future self to his superior, but he would have wished to incite him to solidarity throughout all executive suites with the innuendo that they both spoke the same language equally poorly. For this reason, I assume, and only for this reason, I've convinced myself that in this way and only in this way did my job search produce nothing, not least because there were no more jobs, which left only the search. Every time Bob Hecht went after a job, the cadres eliminated it and established exchange centers, in the knowledge of the fact that he could not work at an exchange center. As soon as it was obvious that this world had run away from him, he became small. He had to quickly betake himself into his interior and there draw consolation from himself, from his unique penetrance, which he cultivated as an insatiable loser. The first thing Robert did was to annihilate his pleasures. He did not make the mistake of demanding all too much of himself, just to descend—given the incompetence that could be expected of him—into the accustomed disconsolation. He demanded *everything* of himself; thus he made his way via a small detour to the same disconsolation. At least it was enough for a disappointment—which added itself to his disconsolation—when his meteoric career came to an end before it had begun; now all that was left was a meteorite. Similarly, Bob, that Hecht, had the opportunity to get to know himself as someone who never pressed onward to his decisions, and they were actually set long before he could make them. At that time he stood before his individual as a threatening example and murmured threateningly that those capable of decisions were pursued by the decisions they put off until later all the way into their sleep, their dream-filled sleep.

"Have you, Roberta Hecht, surreptitiously transformed yourself into a woman?" "I'll start with a tangent: I also subjected myself to the Alfred Hürlmann course. Now may I respond to your question: the follow-up question is: What did you say?" "I'll be doggone, Bob, would you look at that Wattenwyl woman!"

"Yeah, I will in a minute, my thin neck doesn't seem to want to whip around, okay, now I can see the Wattenwyl woman. Is that Ann, the widow, up there by all those Leitz file binders?" "Ann, the widow, Bob, has improved her situation by leaps and bounds."

"I would also like to inform you that I am also regularly attending Count Hilmore's English courses. In England they dubbed him a Sir before he gave back his citizenship and moved over here. Hilmore knows Annie Watt-Wylie and testifies that she exhibits a little talent, har har."

"Annie the Widow sweeps the paper clips into envelopes."

"So that, pardon me, due to the autumn balance sheets I still cannot present a diploma in accounting."

"But Bobby, that's not what I meant. Would you please have the playful intrusiveness to cast an unmistakable glance for me now at Ann Wattenwyl's jumping musculature; that's what's meant by hopping around; when Annie bends over, Count Hilmore or no Count Hilmore . . . I have assigned to her to attend to the lower Leitz file binders, so that she has to get down on her knees once in a while. Please comment."

"Har har."

"I thank you for this fine observation; indeed; you guessed right; that's all I'm thinking about."

A small worry was resolved, and Hecht felt lighter and even a little worse. After money had been abolished as a means of payment, he did not have to suffer so much from his poverty prestige; in this regard, the economic restructuring to which they had not invited him stood him in good stead. He was convinced that the mid-level cadres had forgotten him, and it was equally beyond doubt that they had done it on purpose. No more acceptable jobs were being created, and the people who remained, the leftovers, the not-yet-laid-off bivouacked in the departments, crouched in the leg spaces of the desks and passed each other flounders through the keyholes. The politeness with which Hecht spoke to them bowled him over. He would never have thought he could manage that, but he managed it. Without further ado they intimated to him that they . . .

. . . absurd story . . .

. . . that they were able to get along without him. They spoke right through him or away from him, so that he received their words only after they had banged into a wall. Or with a slight displeasure that clouded their brows—and made Robert, who was dependent on these brows, pale!—they divulged that they got along better without Hecht than they would with him. Thus Bob, in contrast to Ann, had become a useless human being, and now he sought his yet more useless human being in order to kick him and to comfort him, for nothing was so comforting as the possibility of being able oneself to offer comfort, and nothing healed kick bruises better than being able oneself to deliver bruising kicks. Because the possibility that Hecht was not looking for a job at all, and really liked doing nothing, could not be casually dismissed, then the assumption that, if something could still be done, he would have been very unhappy, was at least a possibility. With the value standards that are not yet being passed on to the cadres, Hecht attempted to give himself a meaning, at least a bleak, inept, absolutely traditional meaning, before the spark went out. Behind my chair, peculiarly enough behind my old writer's chair, I dragged him home. Home had fortunately remained a warm little place. At the time, on the tiring way back, it became clear to me that I would go fishing so that I could trade in a small fresh whiting for a small whiting that was at most a couple of months older and rottener; even though . . .

. . . Robert was still young, and the purchase made him feel good. His continuing education had homed in on the required goals, and his temporary stay abroad had lasted one long, uneventful year. Not only were the concerns of so-called "marketing" no longer a secret to Robert, but he also actually stood up for them appreciatively. The markets spread out like towels on a bathing beach, and a host of publications bore the flamethrowers, Robert's main banner title headlines, into the most remote spots; even the locality of Mud Hole South collectively took out authentic fire insurance. Robert did not lack personal initiative; contacts, including those with rural clientele, were easily established; with a few strokes of the pen he knew how to set up distribution plans and to feed his gigantic advertising budget to the various sharks that had divided the public up amongst themselves. Once even two hundred thousand by night and rain, for the circumvention of a functional hierarchy in which no shark was ever allowed to leave his place once it had been assigned to him unless he got promoted and helped the promotion along with support from his own resources. All sharks saved up for self-promotion that was intended to raise them onto a platform into which more resources flowed. But the costs of self-promotion rose at the same time. After the sharks had secured themselves the right to regular monitoring, fewer promotions took place, possibly only in the dimensions of half a billion. Robert was more or less equal to the demands of his job description; when the demands of being a shark had risen over his head, the sharks rose up and Hecht remained below. No! Shortly before Robert was about to give himself up, they sank, the demands did, or everything was delegated over his head; in any case, his tenure was extended, and he was able to keep the roughest business at bay. But what was the roughest? Well, it must have been what the sharks considered to be the roughest; if Robert looked at them, then they revealed themselves to him; the more devastating his gaze, the more the sharks revealed to him; but the more devastating his gaze, the more it invited communication, and they seized the opportunity; if a certain amount of therapeutic tolerance still prevailed—and for them this was not even in short supply, but was something that they never even felt in the short supply or in the shorts supply—then the accumulated complaints beat the path of least resistance to every one of Robert's safety doors . . .

. . . sharks wanted to relieve themselves, by no means change themselves, and probably relieve themselves all the more urgently the longer they wanted to keep hold of themselves; did sharks want anything at all? The question "what do you want from me?" didn't get you anything more than a derailment, followed by a teeth-gnashing silence (one that filed the teeth down to the jaw-bone!); they noticed that someone was listening to them, and the sharks had already gotten to the point where with this discovery they felt caught in the act and looked over their shoulders, wished for a quiet rug under their shoes, and commanded a "do not tell anyone else" into Hecht, which made it impossible for Hecht to pass on to sharks the Leitz-binder-bound emotion-dulling pain that had collected within him and which he had moreover carefully cast off . . .

"You're thinking of your apparatus, boss, which cannot throw a punch."

"You took the courses, Bobby; for gosh sakes, what a good job you did!"

"If I may allow myself this remark; is Fräulein Ann the widow Watt-and-so-forth?"

"For gosh sakes. Her pleasing countenance and the way she stands there motionless are proof enough for me."

"That doesn't prove much. I will speak a tangent as an aside: Where does he obtain the certainty that my motionlessness is a proof of harmlessness?"

"For what I need you for, you can use what Berlitz taught you."

"This heat. I will sob a tangent: You do not know me, and may my movement, which is a deeply personal one, preserve me in a condition of unfamiliarity to you!"

"I'm losing the thread here. Shall we regard this as a casual conversation in an informal atmosphere?"

"This heat."

"For gosh sakes."

. . . was able to keep the roughest business at bay. Used his continued active work on the path he'd already set out on to build up those marketing strategies that should have pumped up the shrinking markets again. Li'l Bobby's battle for other people's markets: they won; Hecht melted away under the hands of the newspapers and advertisers, certainly in accordance with the law. The hectic tone of the fire insurance campaigns in particular (slogan: "Any fire that brings light to the darkness can save lives," with a graphic above it showing an isolated farmstead frizzling in its own hay and a matchstick retouched into the skull of the aggrieved owner, a light went off in his head, and in this "aha" moment he realized that from now on only insurance could cover all of the buildings . . .), along with the serial fire of the series of ads, was slaying Hecht. At a minimum he believed he would have to die squeezed out; at least at first no evening passed without death. Later Hecht noticed that he, instead of dying from this, could actually live quite well off it; the honorarium, a concept that, deriving from the Roman language, had to do with honor, was dizzyingly high. One good slogan outweighed 45 pages of the private prose that Robert produced for himself in the evenings; it was definitely worth it to keep your mouth shut for that much, and to start enjoying those social benefits while at the same time verbally battling against their further expansion, with the honorable threat that the "welfare state will be the end." The threat did not mention whose end was meant; being able to formulate the threat in ever new, similarly rousing slogans was sufficient to get him accepted into a political party that was not content merely to express slogans, but ultimately got serious about their contents; application for acceptance rejected; the welfare state kept its distance from that party even without late-bourgeois attempts at a final solution, and permitted Hecht to firmly establish his mode of operation.

No sooner had he arrived in his new work area, that is, Mud Hole South, than he sent an application to Big Brother, a super-conglomerate that was blue in the face from its appetite, and which not only published the advertisers and newspapers, but also, when necessary, put the brakes on them, extinguished them with foam, or made them disappear, so that Hecht—negotiations were continuing intangibly—lived with the impression that he was ceaselessly investing his budget in a gigantic editor-dump where everyone who had anything to do with Bob's little old mouth had to deal with the bluish Brother the next morning, whereupon the next day Bob carried out the negotiations with someone else, until a slight dissent over the nature of the spongy compromise that these negotiations were to achieve knocked this man too off his chair and bestowed upon Hecht a fresh, if already somewhat used-up, vis-à-vis. There were some weeks when Hecht ate up to five negotiating partners for breakfast, leaving no leftovers, as a sort of fuel for the weekend, when he gobbled up another one and half of them. On Sunday, unfortunately, because he was late getting down to work, he only ate half a one. Everyone who was transferred and finished off gave him the energy for tackling the next one; and on Sunday, in the evening: Robert himself was summoned and then enjoyed the skin-temperature showers that the dominion of the great Merciful Ones let rain down upon him.

Not so tempestuously! His application with the handwritten résumé (he couldn't even read his own handwriting), five bust portraits in profile and two short publications went to the assigned human-resources consultant, who after a week's time for consideration called him into his office to suggest to him in a veiled way that he was, just like himself, the consultant, his employers' man. The authorized agent for handwriting, a manu-scripter . . .

. . . even while still on probation—that's what it was called, wasn't it?—Hecht, now in his element, dispensed with every exam with the manu-scripter. Lightly flowered curtains fluttered graciously over sparse furnishings, and everything that was hollow inside was lockable as securely as a safe. Robert's apples and sandwiches lay protected behind five-inch armor plates. For fresh air, a special key had to be turned in an attached device (nothing mysterious—in the event of misconduct the key was not taken away as a punishment but it was repulsively beautiful). A sector of sunlight cast the pencil-sharpening machine huge and black onto the wall, its crank the crank of a laundry press, immobile on its axle, waiting. The dying storyteller presented the shattering drama of a man who contrary to his own reassurances had learned not to grow old and weak. Presumably, his parents, like nearly all parents, had neglected to teach their youngest and then merely young son how to grow old, how to turn gray with decorum and dignity . . .

"Hechtie, how did it go with the boss in the sauna?"

"This evening, if you can imagine that, he's going to dictate his life story to me so I can write it down."

"Oh, is he still alive?"

"It will be a gigantic tome, written in a completely linear fashion. In his middle age he experienced enough to fill a phone book."

"Are you going to tell him, Hechtie, all the other things you're capable of doing?"

"He played a significant role in the practical adaptation of nuclear energy to the operation of tabletop calculators and he wants to demonstrate the atomically derived cube root of five to me in his room."

"Hechtie, is he going to drive you home?"

"He is an established man."

"Do you like the work?"

"After having attended my courses, a fiasco ought to be out of the question. The rooms and participants of the typing course have been photographically recorded."

"But Robert, you . . ."

"Unemployed before long."

"Like a million others."

Because youth was a good or even the best argument for the sale of the human commodity, the aging author ("I not only set pen to paper, but traps as well") was not only selling poorly; he should have, shrewd as he was even without experience, kept his distance from a sale in which someone who was selling fire insurance policies had to sell himself as well, preferably to someone who was buying him because he in turn had to sell himself by taking someone whom he could entrust with his sale, if it turned out that the novice could be bought for any kind of sale. It was unwise for the aging author to continue relying on the mediation of bought-and-paid-for personnel or on the salability of his skills. He should have turned his back on his current occupation. Meanwhile he amused a Hecht who, as he had sworn in the oath that he had made during a serious illness, showered him with consolation and with kicks, then with renewed consolation and renewed kicks, then with consolation kicks, until Hecht felt the onset of healing, or he pictured healing, or he imagined healing that would become a healing because the illness to be healed away was based on imagination, because everything was only imaginary, but imagination was the world and life . . .

"The hammers of the typewriter. The mishaps, accidents, and the torment when you whack yourself, and the disgusting waxed paper shoved under my fingers, which blots me out."

"He will want to write you off at a favorable rate and get rid of you as fast as a stockjobber."

"Har har. I'm gonna go off on a tangent: I am hiding my tangentialness. Tangent: har har."—"We'll keep our fingers crossed for you."

"Soon it will be all over. In the fall I'm going to quit for good. By then my hated, spatula-shaped things will have become well nourished, standardized machine-typist fingers."

"All the best until it's over."

"Same to you."

"Fingers."

"All the best."

"Come. You like me. Come on, go on with you!"

"I love you, Hechtie."

"Now all of a sudden, though, tears of smiling are commencing, so to speak, to abandon my eyes."

The author was silent. As if he felt he was above asking for help out loud. If Hecht had jabbed him with his finger, instead of "Help!" the scribe would have cried out "Can I help you?" Robert shoved some money his way, across the paperweight. If young folks were cunning salespeople, then old folks were skilled beggars. If at the time of his employment with Big Blue-in-the-Face Brother (BBFB+Co.) Hecht had had the choice between a young author and an old beggar cawing for recompense and redemption, then he would not have known which one to give preference to. Not even after a glance at the sales chart. Since Mud Hole South, in spite of the fire insurance policy that really should have brought on a fire, did not burn down for three whole years, Hecht's position in the Central Slogan Office in the ocean of sharks had become weak enough for a discharge . . .

. . . for the long term . . .

. . . dangerousness with a bright, rather strong baring of teeth . . .

. . . marine prey . . .

. . . all in a row, teeth that is . . .

## 18

The present holds no more work in store for me. That used to be different; when the time that is past was not yet past, everything was different. Two hundred years ago, the eighteenth century wore me out so much that it almost made me neglect the seventeenth century. And yet it had so much in store for me; three hundred years ago, whatever was different was still resolutely different, and there were things for me to do, for me who was gradually sliding into a get-deeds-done fitness with which I custom-tailored all of those crisis-shaken Palão buddies to fit my hungry, now yellowish body. *Tempi passati*, I would have to treat myself again to the carbonated tingle of an abbreviated anecdotal revue and, with all manner of blandishments of a verbal, reminiscing nature, talk myself into a state of unconsciousness that encompasses the twentieth century and obscures my consciousness of this century; it was never bright (my consciousness), and it will never be bright (the century), he will always talk big (the evocator). With no prospects for making a living, but also without the threat hanging over my head of a renewed contact with an outside person for the purpose of reapplying for a job in the working world that at some later point will never open up after all, I performed ("so young and already so historical") a few cerebral moves on the board of past, imperfect possibilities that had never been my own and would never be my own: possibilities that, no sooner acknowledged than seized, taken advantage of, and SOLVED in the sense of a problem, would never take me into consideration in the majestic spectacle of their illustriousness. But I would take them into consideration, at least a representative selection from among them, soon to be three hundred years old. It used to be that a possibility was something that was present, and no sooner was its realization present than the possibility had vanished for ever, until . . . I know what I want to remember again now, it shouldn't push itself to the fore, or in the end, the end . . .

Seventeen hundred and a few odd years. Bob summarized the mathematical theories of combination and probability, and then I invented the electrostatic generator and had a few corrals of gray horses pull on the Magdeburg hemispheres while I was sketching a meteorological wind map with my left hand, worked myself to the point of collapse in theoretical physics, experimented with casting mirror glass, and published my wave theory, which for a long time had been in the drawer to which I suddenly found the key again, when I recalled a double bottom. After that I constructed the simplest steam engine that I could think of ("a most humble piston rod for your excellence, Count von . . ."), then a sketch for a submersible boat which I could use to classify all submarine fauna according to their anatomy: after only a brief time I categorized the whale among the mammals; it probably took about a week, in which I did nothing smarter, nothing less smart, nothing else, and nothing divergent. This classification was fiercely opposed by the ichthyologists, but I was the victor in the end, sitting and spraying the inside of my wig on the stack of my brochures, in which pectoral fins of newly conceived whale young were yellowing.

Overnight ("the nights two centuries ago knew that they were to remain unmentioned for two centuries; likewise the nights three centuries ago") it was unexpectedly plausible to me that plants also reproduced sexually, how quickly?, and the clock with cylinder escapement was already thrown out, it pulsated a few times, and then I also knew that the frog larvae were suffering from a blood bypass, and in rapid haste I described peppermint, and thus eleven or more years had passed. They were active years. I was needed and I found no substitute for myself; I didn't look for one either, for if I had found a substitute for genius . . . what effort it would have taken to make it clear to him, the substitute, that even if a substitute had been found, there couldn't possibly be any substitute for me! Furthermore, it was up to me to finally annul the Edict of Nantes, and there were continents calling for me, I whose reputation preceded me to such an extent that I would have embraced any spot of soil on which I was not yet famous and settled it for further exploitation of its minerals and its resources.

Edict annulled, so that the Huguenots could flee to Brandenburg, painstaking persecution organized, the League of Augsburg had to be overpowered before the personal union between Austria and Hungary was carried out; presumably I came too late, because thanks to my negligence the War of the Palatinate Succession broke out without my assistance; for two years a side effect of my activity was that no one was able to call it a provocation of war; a side effect that took no effect for the reason that when it could have taken effect, I had long since become a war provocateur; what all didn't he do just for the sake of doing something while the period of the century elapsed, indigestible and yet consumed right up until the last second of its existence.

A hope was fulfilled when the Turks were defeated in Bosnia and Serbia; I had predicted this and made myself into an accomplice to the fulfillment of my prophecy. Nothing was easier than prognoses like this, as soon as I got a grasp of the events, and nothing more ever happened without the person who foresaw it. Thus I made every one of my intentions into an announcement. Not only did I give information to the effect that as the bookkeeper of the first East India Company I would break ground for Calcutta, but I actually did break that ground. In return I drove the French out of Siam and, with the utmost urgency, I established the first of January as the beginning of the year. On April fifth, calculated from that point three months later, I edited something compiled; an address book. So that they would be accessible, night and day, it made the administration more effective ("the foundation of all efficiency"), and since I had assumed the leadership of the Quakers, I had to push through all of the legislation in Pennsylvania. I wasn't familiar with Pennsylvania, the laws were foreign to me, but I pushed something through that, if they knew how to put it to use, could really bring the Quakers up in the world, so that one day Quaker crises would become global crises.

My horizon did not exclude a European federation, which could be of value in and of itself; a value that wouldn't profit me in any way, but one which would not inflict damage on anyone except the compulsive carnage and pummeling; before me gaped—as always, as accustomed, as if yawning—the crossroads, on the one hand the spoils of war, on the other the spoils of stability. I won on the red squares as well as the black ones, but still I was aggrieved and aggravated because a double operation on both at the same time was impossible; I consigned a shooting pain in my left upper abdomen, starting at the liver, to a bright, matte carafe that stood on the stone floor upon which I had set my feet . . .

I could not overlook the fact that they all wanted me for Prince Elector of Saxony before I had mounted a hasty, approximate critique of materialism, which would have weakened my position and which unexpectedly made a question of him who had come into question, or *would have* done so, for I mounted my critique *after* I was already Prince Elector of Saxony and had driven Saxony to ruin.

The first bombing raid ("and who was there at the birth of the bomb?") blew the powder magazine Parthenon sky high; sights were set on Schönbrunn Palace with special attention to the *piano nobile*, the *bel étage*, where I succeeded in producing a dozen reasonably lifelike still lifes with poultry, freshly hatched chicks with diadems on their heads, but I do not believe that I pulled off the formula for any and all chemical alloys; two and two made five; this, although certainly correct, was hard to explain to those who, before I was born and hence before the seventeenth century, attached to the sum of something called Two and something else called Two something to which the name Four perpetually adhered from that point on. Attendant on my formula $O_2 + CO_2 = C + O_5$, I solicited a linguistic change with the purpose of a new categorization for the result of this venerable addition; intellectually I did not prevail, for I had been labeled too much a man of action who could be counted on for a transformation of reality, but not for a simple rearrangement in the realm of pure spirit, which, I was given to understand, I "besmirched and dragged down into the tallow of the free spirit."

A number of things went wrong for me in the subsequent twenty years; an imprudent folksy astronomy determined that the orbits of the planets were parabolic while the planets blithely kept on moving on their regulus lines, with the firmament a flat plate on which lines were drawn; a Bernoulli beat me with his geodesic lines on a curved surface. My lines, whenever I drew one and drew from its existence the courage for the next one, always turned out much shorter than his; thus I was right in contrast to him; this hope was justified as long as I possessed the power to detain him in his home and maintain him in his powerlessness.

Furthermore I was convinced that regular meteorological observations would produce nothing but the tedious proofs of existence of rain, clouds, and fog, while their existence was a natural, unprovable one and would remain so. The Prussian Academy of Sciences broke out in furious applause during my inaugural address as its first president. "The Universe is built on sand," I spake. "A cog within the Almighty that leads to a transmission of the Almighty, whose most powerfully transmitted axle drives a worm gear at an excessive speed in such a way that the initial engaged cogwheel can in turn run almost imperceptibly slowly," cried Leibniz, and from a ball-bearing turntable the Almighty, that brass-plate-spinning all-purpose computing machine, cast a bolt of lightning at this fulminator; at this moment I behaved quite atheistically ("one day it will be said, quite frankly, that He does not exist, because there is nothing to calculate") and accepted the disclosure that my magnetic field maps had resulted in the sinking of five British merchant ships with aplomb, by asking twice about their number, when a token of mourning would already have been appropriate after the first one had been named.

The admiralty prosecuted me via Downing Street, where I turned an unpleasant meeting with one of the kings to my favor by means of my cigar trick ("one cuts the tabac, but it be flammable"): I secured continued marketing of my magnetic-field maps and acquired an imprimatur to boot.

The acoustic foundation of music was rejected by me out of hand; I went at aesthetic decisions frontally and without wasting any time; who cares if music suffered a setback, there were other art forms, and for every form of art that was set back, another came to the fore. I also decisively took sides in favor of witch trials after the Turks had lost Hungary to Austria, a signal that shook me like a fever but soon covered me with ice as well and ignited long-licking dark-green flames under my kidneys. In the immediate vicinity of Aachen I was detained by the local heresiarch, who stepped out of some bushes and showed me his tiara, and I spent a pleasant night in which France lost all of Lorraine; although an atheist at the bottom of the layered deposits of my soul, I comported myself like a Catholic, whereupon the Poles promptly installed me as king—as expected, at my scheduled death the Habsburg line in Spain was to come to an end. How were the Habsburgs supposed to continue after the introduction of the first street lighting in Germany anyway? I did still consider water to be transmutable into earth, but even that soon became a fallacy: the four elements were not circularly arranged, so that, for instance, sky could become sea, any more than a Protestant could arise from a heathen, or a Presbyterian from a Sioux. For me two hundred years ago, for example, light was a kind of water, just as it was three hundred years ago; but at that time Newton's regular excretions were reaching broader circles.

I maliciously observed the first parthenogenesis in the Brodendal-York Laboratories; no sooner had the ambisexual subject, a wan cabbage white butterfly who made its own feeler disappear into itself, self-copulated, than I knew that I was born to be an entomologist and had missed my calling in spite of ceaseless activity in the sector of diminution, reduction, and demolition.

"Every seventy-six years my comet will return," I promised and right away I began the cathedral at Fulda. A translation of the *One Thousand and One Nights* restored my equilibrium by taking me away from myself; I was released from having to reconstruct my own inventions, and could prop myself up on the pre-fantasy of a pre-rhapsodist and could devote a few nights in Petersburg to the translation; during the 649th night the Russians produced the first newspaper, in which the English occupied Gibraltar on the first page—it could no longer be defended, although I would rather have seen it in the hands of the Crusaders, or at least in the hands of their descendants; it wouldn't have been a permanent asylum for Quirinus, whom the century incinerated so cruelly in Moscow, charring him and, in the dying flames, turning him over one more time with a grate. His women, possessed by huge quadratic incubuses, howled at the foot of his stake and used felt tips to push hissing embers back into the blaze that he, Quirinus, was no longer permitted to cool by singing his psalter; would not Gibraltar have been his exile, one or two centuries earlier? My next foray with the time machine had to settle his case and clarify his circumstances.

Hardly had Gay Lussac traveled to Amsterdam when behind his back I established absolute zero at -150 degrees, but once again I had not gone far enough; one would, I said, have to employ a ventilator in the mines, and then the miners can pickax away longer at the subterranean rockpiles. Hardly are they back on the earth's surface when I delight them with my new greenhouses and explain to them the Jupiter rotation of the zodiacal light, in order to make amends to them; not all of them could do everything at once; my first perpetual-motion machine got stuck after the first automatic rotation; it was a ruby model I had tried, no fuel consumption besides diamonds in great quantities, laid on a gold plate, and the machine melted them away for the second rotation; I abandoned the experiment because of a shortage of new diamonds; in any case the predictable stone-radiation emission was too small, and on top of that it fell off the seventh cornice of the Kremlin, and the Tsar personally slapped me in the face; the hospital should be in one block, I recommended at the convention of state physicians, while Leibniz, intervening again, put through the pavilion system, which subsequently, in a later period of time, caused me so much trouble; I wanted out, I wanted out, I didn't want any steam heat anymore, I didn't want to get immunized anymore, I didn't want to be hooked up to the atmospheric turbine anymore; what did I want?; if I had still known what I wanted, then I would immediately have been discharged, back into the crisis.

"What is it the gentleman wants?" asked Leibniz, asking none other than myself—there was nobody left there, the round, the last round that is, which I had attended, had broken up toward eveningtime, and only Leibniz had stayed back and was standing immersed in a cut crystal polished with fine sand that bore a pyramid composed of tropical fruits and Chinese berries.

"The gentleman should tell me what is his will, and I shall fulfill that will for him, provided that it can be broken down into three wishes that can be strung together in a straight line that leads to the gentleman's goals." Calm and collected, he carried his amazement at me across the room; what did I want here, two hundred years back, three hundred years back? To win the Baltic States from Sweden? To defeat the French troops in the Spanish Netherlands? To become a materialist philosopher and biologist? To remain a German engraver? To ship myself off to the Helvetian lakes and manage to compose a *missa canonica* beforehand? Hadn't I, after I had become too much in my own times, also become too much in the times that I had visited in search of consolation, and which made me speechless from being consoled? Further possibilities were liquidated in short order, and their place was taken by objects, harder, more destructive of space. The vocational high school was invented, Freemasonry was in its early stages, an encyclopedia was being written, in Berlin they were observing the weather precisely, for fog, clouds, and rain received the designations that were granted to them: "fog, clouds, and rain." Palfijn showed me his childbirth forceps in a private demonstration, and if I had possessed a wench, I would have made use of them in front of the English wallpaper, before Progress cast its first shadows in the form of hereditary property for the Prussian sharecroppers; another forty years lost, as I crisscrossed the landed properties and inquired whether they would let me do something if I promised to do it well, sacrificing all my physical and mental energy and demanding nothing for it but lodging for one night and a crust of bread for one morning.

I wasn't very good at dealing with the perplexity of all of them, which glittered wherever I showed myself. I quickly sketched a map of Europe with an indistinct scale ("no interested party"), took a step toward photography with my silver salts ("the factories have no cart for transporting this rare type of material"), included the aberration of starlight in my calculations ("but aren't you the one who is telling us about the flat plate"), and founded the first independent science of dentistry.

Nothing was working out anymore. Day and night I felt the intellectual expropriation. Others stuck their names under my name as an inventor and shone brighter until it disappeared in the shadow. One morning when dense fog hung down to the surrounding treetops, there lay on the threshold of my house, in which I was living in exile, a pulped copy of my wave theory; the Hebrides were an ugly country with ugly inhabitants and ugly girls; not even on the Easter Islands did I still feel like a human being who was fit to bear my name; all of a sudden, my reason gave out in the face of my own misery. What was the name of the next place of refuge, after ferrous metallurgy steamrolled me, the missionaries were driven out of China, the patriarchy in Russia was abolished, Voltaire exiled himself to England, Greenland was colonized by Denmark, and Law went bankrupt and in his *faillite* caused a wave of inflation to arise?

After having repudiated the appearance of the mirror sextant, I wept tears of crucible steel and heard that in Prussia the landed gentry was appointing the functionaries; I recruited 83,000 men out of 2.5 million and entered the Polish War of Succession fully armed; I had been king in Poland, but the Poles had forgotten my beneficence and the orderly era that they spent under me. A good zeitgeist, which caught wind of my decisiveness, let a long time pass until the Peace of Vienna. I didn't need any peace, what was I supposed to do there, in peace? Find myself again, myself and the period of my life, a life that had happened before it had gotten started? Bob was my only assistant with large-scale production of sulfuric acid in lead chambers; I traveled to the Netherlands, had myself given an electrical shock from the Leyden jar and darkened it—my consciousness—which had never been lucid and could rightly maintain that no remedy would ever be passed its way that could help it become a lucid consciousness. I recall the Netherlands, a yellow soggy plain covered with roads, canals in all four compass directions, between the canals a meadow, an unending meadow. I climbed up out of one of the canals and ran, with Leibniz at my back, who was praying while rocking on a short red rug, rapidly and with those movements that shoulders, torso, and legs always make in this position toward the large flashing smooth lethally sizzling jar, across the meadow, soft praying, toward the large jar that would throw me back into contemporary times; that's how his life was.

## 19

What brokenness! Once she took herself for more important than is allowed. Now she is being broken through and through. He can do something about the fact that he is being treated this way. His understanding is past and gone. His intellect shot at itself, spun around once, and crumpled, and in the lethal pain a face as if someone were offering him a bouquet of chicory.

He is soused when he gets his pension payment. When he has to go to pick it up at the post office, he is even more soused. He is most soused when it doesn't come. Then the month that was just about to end on the tenth is ended for good. It can fail to arrive in case they want to torment him. Then he has to go begging to them. For that purpose he will get soused for courage.

The backs of their necks will get creased from laughing, if he then does a fair turkey gobble, and when the curses that escape him run down his shirt because he doesn't spit them far enough away. Now he's drunk as a skunk without my knowing what form of pension denial has just occurred. And so the pension and the conditions of its disbursement depress him more certainly than his previous condition, which was no picnic either.

Because he is now a little bit destroyed, the reason Hecht gets the pension is because he is now a little bit destroyed. Thus the decline of the unemployable springtime of his life seems to be unreeling into a cycle that is spinning into a spiral. Not only does the amount of the pension for housing, food, and inhaling return to the pension freely and piecemeal, but the pension, its receipt, or its refusal also continue to destroy the person in Hecht for whose sake he was once deported into a pensioner's existence.

They're tormenting him. Is that what they want? The crushed person who earns his pension honestly molts to produce a very definitely crushed person, and every pension-needy thing about him is too crushed to warrant further support or necessitate some subsidy that has not been introduced yet.

No one puts a coin in the hand of the beggar who has a hole in the palm of his hand. Because it falls right through the hand into the gutter. You can tell by the jingle. Everyone keeps his coin for himself, even if the reason the beggar is begging is the hole in his hand. Having a malfunction in a functional sector, one that makes the activation of the emergency sector into a farce, is not recommended. Beggar's hand-hole is an impossible injury. In the parlance of sports that's what they call tough luck.

With a beggar, the coin must not fall into the gutter. Otherwise he won't be getting any more coins. Even the stupidest almsgivers are that smart. Robert is dealing with the second-stupidest ones. By now they've gotten smarter. They know every hole he runs out of. They are the glass through which he is observed and appraised. They want to torment him, martyr him, torture him, impale him; certainly their intention is this: to put an end to him, so that the pension payments can be stopped.

Robert doesn't hold the torture against them, and anyone who knows Robert forgives them for the torment that passes them by. He is simply an all-too-grateful case. He gratifies their desires rapidly. In the office they put him, e.g., in a corner, with his back to the wall, and aim at him with the discharge of an uncorked bottle of champagne. As soon as he takes a first slug and then tips the bottle, they stick a little subsidy in his vest so that he can raise a few more medium-sized ones before his final payout.

After an hour of soggy recreation he shuffles off with a word of thanks. And he takes his stomach-lining rupture with him. They wouldn't have put up with him in their offices much longer anyway. The letters that they wrote to collect his outstanding contributions did not get finished, given all the pastimes that the addressee provided them with. And he was stuck so deep in his condition that he made a convincing impression. They nearly ended up under the pressure of the suffering that they had begotten and continued to fatten up in Robert with such insistence and good-natured guile.

The next dose of pension comes punctually. Stinking drunk, he opens the door to the enforcement officer. He's mislaid his name and thinks he's the first of the month in person. Scribbles an X on the receipt and stamps it with an imprint of his mouth next to that. This is interpreted in the office as a kiss, and they say nice things about him behind his crooked back. And he can use some nice things. Even among pension recipients the principle of competitive achievement prevails. And if he knows he's not producing the highest achievement, way beyond the competition, then he depends on the grace that his achievement will nonetheless be accepted.

There are other failures who are more powerful than he is. They're sober when they pocket their pensions. Regard it as hush money and keep their mouths shut about the shape they're in. Saying anything about that would bring both no job and a lower credit rating. They won't get a loan from anybody. But if they talk about their conditions, then anybody will tell them that he won't loan them a thing, even before they've brought it up with him. That's why they're smarter than he is. They pocket their pension, accept it as hush money, and keep their mouths shut, if possible pumping their money on into investments they've been offered. Almost like bankrupt civil servants, little, hairless, bankrupt civil servants in whom the automatisms continue to twitch a little.

He's not like them, though. The people in the offices like him better. He permits quite a few things to happen to him without ever turning into an incident. Robert's open nature, available to anything intellectual plus interest, has grown on them. That's why they'll hold onto him very tightly as a pension recipient, with the utmost emphasis. Sometimes for fun they tear off his ears. There's a scrooping sound when they start tearing, and a scrunching like wet tissue paper when they finish tearing, and then they sew his ears back on. Lots of pension money if he doesn't scream, because he never screams.

Such silly games for the sake of money! Such accommodations for that paltry pension!

In the meantime they give Hecht something to take home and write that is supposed to drive him crazy. He's supposed to copy things from the office. But he keeps turning in his résumé. They have long since destroyed whatever it is within him that helps him to think it's not just fine. So it's a fine résumé. They mistake him for things in the office. Strictly speaking there is no difference between the résumé and things from the office. Hecht arranges himself in a new sauce. They've softened him up so much that he finally coincides with the coward that he is. How helpless he is! How quick and calculating they are!

## 20

Whispered to the mouse breeder: don't worry about being a little malicious to the mice. True, they won't thank you for it, but they will bite through your arteries so concisely that it will be pleasant for you to know that you have spared yourself the astonishment at an attack like that by the straightforward behavior that has been yours since birth. Proceed more resolutely than your attackers in doing what the course prescribes to you. As a weakened breeder, at least make the prognosis of sudden breeding-animal aggression with subsequent bleeding out. You have to hate the mice. Abhor them. In principle, you can grow to like your hate because of the clarity of its origins: but along the way keep breeding with no worries. The mice know. And they've known your wrists by heart for some time now.

# 21

"There's something I have to tell you," Ann says. Hecht is in the room that serves those who are occupying it, which means that it denies itself to them. "Where are you," Hecht asks. "In the kitchen, cooking," Ann whispers. Robert gets up off the sofa and betakes himself to the kitchen—it is, because it was so decided, a kitchenette. "Now I've ended up in the bedroom," Ann whispers. Hecht pushes the door open; the door—against expectations—opens; he does not appear in the frame. "Would you just say what you are going to say," Robert barks at her. "What are we doing this evening?" asks Ann. "We're going to the movies," Robert says, scratching her on the chin, because he's exploiting the submissive look in her eyes. He can't believe how much it eases her mind to know that he is hanging over her like a house blessing. "Come back in the so-called living room," Robert whispers. "It's nice here in the bedroom too," murmurs Ann, the widow.

In the evening they go to the movies; movies are an expectorant, they loosen up things that get spit out. Often they do it with the suggestion of things that cough fitfully. Some localities are being bombarded; Robert is coughing because of the smokers on the balcony; the film comes five years too late, that is, at exactly the right time; if during the war it had been a government information film, now, after the war, it is a coughing film that irritates Hecht's pulmonary lobes to the point of discharge. "Protest is reactionary," says Hecht, who for variety's sake makes a shift to the right. "What are we doing tonight?" asks Ann. "Think about your first husband," Robert says, "I'm feeling reverent from reminiscing." "Tonight," Ann whispers. "Afterward we'll go to my club," Robert says gently, "men only, but for you they'll come up with an exception." The ears of both of them are humming with screen noise.

Three times they get shot in the face, for muzzles are pointed at them, for nobody should miss the point that everybody should cough up. Ann is afraid and is reminded of ironclad principles; every brandished gun is an archaic upper. Remembering creates desire and changes people for the cheerier. "Luckily I'm feeling sick enough to spew," Ann says. "For eight francs admission you can demand that," says Robert. "I'm spewing," says Ann. "What's the matter, check right away and fix the gadget," Hecht remarks, relieved, and leaves the movie theater with her. Heavy fire from behind.

Later they're sitting in the club. Ann is wearing close-fitting pants and has flattened out her breasts under two pieces of pasteboard, so that she will be allowed into the club as a man; a truss is loaned out to her that has to be lashed tightly around her glottis. "Basically that was fundamentally a pretty nice day," Ann says. "Fairly successful once again," Robert confirms forcefully. They are silent and leafing through periodicals; the serious daily papers are proving not to be equal to the satires they have to publish. Only once in a while does a squib function as the safety valve that it is not, devaluing the surrounding reports to mere squibs. "This is sad, this here," Robert says, wiping the back of his hand generously across a page. "Twenty years ago I knew a wrinkly old man who could reabsorb his tears with the corners of his eyes," Ann says. Remembering puts a strain on her. While the act in and of itself would be fine, it's just that the composition of an uninterrupted stretch of lifetime in which dull moments, without producing a sum, are added to each other until they make a formless mountain of good stuff and nonsense, wipes Ann out so much that she no longer steps up to the counter window of memory, because the bureaucrat there treats her rudely; this explains why she tells the whole thing as well as what's left over.

"I believe the time is not past in which I knew a sculptor," Robert interjects. "It was so weird the way that man sucked up those tears," Ann interrupts, taking the newspaper away from Robert and folding it on the end table. "The sculptor told the defenseless Hecht," Robert says, "that he approaches the time that passes like a chunk of rock, by chiseling away at it, hewing out seam after seam, and he runs around every moment to see whether it's looking good from all sides." Besides Robert's visibly self-unleashing rhetoric, whose chips are all down, Ann is starting to falter, emitting cries and getting her contorted hand halfway to her forehead before she crumples, comes back up, and crumples. Ferrum deficiency. Hypovitaminosis.

"The gadget is coughing," Ann says calmly. "Is it not remediable?" asks Hecht worriedly. He gathers her up and beds her on the sofa that is in the room that does not deny itself to those occupying it. The club is better than at home, but unfortunately it is public and for men only. "What is going to knock you onto your feet?" Robert inquires of the prostrate woman. The services provided by the club are of world-champion caliber. The club doctor is already standing next to her, pulling out the pasteboards, sniffing at them, wrinkling his forehead and tightening up a knee muscle.

"We were at the movies, and afterward we wanted to go home, with a detour via the club," Hecht explains to the doctor, guiltily tracing on the end table the couple's path since they left the apartment. "There's something I have to tell you," Ann groans. "What's the matter with her?" Hecht yells at the doctor. The doctor takes a jump away from Hecht, and relief at the distance between their bodies fills the pleasant room. What? Hecht asks the doctor, who is standing there with the stethoscope, rolling a stethoscope about twelve meters long onto a spool. The club doctor shrugs his shoulders so that his hands shake like leaves, and he spreads his knock-knees apart, and from slackness his upper eyelids crash down on his lower eyelids, which have already scooted down onto his cheekbones. The doctor's eyes reveal an inadequate segment. Are light and knowledge still reaching his retina?

The doctor looks at Ann's tailleur. "So what's the matter with her?" Hecht yells and makes an effort to remove any accusation from his voice. "She is not especially strong," the doctor states, without any contact. "I'm going to pretend I didn't hear that," Hecht breaks in loudly. "There's something I have to tell you as long as I can still tell you," groans Ann, who adjusts to her own situation as fast as lightning, playing last-will-and-testament executrix. A wool blanket has slipped over her mouth. Hecht draws back the wool blanket and before he has time to think, a doctor as swift as the wind has pulled the wool blanket over Ann's mouth again. "They'll see her breasts, in the club," the doctor says. No emphasis on the reprimanding element. "She has to speak, so down with the blanket," Hecht yells. "Just imagine you had a prostate condition, here in the club," the doctor says. Hecht understands obscurely and leaves the blanket on.

"But there's still something the matter with her," Hecht bellows and gives the club physician a shove so that he tumbles over the guéridon. Two liqueur goblets shatter. The club butler hurries over, coughing, straightening out on his way the tassels on the heavy rug with soccer moves, pullbacks and trots. "Come closer," Ann whispers, doubling over and pressing her forearms onto her chest and thus pushing sounds out of herself. "Do you want a gauze gag?" Hecht asks, bending over her. "There's nothing wrong with her," the doctor says from five meters' distance, "at least I don't see anything that I could treat. A treatment is not worth the trouble, and it must be worth it, one has one's little vanities, and just because of a fainting spell we're not going to cut into the roast." "She's only acting like there's nothing wrong," Hecht states, outraged. "She's as healthy as you and me," the doctor says quickly, "I advise you to ignore the fact that she's only acting that way." Now that he has caused the illness to disappear in favor of classical medicine, Robert looks at him pleadingly; that ought to be of some use, even if Robert doesn't know how much.

"What is her name?" the doctor asks. "Annie Wattenwyl," Hecht says gratefully. "A nullipara?" the doctor asks. "She is a widow," Hecht says, scraping a large gratuity from the bare walls of his portfolio. "This is no place to crack jokes," the doctor grunts through a coughing fit. He destroys, stumbling on his way to the microphone that calls the ambulance, the orderliness of the border of the heavy rug. During the transport Hecht sits in the vehicle next to Ann's stretcher, beneath a small restless light. "Is this where you live?" asks th driver, who has a hole in the floor of the car below him in order to be able to brake with his shoe on the roadway. "Get out of the car," Hecht encourages Annie. "Your pasteboards," the driver calls. The doctor, who is tinkering with the small light, grins. "When she comes to the club again sometime for her *évanouissements*," he growls, with his back to Hecht.

At home Hecht is suddenly in a room that refuses those who occupy it—which means that it is destined to serve them. Ann, who has dragged herself upstairs, tried to push the door shut behind her; old loafers left lying around got in the way. Hecht heads for an electric wire hanging out of the wall that is pointed at his face. Robert clears his throat and rolls up in a ball and lies down in the bedroom, quiet and quiet and quiet, no movement gets expressed, the doctor and the club butler stand around his bed, both in full gala with suits of armor; over the foot end of the bed, thunderously powdering exchanges of fire take place; Robert's big toe, shot through for years, is the bridge on the River Kwai, and it's hardly believable how much stamina a doctor like that expends in order to make himself the master of the bridgehead; or is this bridge located in Luxembourg? That leaves the doctor as cold as a winter moon. One of Hecht's elderly neighbor ladies, who claims to have nearly seen him as a child, who in a way placed him inside his mother and pulled him out of his mother and who will certainly lay him in his grave and pull him back out as an urn—she fills a useless glass on the useless bedside table with pale pus. "If'n the wound makes it, the mouth takes it," she hums hexily.

"And with hindsight this moment is going to look damned bad," Hecht groans. An attempt to reabsorb his tears miscarries. No doubt Hecht is not old enough for that. "You poor guy," Ann whispers, running her hand over his hair; his knee is showing at the top, but Ann is familiar with nature. "Who is he?" asks the club butler, made distrustful by Hecht's encouragements, all of which are aimed at the battling parties at the foot of the bed. Robert overestimates the good people whom he—in spite of the fact that they are quite definitely fighting over the bridge on the River Kwai—addresses with "there's your damn bridge, you bugger"; this sort of thing does not get through to them, for their fight is disguised even from them as a nursing-necessitated participation in his breakdown.

"Well, you've still got each other," the doctor consolingly tells the couple, a couple which Hecht doesn't really want to be part of, and Ann even less. "My ass is grass," says Hecht, and a scream follows these edified words. Hecht is lying between the points of his pillows; the kneaded-down feathers are putting on a groundswell of happiness in their billionfold cloth-wrapped collective.

Everything is breathing along together, and the world of things wheezes as if it had climbed up the mountain and over the mountain. Ann brings him egg with spinach, and Robert spoons away, a wax-pale, wool-muffled chubbiness with a shattering intake volume. "Thanks, Mama," he says after the last spoonful. "And now one more for Grandmama," says Ann.

"He's not *that* weak," the club butler interjects with a shout. He is picking up all of the objects in Robert's bedroom one after the other and pressing them incredibly hard with his hands, silently crumbling them if he can; whatever crumbles is not genuine, his big, warm thing-coveting hands say. He knows some soccer steps too, the butler does, and because all of the fringed borders on all of the runners are crooked, he kicks them straight with extravagant fancy footwork; as if he were in his own home, where he can work off his denaturedness. "Well, he's mimicking the sick man of Europe," quips the doctor, who is loosening up because he stands to lose a lot of time that cannot be recovered, so that all he can do now is be happy. "And that's how he was even when he was still little and when I was bigger than him," the elderly lady persists, unfolding before Robert all of the splendor of the thrusting brooch pinned to her chest. Ann, the ape, swings through the room on the curtain cords, letting herself drop down onto his acutely angled knee. Modestly the paratrooperess decides the aerial battle for the bridge and the abyss. Hecht coughs. "There's something I have to tell you," shrieks Ann, the ape.

"I know what you have to tell me in general," Hecht laughs, cheerful and cured. "I will keep your mouth shut in the future," Ann says. "It makes me happy that I voluntarily realize that," Hecht says patronizingly. With backstroke motions he shovels himself free, pillows float toward the club butler who is stumbling in retreat, and who immediately pokes them full of holes and shreds them to bits. All recoil from the wide nightshirt; this cannot be the white swells of acquired happiness; Robert is messing around with his feet, which turn inward and three times around themselves, toward Ann, backward and then headward. "He plays that like an old pro," says the doctor, who has to keep the club butler away from his unrolled stethoscope; he wants to kick the tube; a butler like that can be childish when he feels at home.

"Do you love me," Robert asks. Ann wraps a scarf around him. "That will do me a world of good," Robert says. She pulls him into the kitchen(ette) and leaves the small group in the bedroom, where the furniture is being taken apart. "Do you want a wool blanket?" Ann asks. "Turn on the oven," Robert demands. "I remember," Ann gushes; she's lying. "If you turn on the oven, I'll know that you love me," says Robert. "I love you," says Ann, "because I had the privilege of spending an evening with you." "In reality those are hundreds of rooms that are sunk into the earth with the elevator or which I brought up out of the earth with the elevator," Hecht says sheepishly. So much claimed wealth takes away powers of expression. "More evenings like that, please!" Ann says, "then I'll be a widow again." "You like being one, don't you," says Hecht, who places his ring on her finger. In the bedroom, the doctor—raving coughing fit—splits the digital clock with a karate chop, and the club butler is tinkering patiently with the window latch, and the elderly neighbor lady is jotting down the addresses. "What are you working on right now?" Ann asks. "Nope," says Hecht. "What you working on?" Ann asks. "I'd rather not," says Hecht. "And your work?" Ann asks. "If you take good care of me, there's going to be a lot more evenings like this one," Robert says, scratching her on the chin and letting himself be scratched on the chin by her. As a couple they draw aside into the proven furriness: having a pelt is soothing.

"Evening would be nice, it makes a new person out of me," Ann whispers. Without looking, that is, leaning close and form-fittingly on Robert, she feels around on the paneling in order to rotate the rotary switch; there she is with him and made of velvet and was a widow.

## 22

Suddenly, in the midst of the general unemployment, I have the feeling that Bob has been newly hired somewhere. This new-hiring feeling warmly permeates me, but is put to the test; it contradicts the actual conditions too much. After I have convinced myself by means of contract consultation that the actual conditions have been put aside especially for me, I let the certainty that I have in fact been newly hired someplace get the upper hand. The first day of work is already dawning, and bright sun and a breeze are chasing the fringy clouds into pairs, and I'm driving to work on my first day, an eight-lane concrete avenue on my way to the business, which this time is supposed to be big business for me, even in months that have only twenty-eight days. I'm driving straight ahead, consistently, individual lanes branch off, and then I also know that I will never find the firm that has newly hired me, because for that to happen I would have had to read the bold-face print in the contract as well. I drive for another half hour and then I know that I am way past the company, and I take possession of the inkling that I will never again get to work, and I might just as well start looking for my next position right now; at the upper edge of the car windows there are arc lamps that are moving past me somewhat faster than I am moving past them: they have it right. I drive straight ahead until evening, when they will be turned on, I stubbornly keep going, and then the motor starts chugging. I stop, get out of the car, walk toward a building, turn back to the car, turn on the headlights so that the battery will unperform on me, and walk toward the barracks, a hamburger bar with a sign advertising ketchup in tomato color, how original, almost a gag. Wire-reinforced glass fills the hole in the wood of the door that snaps into its lock behind me and makes a soft cracking noise like a dog biting into a bunch of chicken feet.

I order a mound of kneaded ground beef on a slice of cheese and tell the guy who brings it to me: "It appears as though I've missed work today and spent the whole day searching straight ahead and mindnumbed, but if you think those guys put a sign up on the highway showing the way to their company, you've got another think coming, they think they're too good for that, they probably believe they'll get along just fine without Bob Hecht."

"But man," says the guy serving me, "that driving straight ahead *was* your work, that's what they hired you for!"

"I can feel my spleen jerkin' around inside me," I drawl.

He doesn't go into that, if his pouring ketchup over the ground beef is an indication of indifference. In the barracks interior, the ketchup is canker-red—you could use it to advertise for some exquisite floor wax.

"Did you see the arc lamps?" he asks.

"Yes," I say.

"Did you count the arc lamps?" he asks.

"2,489 of them whizzed past me," says my Hecht.

He stops serving, jots down the number on a napkin, and his voice sounds like crinkling glossy paper in an empty spray can.

"That's great. You'll spend the night here. The lavatory is in the front on the right side. Tomorrow you'll continue driving in the inside-right lane and count the Fords coming from the other direction. Then to the motel in the evening. 2-4-8-9, that's great. Until now we've never known just how many arc lamps there are in this damned country."

In the kangaroo pocket of his white apron he keeps the cheese for grating. Before he grates it onto my egg, he has to fish it out with his hand. Before the cheese is lying on my egg, I have pierced the yolk and that does not shake him up, because he grates the cheese over the leaky egg.

"With regard to arc lamps," I drawl, "I think you have built this country here lock, stock, and barrel."

From deep down under the grating cheese he pulls out a rolled-up piece of paper. I want to give him the tip right away and wait to pay until I get back from the gas station. He signs the bill for the meal and holds it out for me to sign it. I dip a fork tine into the red flesh and sign the bill. Then he erases his signature with the corner of his apron.

"Your contract for tomorrow's workday," he says, "and keep on going straight ahead but always get a good look around you but keep on straight ahead."

"With regard to the stupid arc lamps," I say, really drawling it out. I conjecture that I take twenty minutes just to say this one sentence; whether from exhaustion, whether from imbecility, it doesn't come to me, and this not-coming-to-me is certainly just exhaustion, nothing exalted.

"The arc lamps have multiplied enormously since then," he says. I hear his laughter. He's served it to me. The joke was just waiting to be told. Where is my room, I will ask. In the front on the right, he will say, I've quartered you in the lavatory. As soon as I think what will happen his laughter will stop. It was, to hear honestly, never very loud.

"Where is my room," I ask. When he answers I will beat him up and pour ketchup on him.

"Follow me. I will show you your room. The windows look out on the park in the rear courtyard," he says.

What was too much for me until now actually does add up to a great amount. I'm all topsy-turvy, but mostly turvy. At the sight of the tire pump machine in the rear courtyard I'll be stricken with melancholy, even if it hasn't been used in a long time. We climb up a stairway with cork tread covers; in the barracks, which seen from outside only had two floors, the light switches are mounted on the stair treads.

Sometimes a happy impulse, which I pick up in the palm of

my hand and scan from the wall closing me in, shoots through me up to my neck, and I bear this with calmness, at the edge of calmness. He's given me a room till tomorrow. And at least shown me a contract with legal protections.

"As a waiter I find you appealing because of your complexion," Bob says.

"I've been let go as a waiter. This is my last evening with my last customer."

He leaves the door open. So that I won't feel so lonesome. And he won't either. He has to have company for going down the stairs. My company. That's why he's descending so quietly, as if he's listening for someone who's going down the steps behind him. I look through the window and hear him flipping the light switches on the landings. The two headlights on my car shine into a face and go out. The battery held out a long time. It delivered for a long time. Down in the rear courtyard, outside the second window: blackness licks at a pan-roasted potato poster. Tomorrow it will be hung over the front door: the supply depot is changing its specialty.

"Where do you keep the tire pump?" Hecht shouts after him, one of his more spontaneous questions. Then suddenly, but expectedly, very expectedly, he turns out the light downstairs, in the window frame something white explodes in front of my car, a viscous scorched-earth-red slurry runs into Hecht's field of vision from above. Nothing in the field of vision permits the conclusion that Hecht's two eyes and two of Hecht's eyes can perceive only sectors; his eyelashes are damming as well as they can, and Bob throws eyelids over them; I still think of something lasciviously sad and hang up my tears to dry and decide to release my Bob from himself, third door on the corridor. Everything will look like he killed himself, but there will be no self to be found. Speak, Hecht, the last of your brief complaints.

## 23

Deep within myself I feel that this is our end. I feel that pretty deep within myself, not all that deep, but pretty deep. Even deeper within myself I feel that this is our end, but I see it not only within me, but also when I observe the pits out there. Even deeper within myself I feel that this is our end, but I'm not content with just feeling our end, but I also talk about my feeling, visibly more and more freely. Even deeper within myself I feel that this is our end, and I'll wager you feel it too. Even deeper in myself I feel in concordance with all other feelings that this is our end, but . . . this feeling is not an all-is-said-and-done feeling, it's less final than that, a deferredness feeling, a having-gone-too-far sensation, an impression of been-there-done-thatness. Our end, déjà vu. I claim it is our end, but at the same time I feel my own only vaguely, and in addition I feel that because I feel pangs of guilt when I threaten you with your end, for your end could bring a gain for me: your job, your inheritance, your home, the affections of your young widower, the paternal love of your tiny child, the rights of disposal over your library and record collection and the binders with your lecture notes, your six pairs of light brown shoes whose size, as you know, is the same as mine: 44. Even deeper within myself I feel that this is our end, but everything and everybody can become our end the way things now stand; that's how much we're already drifting; just the poke of a finger is all it takes; and the monuments fall down. Even deeper within myself I feel that this will be our end, and I also hope that afterward there will be no more beginning, for it has to be definitively over with us. Even deeper within myself on the other hand I then feel that this means an end; but tell me, whose end? It can't be mine, now can it? How unpleasant and unjust; I will submit my veto to the District Association against the distribution of burdens.

And then: the final feeling. Really extremely deep within myself, that is, back on the surface, I feel with a cold shiver that this was our end, but it's possible it is still yet to come, it can also stay our end, because every end that IS is an end that STAYS. And every end that STAYS stays an end that finally draws a line under it. And a line over it. And a circle around it. And a parenthesis on both sides. And the end cuts our life out and sticks it up like a little picture. That is us. That is how we will have been. Amazingly cardboard-mounted in our little frame. Painted with gold leaf. Deep within myself I feel that this is so and hardly otherwise.

## 24

Whenever I look into the breadbasket, I think of the time when there was still some bread in there. Whenever I am served bread, however, I remember the years when there was still a table under the breadboard. Today the bread hovers in the air and has to be supported with one's bare hand. But when I stretch out my hand as a support I gratefully recall the time when this hand was still firmly attached to an arm. Back then I was twelve, and my hair growth was sparser. Today I am thirty, somewhat hairier, and down four teeth. As of this morning I am relationship-free with my hand. It does what it wants to and it wants to get attached to the wall. Otherwise it would not have run itself across the wall for hours until the wallpaper, gray with grease, came unstuck at a seam and started to hang out into the room, into the room that was incidentally painted totally black. My hand, I recall, was firmly attached to my arm, and then this arm was firmly attached to me, once upon a time. Now this hand decided to become firmly attached to the wallpaper. Otherwise it would not have suddenly stood still at one spot after having moved tirelessly back and forth across the wall since the morning like a rolling-pin-shaped windshield wiper. The incarcerated man felt tenderness for his little dividing walls, and he yields his hand to that little partition.

The wall that is closing up in front of me is made out of bread. And when I look at it I am fearful, to the point of feeling graupelly, of a future in which my entire house will be built of bread. True, then it will be edible, but on the other hand it will collapse right away. I see myself buried under a mountain of bread, moist, weighing tons, with drips coming out of me below. That hardly increases one's appetite. When I think about all that, the era reemerges—it must have been the writing crisis—in which I could not think and could not say anything, even when I wanted to say it. It was preferable, that era. Things move ahead, toward the stove. Or is it the kitchenette? Dough barriers protect me from the great heat. It's like in Holland when they're expecting a hundred-and-fifty-foot surge in the Zuyderzee. As the Dutch fellow said, *nix understand*. When I think globally, beyond the country's borders, I come rambling back, out of patriotism, for example to the butter knife that's lying next to the bread. Once upon a time it was furnished with a grip, and I give the wall a signal that it should hold out my hand. My hand doesn't want to have anything to do with me anymore, and so the wall has to take care of it. The wall is supposed to hold out my hand. Don't hit me, wall, with my own hand. My hope that at some point there will also be a butter-knife grip lying there, but without a knife blade, is counting on different facts than there are. Even if no sun is shining, the facts simmer. I would have thought that the black walls absorb the heat; but no; they give off heat.

Keep your cool, for psychic oscillations that originate from the grinding of the clockwork only occur because the winding key has not been turned in its hole for a long time. I rub pain-relieving machine oil into my oscillations, and I know there once was a day, in a particular year when the writing crisis was past, a day that is no longer absolutely present to me, and on that day in the course of just a few hours which I cannot absolutely recall, these oscillations distinctly occurred in spite of the soothing machine oil. I was frightened about my psyche and held my face in both hands, and I scrunched my cheeks into shape. They kept their shape, each cheek its own. No sooner have I called up from memory storage, for the sake of recall, the fact that the balls of my hands played a role than the year emerges in which my arms still belonged to me. And the year in which I myself could still command my hands to grab my face and knead it into a humanoid form. Today that doesn't work anymore, at least not so quickly. Just the humanoid form of the face . . . what else did I want, since I had assumed the habit of circulating among people? They didn't ask so many questions, those people, they preferred to come right out swinging. Me too. But I was protected and had barriers of metal that descended wherever I found myself and formed a breadbox, a chamber, around me. Almost impermeable, God knows. I must once have petitioned to be let out. It was not granted to me. Nothing was granted. I should have petitioned for nothing, and then everything would have been fulfilled, which is to say nothing, but at least something would have been fulfilled, which is to say nothing. I eat bread, and I think of the time when there was still a breadbasket around it, but now the bread is alone, naked, simply as-is. And the notorious butter knife didn't disappear after all: it was simply never there. It's dismal when you're sitting there enclosed by the dark, assuming there's enough room for sitting; but even if there's enough room for sitting in the dark and the sliding door doesn't go up, then it is dismal to have to watch the objects gradually dissolve. Certainly I petitioned to have myself spared from this. That wasn't idiotic at all, back then. I have to realize that over a small distance I have become a big idiot. The biggest. Unfortunately. I can definitely still picture—especially when I'm eating—how it takes a little bit of mindlessness to be an idiot.

I'd like to be mindless, still. Not thinking anything: you can keep that up for a long time. In this regard I've achieved a certain grace. But not saying anything . . . the best thing would be . . . to stop . . . let it take its course, which is inevitably that of putting out the light . . .

# 25

Strictly viewed and strictly speaking, it was the bathroom; a microscopic room that contained a sink fit for an ant and a warmly filled bathtub fit for a cleanly microbe. From the terry-towel fluff to the cold-water-faucet handle to the crack in the tub to the nail-brush cord to the electric-toothbroom outlet to the soapholder-grate-hook detouring past the water-heater pipe nut pin on some shower-pipe riveting clamps to the toilet-sheet-roll packages and hairbrush-bristle beds plus cotton-bag bottoms to frayed-cotton-ball fuzz and thirty pointy stuck-in-and-pulled-out ear cotton-swab cellophane wrappers to the aftershave-cap threads and the machine-oil can spout cap to the good old soapdish-bottom in a circle around the edge of the armpit-sweat spraycan nozzle to the local post office business hours sign almost pajama-bottom cuffs unused to the hand-towel hanger stand base crooked and the nailed-up washcloth-loop and the Bakelite-sink soapsuds remnants back to the terry-towel fluff, garish orange. Under the rear bathtub feet there were wedges, and over the incline Bob Hecht's water ran through a cannula into a funnel floor drain that was too small to swallow up the immersed person; a medusa suction cup, conical; diagonally across the bathroom crawled an early gray rug, flowing broadly under the dripping washcloths nailed to the wall (tiny—even a trained circus flea would have been crushed between the floor and the ceiling), and stained with bodily fluids. With his elbows, Robert H. bumps gently and listlessly against the tub faucet, which presses into his flesh, at best an electric jolt and a tingling musclescape. Cranked up high, the fear of his head breathes down his neck, puffing the skull toward the pitched ceiling, circling, dangling, it's still possible bubbles will form, cement, plaster against cement, basin scrub brush blocking the way, otherwise it will snap downward in its hanging bracket, the drainage pipes of the ant sink, the microbe tub, and the tick toilet empty into the same collecting funnel, cloaca, platypus, olet, Domitian. The redness flowing away is gushing from my bloody white undershirt, wadded up in the tub, in which a salmon-red skin shank with dark hairs has stopped convulsing. On the shower head, on a tattered men's garter, hangs the head portion of the unfortunate man. His last tongue won't cross his lips, a nicked-up piece of aorta extends down with progressively larger notches in the arterial wall like a blue rope ladder into the Bakelite ant sink, underneath which the largest still-intact piece of a torso, the surface of the abdomen, shaved in concentric circles around the navel, forms a pulsing deposit upon which I stood and was effortlessly able to reach the garret-window-brace locking pin and open the dormer out into the late evening. Yes, I was capable again and have been capable again and again.

# WIFE

In an especially hard winter on the Thur River—his thirtieth birthday had passed devastatingly, the tea tasted bitter that Robert drank while awaiting a thing that never happened, the wood stove was in operation; in this winter, which put a radical end to a number of things, Robert found creative pleasure in ceaselessly repeating to his wife that the endless carrying of wood from yard to stove was completely dissipating his sexual powers, which had always been meager anyhow; now the moment had arrived when he basically foresaw their termination; surprisingly, he had predicted their termination a long time ago and intended, once it did set in, to refer to it simply as Snowman's Impotence. In addition, Robert tried to substantiate this Evening News of all Evening Newses with all manner of anatomical evidence, drawing hopeless sketches on the walls of the suffocatingly narrow hallway (that terrible house-entrance vagina) and on the wallpaper of the vestibule where the coats hung, elaborately accrediting himself with rudimentarily eloquent gestures after he had urgently asked his wife not to interfere in his condition, not to investigate what the precise truth was, not to inquire whether he was deliberately lying or boldly allowing the facts to speak or remain silent, either in order to get out of having to carry firewood or in order to escape the hallway in which their jerky unions took place; furthermore; the wife must be so good as to clear up whether it was nothing but the strain on his back from carrying wood that was to blame, or else some inexplicable but practiced compulsion during those unions that could cause him or her distress, so that undeniably even the one who at first was not distressed would have to feel distress when he got intimately involved with someone who was distressed, or it might simply be lack of enthusiasm for the one as well as for the other—in principle, anything could be true, but of all of this stuff, only one thing could be absolutely true, and he expected his wife not to dare to find out the absolute truth but just to say it. "Everything is true or can be true by having become the reason for one's incompetence"; she should consider this before accusing him of scatterbrained fantasies and subjecting him to ostracism with shards from his pitcher, which was irrevocably broken. Robert's wife, who came from a strictly bourgeois clan, was ascendant in Aries, baked creamy quince tarts with a pounded-almond crust like crazy, wore drapey things around her pampered hips (probably gauzy chemisettes), read novellas in her free hours and in her working hours wrote novellas; even though he had advised her to do so, she never checked the validity of his statements that concluded their cohabitation, but she reached the point, between smiling and halfway regretting, where she hired a full-bodied maid for the household who cooked at low heat; her job was to carry the wood from the yard to the stove and carry the ashes from the stove to the bucket and carry the bucket from the kitchen sink to the yard and come back to the kitchen with the empty bucket and fresh wood and put the empty bucket by the kitchen sink and the fresh wood by the stove and stoke the stove with fresh wood and fill the empty bucket with fresh ashes and go through every imaginable motion dictated by this endless circulation for whose dizzying exertions she would be properly remunerated and from whose soul-destroying stress and strains she would be able to recover in a place of rest that looked like a birthing chair, though that wasn't supposed to mean anything; Robert's wife succeeded in hiring this maid, and she gave her the task, easily communicable from woman to woman, that released Robert, as if in passing, from that one burden, namely the wood-schlepping one, but led him all the more inescapably to that other task, namely the twitchily tender one; this was not difficult as long as the daily household discussion between her and the scribbling Robert would soon revolve around the straight, thick, indestructible firewood in the woodpile; from which a high degree of inevitable innuendoes could arise; in the worst-case scenario she would simply talk about the winter on the Thur and about the drift ice and the rural snowmelt, a topic that was so abhorrent to Robert that eventually, as a way to get off the topic, he would even greet the partial reenactment of a huge, stiff firewood log pointing slantwise at the chimney as a merciful deliverance; in any case, such unruly topics would turn out for Robert to be the downright unruliest thing imaginable. Let's talk about shutting up, he would shout, let's talk about the sun, he would freeze, let's talk about impossibility, for which he said he would need three seconds; and that is what, at the mention of death by wood, could easily give him back his rare proficiency in rehearsed, carefully pilot-tested and almost aesthetically and pleasurably induced moments of lust. In the temptations assigned to her, the maid fluttered her skirts . . .

Imperceptibly precisely in tandem with his garden, Robert's life also developed holes when the snowmelt, to the extent that it occurred, occurred suddenly, if it hadn't already begun the day before, before Robert had managed to get his various shovels, seeders, raffia rolls, cloth gloves, support stakes, rakes, three-pronged digging forks, jackboots, crates, and hoses out of the garden cottage. As soon as the overflowing Thur tried its hand at woodcutting; as soon as unmanned and torn-up rafts embarked on their own to reach the sea and at the first dam were pulled out of the grating in front of the floodgate, already reduced to plank-sized firewood, Robert got down to some extensive excavation by spading a hole in which to plant a tree with a clod of soil on its roots. Above those tangled roots of the tiny elongated bark-covered trunk, around which Robert's leprous hands tautened, a young, trampled-down sapling stuck out of the earth; and beneath Robert's soles the last snow spread out evenly; snow had always stirred his heart, simple snow lying all around; suddenly Robert could not find the planting hole he had dug the day before the day of the snowmelt; it had become lost in the ground, and for a long search the Thur, which was putting vast gardens under ice water, was climbing much too quickly . . . plant during the thaw . . . get the tree into the ground, sun scald and all . . . trunk rot was also to be considered . . . the possibilities of forest pathology were unlimited . . . a few seconds later Robert felt his sweating soles sink half a foot deeper, heels first, which caused Robert to extend those notorious knee joints. The snow was still deep enough to give Robert's poverty of imagination, which was now showing itself, a definite chance. As long as no ideas came as to where to plant the tree, Robert was a horrible failure; the higher the sun rose, the tighter the root fungus and the toothwort closed ranks in order to destroy the tiny elongated trunk that was lying in Robert's leprous hand. The thin strip between the rising Thur waters and the rising sun was shifting upward without lifting Robert along with it, and he had to survive in it. Robert, who had at first been standing on a low earthwork, sank down, as was to be expected, into a shallow hollow in the earth, and gave up, as was to be predicted, any resistance to the events that were closing in wrongly and terribly; sooner or later everything would no longer continue—hopefully sooner; soon Robert more or less fell from the garden into the well, from the well into the bucket, from the bucket into the garden, and now he stumbled into one of the deep, narrow, etc. river beds of the Thur, which, if wildly proliferating lock-ring plants didn't happen to be dying there, were lined with ropily rampant marsh marigolds in vegetal fatness; the Thur between flowers, flowers all around the Thur . . . maybe later at some point . . . consummate Thur-bed vegetable gardens, as the sadistic Schreber method demanded; the method of Daniel Gottlob Moritz Schreber, father of little mentally deranged Daniel, who as a psychiatric patient was able to have a go at his Dr. Flechsig; as the methodology demanded when Schreber senior, the inventor of torture apparatuses, was still alive. Without evasion, Robert ascertained his failure at finding the planting site; his lack of imagination was functioning flawlessly; ice-crystal thoughts fastened themselves where he was standing, in the midst of a thawing geological lineament which just two days ago he would have called "my natural surroundings and homeland . . ."

The maid fluttered her skirts while performing the temptations assigned to her whenever she walked up the steps from the yard to the kitchen, just as she made her legs go back and forth in a particular way, like snatching pincers; which, if Robert hadn't been busy with his unbearable arguments from evidence to the point of an absence absorption bordering on autism—an unbroken chain of evidence, grippingly presented in every detail, seemed to him the halfway-most-certain means of presentation—those legs would have led Robert without any teeth-gnashing and hair-raising shame to her lap, even more, they would have led him to her room, even more, they would have led him to her place of rest, that very particular chair, which wasn't supposed to mean anything, nothing at all. Robert, occupied with himself, as has been demonstrated, all day and all night, but citing with no visible effort the most monstrous impotences in the history of the world along the lines of his example; Robert found creative satisfaction and relief from cramps when, in the sparsely sown moments of diversion from his sketchy magnum opus, which flogged him through his wayward life, he looked up and observed other beings, but only briefly, to keep them from affecting him, for he had already included them in his flogging magnum opus before he observed them; so that he, if he nonetheless accidentally lent them an eye or an ear, demanded from them absolute fidelity to the text; their optical appearance had to correspond to the description already chosen by him, and the disloyal were nailed down with pointed expressions of contempt for their mortal sins against Robert's evidentiary work; Robert threw them out into the vestibule and clamped one of their arms between the jamb and the front door, while covering them with a sacklike garment and making them do hairy penance. The pincer-legs did not hold still, but pursued their task, with a counterproductive gait, that is, scuttling very massively, in an unnatural general bearing, that is, wearing makeup a palm thick, in a simply unbearable condition, that is, trained for bloodthirsty wildness. After everything he had read about Keener, his predecessor with his wife, in her hate letters and his desperation letters, Robert was inclined to answer excitations of a pivoting nature, which tried to wed cheerful female pluckiness with pathetic male angst, with a reference to how cold it was in the house; whole swaths of the Thur, gurgling in a steaming evaporation fog, are surging in from the yard through the woodstove chimney into the kitchen and the stairwell; the cold in the house, he said, was cutting him off from whole parts of his ample body, like a blood-vessel stoppage; he was still himself, but no longer entirely so; to his amazement, every morning he found new pieces of himself and, when he reached for them with his hand, lost other pieces of himself; a part of Robert, he said, was sinking into the Thur evaporation fog, while another part, which was already nearly drowned, was rescued from the Thur; with a few analogizing narratives, Robert reshaped excitations from pivoting leg pincers till they were ripe for the slaughterhouse. Among other things, he had never informed the two women living with him that he lived in the slaughterhouse, or, not to put too fine a point on it, in a madding house, where in a row on the wallpapered walls there hung coat hooks made of wire, but the little Roberts hanging in a row on the hooks weren't being unhooked and taken down, and so they weren't able, with little teacups in their little fists, to crowd around the woodstoves that for a short time now had been standing there in rows and burning. But whatever Robert had not yet brought to the attention of his household by taking the detour via innuendos and winding-pathish analogies, would sooner or later—more likely sooner, that is, as soon as the great impotent evidentiary work endeavor had come to rest—definitely be hurled at his household . . .

. . . the Thur area, the entire population, remained instantly unaffected; they did not let themselves be dragged by outsiders into unknown maelstroms; this in spite of the fact that the snow, which during the winter on the Thur had been hard for a long time, crunched under each one of them: now. To the extent that collectively-made and collectively-interpreted perceptions had a calming effect, every perception and every interpretation that was exactly like every other perception and its interpretation was assured to calm every denizen of the Thur region who perceived what was and compared that which was with that which another and then a third denizen of the Thur region regarded as existent and present; this selfsame thing, certainly the catastrophe, was once again not a catastrophe that brought any solution or answer; and yet the collectively arrived-at conclusion—that the catastrophe to be perceived was one single collective catastrophe—was extraordinarily calming; the mental exchange of the news, which would soon no longer be new, was now almost enough to put you to sleep, and everyone was everyone else's narcotic, not blind, not blind at all, not even snow-blind, the reason being that no conscienceless disregard of the natural phenomenon was gaining ground; Robert did not dare hope that in the following hour someone would take up position next to him, peer out, and after a successful peering, shout

THE THAW IS HERE!

No motion moving. The house deathly pale, gently smoking from the chimney. All three were standing where they had stood still. Nothing changed. For any alteration there was not a trace of hope for a reason and not a grain of expectation. Omnipotently, Robert was living high on the hog; with arms crossed, his wife rummaged in old Frenchmen and had the maid bring her the almonds to be pounded for baking the quince tarts like crazy; the maid strode in, wearing a hip-length smock with a broad, plunging rolled collar; her legs were inserted in long, tight sleeves, and what was sticking out of the sleeves was wearing green velvet boots with black zippers that ran along the inside of her calf from the maidknee to the maidinstep; Robert's wife had had her entire face lifted, somehow, in a not-unnatural way; she'd become younger, and she looked younger in her chemise dress with a narrow lapel collar under which long cuffed sleeves led past two breast pockets, once sewn up and now torn open, neatly and as if drawn-on, past the warm brown polecat eyes of her cup-shaped breasts; eventually everything flowed into the slender hands, which tapered funnel-like toward the fingertips; the hands left a tiny square open where all the fingers were attached; Robert knew there were five fingers, here too; the maid had aged with ghastly rapidity, far outrunning her lifetime; not long ago she had grown nearly as old as the northernmost tip of Finland. One morning—Robert was drawing a horizontal line on the side view of a stairstep when suddenly the line bent downward as if on a picture drawn by a severe schizophrenic who, working with a long, thin ruler, is constantly drawing circles—one morning things went downhill, in the direction of springtime; barkless birch blocks bobbed in the eddying Thur; three quarters of an enormous seven-hundred-year-old oak tree had found its way into a so-called glacial mill and, not far from the Thur embankment, was expansively swinging its terrible mass around in circles with a tremendous destructive momentum, beating froth like a generator into the dark current that was whooshing into the depths and with its suction dragging everything down to hell. All at once Robert's line moved downward; Robert's hand, which was holding the pastel crayon he was drawing with, ran after it; without any effort, Robert broke his arm with one blow down on the staircase and, even while the arm was still hanging down by him with the hand significantly twisted outward, began to scream his now conscience-stricken remarks, which were located on this side of proverbiality, in purely oral form into the hallway; Robert seemed to be assuming the presence of a dictation machine, two nimble tape reels that were turning; a dictation machine next to the wood stove . . . Robert was overtaxing the weary props manager who had furnished the house for him and his wife . . . there was certainly a wood stove there, but there was certainly no dictation machine next to it; in a plaster cast up to his shoulder, Robert screamed at the kitchen his "I won't ever be able to do it again!" in every conceivable masquerade and costume with makeup; from time to time he broke out in a hoarse sentimentality along the lines of "shipwreck swim to the shore with me we will join together on the lonesome desert island under the pale Caribbean moon" . . . Robert broke out in such emotionalities if he didn't happen to be playing the Simplicissian hermit aloof from the Thirty Years' War or else burdening his wife with two to five pages of non-intellectual reading with the approximate command "there take that read that it's written by a guy who was also incompetent" . . . his wife took the papers under consideration with a nimble tongue and yellow, oval eyes, or else she didn't; and the maid dropped a log of firewood at her own feet . . .

THE THAW IS HERE! That person could have shouted this who unfortunately didn't turn up at Robert's side when Robert was hoping to find his planting hole by digging, or, in case he didn't find it by digging, wanted to replace it with the new planting hole; the person who had not turned up had perhaps been there anyway when Robert had bent over in such a way that he had to overlook him . . . then that person had run head over hands out of the garden plot and had burrowed into the earth outside the fence gate, speedily dredging with what were nearly mole's hands. Robert took this as the sign which he, himself already half-drowned or burned up, had long awaited, patiently and without quarreling with anyone, no matter who; his hands, on which hungry white leprosy was eating its way backward, dropped the tiny tree trunk . . .

And while she was carrying firewood from the yard to the stove the maid accidentally dropped a log in front of her feet; she was still on the steps when it fell at her feet; the thin sleeves in which her legs were inserted under the smock, the legs that were flicking back and forth like pincers, stood still; the log of firewood fell in front of her feet, and at that point she had not yet gotten past the stairs that led from the yard to the stove; outside the kitchen door is where it fell in front of her feet; in front of her feet the log of firewood fell onto the steps, next to the bucket that she had not emptied, so that she could not fill it up any more with the ashes that she had to pull out of the ash pan on the stove when she shoved the new wood into the stove; and there lay that log of firewood on the steps in front of the maidfeet; every detail that could still have made the maid into a particular unmistakable being was extinguished; in Robert's creatively crushing work field she will-o-wisped, this grand new woman standing still; and since she had been an old woman and was also losing her eyebrow hair and was approaching a lusterless pallid never-again-oily woman's pate without even the smallest wig-like-nestlike-concealing secret compartment, she phosphoresced even more nocturnally, even more piercingly, spectral but present. No sooner had the maid noticed the piece of stovewood at her feet (just as surely as she deigned to overlook the unemptied bucket and the halfway-pulled-out dust-emitting ash pan), than she repressed any surprise, so ineptly so that she made an ashenly horrified impression on that very Robert in relation to whom she was hoping to put herself in the position of the stronger one by showing utmost fortitude in adversity; hadn't she watched many times, softly stammering, as Robert, on the leather leash that he asked to have put around his neck, sniveled weak and short of breath and spoke of mercifulness the way people do who often get beaten, but hardly ever people who often do the beating; or else people who often get beaten are too beaten up around the mouth to speak of mercifulness, and people who often do the beating are afraid (usually groundlessly and in misplaced excess anxiety) of the bloody revenge of the people that they beat, and so they talk endlessly about mercifulness; hadn't the maid often stood by watching mutely as Robert, almost strangled by the leather strap that was looped around his neck, and beaten almost senseless by the diligent little men who ran around in his brain with nasty threshing flails, sniveled weakly and breathlessly, trying to discern a sensitive side of his slaughterhouse; mustn't she have noticed from his frequent goal-directed jaunts that he had long been suffering from loose and extremely painful stools due to a highly cultivated digestive-tract cyst? In any case, by making her legs under the smock that covered a lot of things move back and forth in that particular way, she called for Robert just as loudly as she would have if she had possessed a really loud voice or if she had actually been possessed of a resonant, operettic voice that carried. No voice that carried. Every word with which she called for Robert's help was left uncalled. No one and nothing communicated. For a speaking relationship there was not the shadow of a suspicion and not a drop of promise. Whether the maidvoice would sound, was decided; how should it have continued to sound after it already died away at the point of its gurgling origin? and yet; the maid's shrill throat voice reached Robert in the corridor, at the foot of the staircase, where he was gloomily brooding over fresh drawings that had come to him overnight, for the drawings remained undrawn; Robert was afraid of breaking a bone in his other arm, and instead raised his broken wing from the supporting plate; his hand was still turned upward; his upper arm and forearm, instead of healing up, were growing apart; Robert no longer took up a pastel crayon with his healthy arm, but cried out at the pain in his joints, giving the confession of his incompetence a new connotation. To a day he heard the maidcry, rushed in great confusion (which set suddenly in after energetic cheerfulness and had an easy time of it with the preceding fluctuating emotional state) outside through the kitchen door, past the full bucket, ran as if there were no stairsteps out from the raised threshold flat out into the air and was borne up by the air; and from the way her legs formed the pincers Robert recognized his own situation, namely . . . he recognized his own situation, namely . . . Robert rather painstakingly pondered the log of firewood lying on the steps with the maidfeet behind it, both lying on the steps from the yard to the stove; the feet adhering to the wood, the step swallowing and cementing-in the maidfeet up to the maidankles; agile plaster fibers, penetrating-hardening, blocked the zipper tracks on the inner side of the ancient shanks; everything on the stairstep; the stairstep swallowing everything, already close to swallowing the maidsmock; and the air carried Robert, who did not sink down onto the stairstep; it would have absorbed him too like a wanderer in a foggy marsh and the wanderer is wearing no snowshoes on his feet to prevent sinking; and the dreary nature of the excitation to the most terrible of all unions hung the little Roberts in rows from the bewildered hooks and clothes hangers and then forced them to drink to the dregs their dwarfish little cups filled with a colorless liquid; the dregs were bitter and tasted like almonds. With the same tenacity with which the little Roberts, severely mistreated and hard-bodied from lifelong thirst, slipping in the direction of the distant wood stoves in the frothing Thur, so grew the big Robert's bumbling desire for fleshly proofs of his incompetence, which up to now he had given form to on the wall of the stairwell, without his wall sketches having proven anything other than the stoic equanimity of walls and their immense bearing capacity . . .

Robert's sickened hand dropped the sapling on which progressive mottling and soundless twig dieback were making themselves noticeable; at first the interruptions in exposure to light were bearable, and then light exposure went on without a pause; cold light began to shine on Robert's small tool shed three hundred meters away from the garden cottage, and the endless snow surface glittered as well; in it advancing tongues of brown earth were visible; the microbe landscape had become pointy and vicious; every crystal started dispatching its own kind of piercing light. As if carousel balloons were tied to it, this strip of existence rose and lifted Robert up with it, who was pleading vociferously and hardly convincingly for his expiration, his intimate expiration: along the clot fiber by the name of Thur, Robert was running a race with the rising sun, leap for leap; he did not have the slightest prospects as soon as the hot light made him sparkle and radiated him to bits, if it did not intend to cook him maliciously until the bouillon cube Robert produced meat broth, even while his notorious knee joints carried him away from the Thur sun, which remained hopelessly near. Up to his knees he stood in the clot fiber Thur, at forehead level the sun raged, let off its leash; the strip of existence was narrowing, it was not rising but narrowing, the riverbed rose, the sun ceiling sank, and in between no Robert was needed any longer. That horrible sun; it was brusque, heating it up, fast and red, heating everything up; Robert's lips, drawn into a straight line, could tell you a devastating thing or two about that; no voice; and yet; as if after a bereavement, his voice was coated with fake sympathy. Once he had gotten up to speed, Robert was roasting with fear; a chest muscle contracted; his heart did a pike against the contracted muscle; nearly infarctious heartbeats; piddling flight-haste threatened by apoplexy; the fear pulled one of Robert's eyelids upward, but at the same time his pupils were closing; Robert wanted to get out by his fence gate, whose opening he guessed was two shoes away from the fence corner; incorrect; it was eighteen shoes; when Robert collided with the fence the first time, he still had fifteen shoes' worth of fence collisions ahead of him; eighteen wounds in his wire-pierced pelvis. Robert's sapling had gotten hung up by a hook of bark in a shoelace, branches on hand forced their way into Robert's shoes, and he got stuck on the gatepost and wished his vexing implements to hell with a banal curse originating from the lower vernacular. The Thurian hell broke over Robert, who spent days tearing himself free and was able to detach the tiny tree trunk but not himself; Robert, who eventually left all the branches hanging on that damnably distant fence gate and headed for those monsters, namely . . . toward those monsters, namely . . . toward those monsters, namely the Thurian high-rise housing complexes. Before he made his way into the shadow of the housing blocks that went on for kilometers, he could not consider himself rescued; when he heard the hoarse roars of distress of the tenants lined up for kilometers on their verandas and ready for the roll call, coming from the more-or-less sunny side—in a slightly hissing vapor cloud the entire Thur had evaporated into thin air—Robert considered himself rescued until further notice. Others were boiling in his stead. Seething, the springtime sun rolled down behind the apartment blocks . . .

Robert peered back. He surprised himself by not having gotten out the kitchen door yet. Several things occurred. Robert saw his wife, in red shorts with very short cuffs, standing very erectly way in the back behind the stove, over the ash pan far in front of the full bucket, in the half-shadow of the walls of the hallway, almost in a niche of the staircase, out of which the riser crawled forth. The hallway opened out way at the back, where it was narrow and ended in the cooking area, enlarged into a sunken space that opened up on all sides into the distance, into the stove area in the middle of which the stove stood with the ash pan hanging out; the maid on the way from the yard to the stove had grown quiet; the log of firewood in front of the maidfeet; the step covering on the kitchen stairs engulfing the maid, starting with her feet; Robert entrapped in between; Robert's wife, one side leaned against the stove, both boots with zippers ripped open stretching away from the stove diagonally over the stove area—so that Robert will never escape from the mesh of the net—Robert's wife, her breast pockets hanging down to her belt, reading out past the pages of the novella as if the lines of the novella went on to the right past the page margin and as if the stone floor and the wall seams also contained novella text printed on them and as if the all-covering wallpaper was nothing but a never-ceasing novella text smudgy with fly-foot specks . . . Robert's wife, reading text lines three meters long—to judge by her swift, squinty eye movements—waiting with a stony mouth for Robert's ultimate befuddlement. Steaming slaughtering days with jerky unions in the hallway would bleed Robert anew. The time of the maid was over. The maid, who in her green velvet boots zipped all the way up sought refuge behind her venerable suit of armor, which had become as hard as chitin in the domestic service that she had performed from time immemorial ("That totally ridiculous firewood log that has just fallen down at my feet!"), when the anthracitic tongue of her mistress denied her any further justification for carrying wood, picked up that "totally ridiculous" splintering log from in front of the maidfeet that were alien to her; her eyes closed themselves . . .

The spring sun pushed its way behind the apartment blocks. The end of winter on the Thur. The thirty-first birthday would be an occasion for celebration. The spring sun grabbed at Robert, who was binding up his raffia rolls, oblivious and yet leisurely, while he was making it clear to himself that the springtime and the resident population that was spit out by the rest of the population in and of themselves signified an end like oak fungus; as often as Robert fell onto his back in the empty channel from which the Thur water had evaporated, he completely hyperextended his knee and burned up and drowned like his shovels, support stakes, rakes, crates, etc., just the way the snow vaporized, just the way the skin on Robert's face became the garden-variety suntan, not one degree too dark; the hole in Robert's Thurian life, which would later be his whole life, had finally expanded, far too consistently and forcefully to be called consolingly small, imperceptibly small; in Robert's future, Robert planted for decades—until from leprosy there were no more hands there and tiny tree trunks could no longer be grasped with the stumps, which were already sick again—in the eternally determined future Robert planted without a single planting hole, according to the unnatural Schreber method, as the inventor of torture devices had laid it down in his apparatuses; in just this way Robert planted a green, branching, tough little sapling in the center of the brown spot, which was later torn and broken wide open . . .

With youthful maideyes, still skilled but half-closed in childish pride, the maid ran past Robert and knocked over a full bucket on her way to the kitchen; the maid climbed over her mistress, stepping on her knee, stepping on her book of novellas, stepping on the crown of her head, and threw the firewood log, which she had gathered up, into the stove that was glowing with a blazing flame; she could still have followed the orders that assured her a livelihood by hurling herself at Robert; at least she might have emptied the ash pan after emptying the full bucket after going from kitchen to yard; and after setting down bucket under sink, she might have pushed the empty ash pan back into the yawning maw of the stove under the log of firewood that was catching fire; Robert's companion cost herself her board and her job, while Robert, with a cold, impassive gaze, straightened out his arm cast, which was pointing horizontally from his shoulder toward the staircase; the maid was running toward the debouchment of the hallway (that terrible house-exit canal), in a panting geriatric run as old as Finland; in order to rescue from the flames that which was not charring, Robert ran after her, she who in the following, eighth month was already laid off in shame and disgust and naked under the scratchy hairsmock and put out on a street where the overflowing Thur raged and severely injured her with the oak sweeping by; the maid climbed over her mistress in the reverse direction, stepping on the crown of her head, stepping on her book of novellas, stepping on her knee, from kitchen to yard. Before Robert, in pursuit of her, put the house kitchen behind him, he had snatched up a goodly number of hot logs out of the burning stove and thrown these firewood logs, replete with their unsteady smoldering, onto the floor in front of the stove; the logs piled up on Robert's wife's open boot flaps, which were moving across the floor; and Robert fastened his broken arm and the flesh of his pelvis, which had outgrown itself at every point, to the glassy cheek of his wife; all of this of course while hanging up the little Roberts over the little stoves, the gaze of the dead, shut, lidded eyes of his fanatically loved wife behind him, the living but ancient, bald, monstrously essential maidgaze on his chest, flinging the still flickering log from the floor back into the stove, stepping twice over his wife, stomping on her knee, stomping on her book of novellas, stomping on the crown of her head, standing still and listening to the whoosh of the wintry Thur; from the crown of her head down, trampling her book of novellas, down from the book of novellas, trampling her knees; slowly, moving his one side away from the stove and cattishly floor-skulking from the stove area to the middle of the kitchen, tore from Robert's wife's blouse her breast pockets, hanging down and fluttering in his wake; no more new pain arose, at most the same old severe one a hundred times over; all this after Robert's finely drawn-up plans for all the rest of time had become meaningless due to Robert's profound incompetence, and now he was actually awaiting nothing more than deliverance and the death of sleep until he turned a year older.

# TOTEMS AND TABOOS

Nothing more . . .

Nothing more . . .

What was to be written is written. I'm not getting any more ideas. The book has to be longer. God help me . . .

Cost what it will . . .

Sitting here . . .

Not a single idea, no ideas . . .

Over. Done with. I am now experiencing how I . . .

Help me, God . . .

Nothing more? . . .

What was to be written is written? . . .

Shall we start something else? . . .

A very homey inspiration for once. It begins when you're picking your nose . . .

Nothing more; only . . .

I'm bored to death, picking my distended nose and sticking the snot on my eyebrow hairs and on my backside, and the harder I pick, the slower time passes, and the more mischief I can get into in the same length of time. What goes through my head that my finger can't dig out? So let's just write haphazardly—what's hazarded will happen—like the following . . .

I was a young author; pretty pauperized; there was a connection there. From my own bed, when I was in love, I had taken a pink sheet. When I was standing under Ann's window, I threw the sheet up in the air, toward Ann's illuminated room. She grabbed the end of the sheet, tied it fast to the hinge, which grew in the darkness and stuck out from the wall (west window), sticking out a little. The lamp in her chamber shed light on an opulent philodendron with enclaves in its arching leaves; vegetating teeth; the plant had a proclivity for the Amazon rain forest and surrounded itself with branches like a Creole woman with crinolines. While I observed Ann's hands handily smoothing and stretching the bed sheet I thought about my social status, which, although I had become the manager of a writing business, hardly stood above that of Berditschewsky, a foreman in whose tract house on the edge of the city she occupied a furnished room, to which she made an exceedingly courteous invitation after I had made her aware of my crippled condition (stage one, totally non-venereal). It was to be free of charge and not touch the reserves; moreover, in possession of a young, marketable portfolio, I had my sights set on a change of career: pimp, white-collar. In her curled hair Ann wore a blue rose, and with her piano fingers she fondly fondled the feathery fluff; I saw before me nothing but interstitially interlocking rooms in which bare, flesh-colored parrots lay on their cage floors next to their perches and could be pulled out through the feed tray. It would never have occurred to me in those days to shave twice a day; the razor had fallen on the floor; then I let the noon hour pass unused, ingesting at most a Salisbury steak with onion rings kneaded into it; the phonetics of the pathological interior monologue were chewed along with it . . .

That was bad. And now a quip that will be told again about ten more times . . .

"Something is tormenting me. I'm writing about it," I told my subaltern Peyer.

"Writing is *my* job," he interrupted me.

"The agency is supposed to write along with me," I sighed.

"Have you already started it?" he wanted to know . . .

Shaving in the evening. The razor's vibrations were massaging the fat off my jaw. Pushing it into my earlobes. Suddenly my eyelid seized up. My dubious winking petrified. The shape of my chin before and after shaving was not the same. That could not have come from blood loss alone. The same thing on my abdomen . . .

If it has to be, then at least as quickly as possible . . .

Robert stood by me, my spiritual father. Otherwise, pragmatically speaking, I had my nimble, somewhat chittering assistants, male ones, who wrote the manuscripts for me, and now and then even let me insert a word myself. Ann, when I hoisted myself up by the sheet, was wearing her blue rose and glowing, the bartered bride. The unkempt bartered bride, when I the puritan got up there, was smoking a cigarette with hints of barn animal, radiantly white and clear in front of the black backdrop. Stupidly, I was wearing thick sunglasses. A tortured laugh with my tongue tucked back, for I knew that there was an expanse of snow below me; the streets were frozen over, and for the sake of credibility I had flitted to the periphery on the ice skates (propeller steamer: there is no more slippery vehicle than prose) to throw the ice skates through a hole in the ice on the pond; better the skates than myself: that much at least seemed clear, in this highly romantic side note . . .

With a scrunched-up sheet I stood in the winter night and . . .

She's constantly putting the squeeze on. I'm afraid she'll just get mad at me again. I beg of you. I'll give anything just to have my peace. She won't give it to me. And so I have to give more. I give. But I don't know if she thinks the dose is big enough. On that point she leaves me in the dark. That's a state of suffering for me, do you even notice? No sooner do I think I've bought me some peace with her than she lets me know that peace expects a new gift on my part. How long can I keep on delivering? And am I allowed to talk about all of this? I assume that by having talked about it, I've forfeited my peace for the most part. The worst thing is that you get used to the squeeze. I love peace, and my inhibitions about paying only a limited amount for it have vanished. I am completely uninhibited when it comes to paying; "squeeze," that term from the orange and apple juice industry, fits perfectly; yes, the affected fruit, that's me; I'll pay whatever it takes. And that's probably only so that at some final unpredictable end I'll get peace. She'll withhold peace from me as long as it suits her. That's what I call a lucrative investment, a chain of gifts from one company to the other that never quits and never pays off. I'll never be able to pay it off—the investment, I mean. And the miniature, as well as the cosmic, quirk consists in the fact that she delivers her monologue about me in the same words, because her galaxy sends out the same message via cosmic rays: "He's constantly putting the squeeze on. I'm afraid he'll just get mad at me again." This much symmetry is madness, or else will lead to it; the logicality of both systems amounts to their mutual destruction; but let's wait and see, let's just wait! Until further notice, everything is changeable . . .

I had clammy hands, clamping my end of the sheet threaded through them, and then the sheet ripped, in the middle. I landed with a thud on the glazed cobblestones; her landlord, the foreman, was sound asleep. At this moment, on the other side of the city, at the foot of the first suburban church, Peyer was dying; Peyer, who hated me and had never converted—at most once, when I deferred to him the right of way to her. While I was lying on the ice and thinking things over, she came down the outside staircase, took off a glove, took off two gloves, and took off a third glove in order to create a certain suspense before promptly rolling up one sleeve, under which appeared the brawny arm of a boxer. As soon as I started screaming, it was opened to me, just as if it led INTO the tract house, the door. A man by the name of Peyer had probably shown a man by the name of Robert a few immanent space tricks that could be used to expand the tract houses; as interior designers, they were both just about equally good, except that Peyer earned incomparably more money: he had made his career with his front doors, which did not lead INTO the building, but AROUND it. You could expect anything from that kind of architecture . . .

In one room, all of a sudden, more stuff was found than we had put in there . . .

With the scrunched-up sheet hanging down from the window I stood bent over in the winter night and said: “As you can see, I brought the most essential thing right over.” Ann showed me in and we ran around the house four times before we entered. She offered me a scotch, an easy chair, and a small white lightweight ball; it happened quickly. “Hirsch wants it that way, so that you know what’s up when he calls on you,” she said. It came as a surprise that he wanted to interfere. I hadn’t been planning on this interference. Never before had I tackled a homeowner. I laughed gratingly and said: “Up till now I’ve played ping-pong.” His breathing was audible; we were grinning. I plopped down on the mangy, forgotten seat in the lobby. She leaned over me, I leaned over the philodendron, Ann leaned over the sea-green floor tiles, both of us leaned over the newspaper rack and waited for the Count to surprise us; end quote . . .

In the laundry room Ann had set up ten little men, in ten little cages, all in a row . . .

Outside. Divided from Inside. Windowpane in between. Birds that didn't figure that out. They flew into it and . . .

On the same evening I suddenly got sick. My ear was whirring as if there were a zeppelin tearing around in my auditory canal and trying to get out, and I pulled two metal rings over my arms. That didn't do much good. The rest of my arms swelled up as far as my shoulders, where two bloodshot pouches formed. Then it came to mind that I was just imagining all of this. I stripped the metal rings off my arms and the flesh redistributed itself quickly, down to my wrists. I let myself fall forward and Ann's hands tried to catch me from the front, but with an effort of will I knocked them out of the way. My hair flattened backward in the draft of air; I caught a glimpse of a field of sharp pebbles quite close to my face, and then I lost consciousness. I was not aware of the impact. When I woke up again, I was still lying down as I had landed, and the whirring in my ear no longer mattered to me. Nor was I sick any longer, just badly injured on my face. Granted, I was now doing much worse than when I had the zeppelin in my ear, but I had become much calmer. I knew what was wrong with me, and from now on I didn't miss a thing. The injury was impressive enough, but at least no unexplainable symptom was announcing itself anymore, and the next morning I was more or less scarred over . . .

Now she was ready for anything . . .

In the restraint room, which due to the length of our stay there was taking on the character of a living room, there were suddenly two desks . . .

One room we protected from intruding eyes with white hovering soffits. There were no nosy people, but we imagined to ourselves that there were; I suspect that I talked to her for so long about nosy people, describing the rheumy prognathic eyes that they directed at our feathers with such powerful visuals that I convinced Ann—right out of the blocks and without further argument. "I would never like to be seen," I said. "All lives and all life processes run parallel," said Ann, "and so they're doing it if we're doing it." In this room . . .

All the time, ceaselessly, birds outside flying into the windowpanes. They wanted a shortcut and got suckered. We heard a soft thump whenever the panes let one through; as if a slipper had fallen right side up onto the rug. Then they would lie on their sides, with their little legs sticking crookedly up in the air. She laid them in a basket lined with cloth. Gave them water to drink. They went and got it, putting their heads in the salad bowl and scritching their beaks across the glass, which did not retain a trace of them. They turned away and took another short cut . . .

In a fireplace there was a niche. Then and there . . .

In a corner between the chairs . . .

In the room where food had twice been spread out on the long table, and which therefore, once we were well trained, was called "dining room," a dark-brown roll-top desk showed up in the vicinity of the curtains. They were made of red tulle. The roll-top desk created contrast and deepened the roominess of the room, which at 11.5 by 13.5 feet really could use some roominess. An airiness emanated from the desk, as if Ann, more powerfully than expected, had performed swimming movements in the junk in our apartment for several weeks and eliminated the worst of it and then rinsed her elbows up to the base of her neck . . .

The big lamp assumed us into its dome of light. Ann cast a shadow; I cast my own . . .

She was lying very close. She was pretty warm. I tried to enter her . . .

In the fireplace there was a niche; the decorator had a skewed imagination; in the niche there were rolled-up rugs, enough to line a train station concourse. Bumps protruded from the walls; each room had its own small tile stove, a guarantor of equal-opportunity freezing. In one corner stood a shaft like the cleaning rod of an air rifle. With a shoe I knocked on her door. At this point Peyer first became aware of the problem that there was no connection between his reading and his understanding, unless he had suddenly—disgusting!—consented to the purely additive, for which, in his own critical words, "not even a binary slide-bar adder" was necessary. In his dungeon Meyer Hirsch Berditschewsky was snoring. Coming from the men's dormitory, he had taken his week off; no hammering alarm clock, no cacophonous bell, not even a mild explosion could have rung him awake; by a wallpapered wall there stood, six feet out of place, the filling, brimming armoire of pear wood, upon which stood a child's bathtub; a spiral staircase led up through the ceiling to the separate toilets in whose bowls there were actually table bells floating and, if you tore off a tissue, they rang hollowly. When Ann said that the cost of living had gone up since the oil (the housewife and the collapse of the global currency system), I said: "Make me a steak, a small one." Upon which she scolded: "That's just it"; no, she didn't scold, she just fondled the handle of the ladle ...

She was lying pretty close. Compulsive attempt on my part. I tried to enter her ...

The tension was moving toward such an unbearable climax that we both cried out loud in distress, out the window which had been thrown open, out into the steamy summer landscape, where even the straw woven into hats became long and hard like the rotunda of the sanctum semen bellyward on the bull ...

In the dining room ...

"May I ask you a question," I asked.

"Later. I'm suffering. On your account. Ask me later," she said ...

Now I was ready for anything ...

A single large feeble pale lamp that stood on the fourth desk illuminated the room from the window recess. From the window, when we were lying on top of each other in the frame, in a habituation that in spite of everything was not disagreeable, we could see the city. From the window we could see out onto the city. Assuming they had torn down the ten or fifteen houses that stood between us and the city and leveled the empty space, we could have looked out on the city from the window. In this case it could have happened that we lay down together in front of the window in order to look out; whereas due to the habituation there was nothing more to see ...

Have a heated exchange of words occur. The almost normal prelude to the emotional degrees of hardness that reached deeper into the other, if only everyone would just take matters sufficiently into their own hands . . .

"I've started your report," said Peyer.

"Where are you?" I asked.

"I'm up to 'Robert stood by me,'" said Peyer.

"I'm about eight pages past that. Keep it up!" I said . . .

In the laundry room Ann had set up ten little men, in ten little cages, all in a row. The cages stood on a table, and the table stood on a stone floor, which disappeared in the middle, at its lowest point, into a drain. The arrangement of the little men was such that Ann could stand in front of it and put all ten fingers into the cages at the same time. Ann did this, and ten deep but tiny cries echoed through the laundry room, and ten jaws closed on her fingertips. Then Ann abandoned herself to various malicious games, pulling her fingers toward her, pushing them away, always with the little men on them . . .

The fiddler crab, also known as the calling crab, is a crustacean that feels itself in possession of two claws of unequal size. With the smaller one it props itself up on the sand—which gives way beneath the claw, so that the animal has to keep repositioning it—and with the larger one it waves at or "calls to" the female: she is distinguished from the male in that her claws are also of unequal size, but the bigger one is only about as big as the male's smaller one. With the smaller one the female props herself up on the sand—bracing herself anew again and again—and with the bigger one she waves at or "calls to" the male. The male redoubles his waving with the giant claw, but the female waves at the smaller claw that is as large as the larger female one. This waving does not stop until the male pulls his smaller claw out from under him in order to have his attentions requited. They are requited: except that the support collapses, and the male digs with his mouth-shovels and feeding filters into the sand—which readily gobbles him up—and in conclusion he lets the large claw stick up over the dune ridge. Immobility is now the signal that drives the crab's eroticism to new, hardly socially acceptable manifestations. The feeling of being in possession of different calling claws, in a wise assessment of the dug-in position, no longer pays a visit to the centers of affect; where a moment ago full possession prevailed, now the absence of appreciable physical—tough-as-shells—fields of application is gnawing. The female, tiny claw and little claw, gets off a dismissive wave at the sunken male ruin, for whom this whole business is now long since only a faint call not to come out again, but to call that which he is sinking into "boundlessness" or "ocean" . . .

One morning, in bed of course, in no particular context, I thought the following: "That which I believe will occur, and that which really will occur: these two things are separate from each other, have nothing to do with each other, each occurs by itself, and it is totally impossible to derive one of them from the other. At most I am allowed to guess the one on the basis of the other. Every prognosis that I posit with regard to me and Ann, and every analysis that seems to work out right for me, deserves to be called GUESSWORK; any other designation would be fraudulent; it is I who am putting an end to fraud; I know that what will probably occur and what will have definitely occurred, that these two things lie far apart from each other and that every conclusion or every extrapolation of thought beyond the present condition is a GRAND ILLUSION. It would be best for me to stop thinking about what will happen someday. Although I don't know what is going to happen, and thus also don't know whether it will be good or bad for us, it is a relief to decide to no longer think about what will happen, whether good or bad. To stop at each and every thought of what is to come! A weight is lifted from me; I can breathe easier; or at least I feel like I was previously breathing under a heavy load that is no longer pressing down on me; even though I haven't actually removed anything from myself; for I, if I stop thinking, don't know whether I am omitting things from my thoughts that are good for me or things that are bad for me; there is no way I can know that, since I'm not even thinking them; that I do not know the contents of the omissions, that I only know the omissions, well, that's just the risk one takes with these omissions; a weight is lifted from me. I only know that if I were to keep thinking and think some more, I would definitely be able to think up many more things concerning what is to come or concerning what in my estimation will come. And so if I don't think, I omit so-and-so many possibilities of thinking. If I don't let my thinking come into play for even just one short moment, I will forfeit so-and-so many possibilities. That is definitely of evil, considering how the supply of life's possibilities is already extremely reduced, and anyway, even if you're putting a lot of effort into thinking, the supply keeps melting away almost hourly. And so, by continuing to lie limply in bed today I am voluntarily forfeiting more of life's possibilities, of the few that remain. An oppressive idea, no doubt; hopefully the oppression will get recast into sleepiness, and then I'll be rid of the idea. The consequences of a voluntary renunciation of further possibilities would have to put me in a gloomy mood and deprive me of any lust for life; and of course that's exactly what they do. There is no other possibility than their putting me in a gloomy mood and depriving me of any more lust for life. Of course it is the end of any life whatsoever if I stop thinking even just a little bit. In general (here I grew bolder, because Ann had slipped into my room) it is the end of any and all life if there is an end to thinking about what will be. But luckily not every life is over after all (Ann instilled hope in me with small acts of kindness and influenced my magnum opus), and the way I hear it, in every life, thought is ceaselessly given to what tomorrow will probably bring, and it is also firmly assumed that what then does happen is something that probably had to happen anyway. This assumption may be wrong (here I wondered about the Kantian locus of philosophizing; whether it also applies in the morning with an Ann who influenced it with small gestures?), and this life might be a falsely conceived one: in any case it goes on, it lives. My life, on the other hand ("Get up!" Ann yelled into my mind, which was instantly darkened by torment), has just been relieved of the heavy weight of total prognosis, which weighs down on me and completely crushes me; but the distance from thinking comes at the price that my life ("Shower's cold!" Ann called through the door) will more or less stop continuing or, more likely, will probably not continue much longer. I got up very well preserved, too well preserved, and I washed up and for several hours I could not discover a single sign of a serious illness in myself . . .

"How much do you earn now?" I asked.

"I don't understand," she said.

"Per man," I asked.

Turnabout would be fair play.

"As for me, I cannot live off your earnings," I said.

"That's not important," she said.

"I can't live off MY earnings either," I said.

"Most of them pay me double," she said.

"That's not important," I said.

"But it is interesting," she said.

"Suddenly the stillness was broken by soft sounds of a beautiful unknown voice that seemed to be coming from an ancient oak tree . . ." (Novalis)

The agitation of our exchange of words seemed to want to prelude psychological brutalities; a minor key was already hanging in the room. I clumsily raised my hands (several of them), which let drop what they could not express and trampled it underfoot, my foot. Words and phrases had broken down, and I personally pulled the plugs on the audio contacts. Something on my nasal septum had shifted. I whistled when I inhaled. When I exhaled all that happened was exhaling, without a whistle. Even though this was normal, I thought there should also be a whistle when I exhaled. Whenever I didn't breathe at all, nothing happened either. Constriction of the health districts—weird. Exhaling and inhaling were both healthy, but unfortunately I couldn't stand either nothing but exhaling or nothing but not breathing at all for very much longer. There was supposed to be some kind of inhaling in there too, that's how I was built. In this regard I differed significantly. To sing a song: "Only when the mantle of air has dropped from my shoulders, tom-tom, then it will rattle like chains, iron links." . . .

In the dining room . . .

I would rip into the interior organization of the house. No matter what particular state of mind I might find myself in—our dining room always seemed to me to be the most repulsive of our rooms. Ann loved it. She liked to sit at the table with the green tablecloth, under the lamp with the straw-hat shade . . .

"You know a lot of people," I said.

"A few besides you," she said.

"How are we going to beat this problem?" I asked.

"What problem?" she asked back.

"Our problem," I said.

"How are other people supposed to beat our problem?" she asked.

"You're making my questions look dumb," I ranted.

"You," she said . . .

Now all of a sudden she was lying very close. Her smell reminded me of her, but also of all of my exes. Of course I became possessive when she took possession of my member . . .

"The money has to come from somewhere, you know," she cried.

"I will sell a piece of prose," I said.

"Nobody's going to invest in you with this recession on," she said.

Respectable.

"We can have ourselves coffined together," I said in a hushed, sing-songy necrophilia . . .

And why not, anyway? But I could just as well have . . .

To Ann's amazement, and in order to hurt her, one morning I shifted the dining room upward. With a block and tackle I hoisted the room cube, knocking a hole in the roof and pushing the cube up onto the beams that still held. We had a tower room. First breakfast with an unobstructed view of the city. Breathlessly you came climbing up the rope that I hung down; I saw nothing but restlessness and cramping in your sitting posture during breakfast. At my side a plummeting with an undetected impact. At the same moment it was standing there: the fifth desk with the teak leaf, merging seamlessly with the dining table. The first thing I did was to insert a piece of jam and bread into the typewriter. Refusal to continue from the point where I had stopped. Shortly afterward—I was not observing myself—she discovered in me the same posture that she had discovered in herself. "How cramped," you said. "My muscle is cramping from hauling the dining room up to the roof," I said.

"On the other hand, you're restless," you said. "You're projecting that outward," I said. "Please don't throw everything off of you onto me; I could start throwing back . . ."

"Everything is due to the recession," I said, in order to provoke Ann.

"Economic being is consciousness," she asserted.

"Does Meyer Hirsch know that?" I asked.

"He's sleeping."

"If he knew that, he'd throw you out," I said.

"You'd fly out of here too, far away," she said.

"Everything is due to the recession." I was provoked.

"Provoke me a little bit," she said, cheered up, tracing the edge of my body. It did not refuse it . . .

"The difference between Scottish bagpipes and Irish bagpipes is that the drone pipes, the ones without finger holes, can be adjusted. Stupidly enough I no longer know which one that applies to. But they are not the same bagpipes. And one of them is even called something completely different. Not for nothing, not for nothing. (Pause) Do you know the master? His name is Finbar Furey. (Pause) Now that lazy memory actually is starting to set in: it's the Irish bagpipes! What are they, I hear you ask. In fact, the bagpipes whose pipes are adjustable are called Irish bagpipes. (Pause) On the other hand, I don't know which bagpipes this Finbar is master of. How dumb . . ."

"Your Peyer," she said, "one of my best acquaintances, son of a bank employee and a sales trainer, came by yesterday, because he is in love with me just as you are; in mean-spirited circles he's known as a slight syphilitic; sickly intellectuals aren't the only ones I take care of. When he sat down in the chair you're sitting in now, taking it easy, the philodendron threw a flesh harpoon that sank its barbs into his gums. Later—it was almost like dentistry—his tongue was injured, he was swallowing blood and threatening me with an embolism if it did not happen that night. At least that's what he told me at dinner. After dinner, as usual, shaving was on the schedule, forty-five minutes on setting number two. Peyer ran away and in the garden he injured his head on a stone bench; my landlord had to get a new lawn put in just because of him, which isn't as easy to do on the outskirts as a country bumpkin (glances at me) might think." . . .

My cooperation with Peyer dated from the time when we had started out with small adventure models that increased into a sum of the collected trivial holdings of our poison cabinets. Peyer was brilliant in high literature, which I was forbidden to enter. "How's your novel going?" I asked. "You're familiar with it," he said. "I've forgotten it," I said. "That's not possible, it's so similar," he said. "Similar to what?" I said. "To yours," Peyer said. Somehow that seemed insulting to me; even more, it seemed disjunctive. I had considered mine better than his.

"A family doctor, who is a forest ranger in his free time, straps on a Colt, wears a Stetson, and stands at the ready around the clock up on the Wörgl, takes a robot who reads Perry Rhodan as his sidekick, with whom he chases extraterrestrial time-travel crooks, poachers, and diabetics. On Venus he becomes a forest ranger again, raising amphetamine berries, and under the pseudonym Dr. Thomas Bruckner he feels billows of yearning for the distraught daughter of a stocking manufacturer in southern Baden; she is a nurse and has an illegitimate brother who is a drug dealer in New Jersey being sought by the FBI, but who in reality is a disguised head physician of a cancer clinic that operates on robots to remove rust, and on Alpha Centauri he has a family doctor's Colt beamed to him and rematerialized so he can aim it at any and all forest rangers; the unlucky shot goes off and pierces the doctor who has programmed into the robot all of the Lore pulp novels in order to turn him into an alcove butler; this is exactly how things happen at the Rosamunde Pilcher estate. Everyone's eyes are full of tears; only the FBI keeps on doing what others don't have to do, namely: to make necessity out of the purest virtue; it plants whitish fungus cultures on everyone who is not rich, satisfied, promoted, or married at the end. So when it's over even the dead robot is laid to rest, after a vivisection by the forest ranger, under the Tyrolean linden tree, and the priest intones a hallelujah." . . .

But to err was nearly human. All of a sudden he thought his was better than mine. "Well, that's now very similar after all," I said. "I stand behind it," Peyer stated. "I would be happy if our relationship as fellow employees were to continue," and I looked at him so amiably that he could gather from it a token of my affection. "Maybe I'll strike out the part about the fungus cultures," he said. "Then it would be only half of the story, but life always wants the whole thing." I had no idea how I had suddenly become so wise. "The Whole Thing," that's going to be the title, and "The Whole of Life" will be the theme of the jacket blurb: Peyer roared, and once again a piece of wisdom had brought me a hard, well-intended whack on the shoulder so that I flapped my lips like a bottle being uncorked; and I . . .

The millionaire's daughter's dog has eaten a twenty-dollar bill. A few minutes later he throws up and barks: "Fifty dollars, please . . ."

Eternal pain: that amounts to eternal anesthesia . . .

Christmas. Venus was radiant in the evening sky. Keep on until August, hang in there . . .

"When the price of a barrel of oil in Kuwait goes up ten cents, the taste of the audience in Freiburg im Breisgau gets ten degrees more reactionary," I quipped.

"I really couldn't throw you face-first into a mush made of two-stroke gasoline and autumn leaves," Ann groaned.

"It's winter," I corrected.

"Your face is expressing a pain that makes me strong," Ann decided.

"Tomorrow is Christmas," I asserted.

On a tenement wall in the city you could see the attempt to sell to some Chosen One among the residents a HOUSE ON A POND IN THE COUNTRY. Some Chosen One whom nobody knew yet was being offered a house—which he did not have—on a pond—which he was doing without—in the country he was wishing for; however, not totally for free. He would not have been a Chosen One if just anybody could have bought it. The price, about which I made inquiries, was so unattainably high that even the brashly dishonest promotional language on the wall of the building did not reveal it. It did not do this, as you might think, out of shame at writing the price of nature on the tenement wall, but because the agency charged with the sale could not deal with the "discreet incorporation of the asking price into the general advertising image." And so the whole "House on a Country Pond" business made a first impression of being gentle and flattering. Only on the telephone did I experience the contours of the hard sell and buckle under. "Interesting," I lied, and when I now lied with reference to the ad as well, everything was suddenly correct again. This system was the epitome of honesty, if everybody always tightened up the little screws and bolts of his speech and adapted them to the machinery. "Now I know," I said, entering the tower room rubbing my hands, to Ann. "What do you know now," she asked, staring through binoculars at the not very distant wall of the next house. "A pond in front of the house would solve our problems," and my hand rubbing grew slower. "Because someone will buy this house, someone else will suddenly know what he's missing," and at the exact place where she set the binoculars upright on the table, the points of two thumbtacks were sticking up out of the table top and scratched up the fine lenses: so that if she put the binoculars to her eyes again, no more gaze could fall on the house wall . . .

Gradually it was no longer worth the trouble to stay wide-awake for what was coming. After I had agreed with Ann to let pass over us as we slept the tepidly brewed, humiliating dreams that in the future were more and more scurrilous, cruder, and more disgraceful, we immersed ourselves in the sleep of the wish that our shared bed might soon grow leather straps that could fasten us to the numbing rest that prepared us to be willing sacrifices . . .

Christmas was long past: M. H. Berditschewsky had still not woken up. A prose piece about the events was coming due. A few assistants were plucking at me on the telephone, trying to rip out a couple of my pages, or in case I didn't hand anything over, to write a few pages themselves under my name. The daily grind on the outskirts of the city was eating at me; that's why I found this extremely kind of them. At that time there was nothing more practical than getting one's manuscripts, if one was not writing them oneself, written by the most eager aspirants. Even though I remunerated them for it, I felt grateful, grateful without any further feelings of obligation. I no longer knew where to get fresh supplies. The daily grind was brutal, but not inexhaustible. Ruinous swill. Gluttonous night-and-day. Uncanny what-was. Scary what-will-be. Bone-crushing just-the-way-it-is. Grueling could-be-different-and-better . . .

Then later . . .

Once in the city. Violating a traffic sign, tripping; the car was parked, two others front and back in the scrunch zone, bumpered flat, until the gap was wide enough for my low-rev car; tripping; with my face, which was tensed up inwardly in the area of the cheekbone (and outwardly my face said to Ann: "you look blurry!"), I banged through the round panel of a rough-road traffic sign. Ann laughed. Pretty honestly; although I had suggested that morning: "Laugh again for once, and at me too!"; pretty honestly, considering that laugh suggestion. A wreath of splinters from the wooden traffic sign around my face; two nails quickly through the palms of my hands, the loincloth, off to Isenheim and into the side chapel. Peyer freed his arm from her and pulled me out of the sign. "How's business?" I asked. "Not here, keep quieter, you can be louder somewhere else, then it can be talked about," said Peyer, who, wafting discomfort, started to quease unobtrusive onions. I flared my nostrils. Shopping, Ann had thought; that's how she was. I'll never go to the city again, I thought, and: it's all their fault. Compared with the fact that the blame for my coming down sick was fully attributable to Ann and Peyer, the two of them were moving like an elastically springy twin who was growing together out of athleticism into a single individual. I almost knocked Peyer into a construction pit. His open sandals caused pity. Brief pity. When it had all passed, we had passed the construction pit too . . .

Before that, the following had taken place . . .

A few times we had been overcome by the insidious fatigue in the tract house. It ambushed us from under the rug so suddenly that we had no time to change rooms. Basically I would have had nothing against spending the night in the tower, but as chance—a coincidence that was certainly of benefit to others—would have it, we fell asleep in an empty room. It wasn't empty for long. The next morning the sixth desk was standing in the bedroom, light finish with the body on the right side, lockable. Ann seemed martyred by depression. I did some gymnastics with a hand towel, not letting her participate in the exercises. She stammered slightly, and had to get through her prescribed speech exercises. "I must n-not stutter, or else people will be cruel and laugh at m-me." I sat behind the sixth one, tenderly tearing up a pad of airmail paper and scattering the scraps evenly across the desktop. "D-don't," said Ann, and self-absorbedly I smiled humbly at an address that was vaguely familiar to me. The addressee who brought out the humility in me was a conniving wimp. Pit diggers made me nervous—and I was nervous and lay down right away. Luckily I was sitting behind the sixth one in the bedroom already, so I was situated in the proper surroundings. Ann, in her depression, had installed lace curtains here too, as on all of the doorframes, so that no eyes had to look outside when it had gotten dark out there. I showed her my gratitude for this by regularly closing my eyes earlier. The completely symmetrical darkness made me so homeless that I was no sooner lying down than I was immediately out of it. Sometimes she was also out of it before I was lying down; then I probably fell on top of her, in case she had the misfortune of becoming motionless in her depression and continuing to lie beneath me. Under the desktop of the sixth one she then lay, covered up, and in the course of the night she worked her way out from under me. Multiple times. Everything was conniving . . .

Then later . . .

"Come over and see me sometime," I said to Peyer, to whom I wanted to pass on the documentation work for the Ann/Me Report. I was still hoping that my language would one day tell me what I was actually thinking; but all it ever said was what I should imagine my thinking to be. The thinking was even more pauperized than the rest of me; that's probably why I became an author: if nothing else is working anymore, neither life nor thinking nor love nor speaking, then at least writing still works, as it has been for a long time now; this writing was working practically constantly, on and on, even if ruin was raging all around it right down to the lamp with the straw shade, which was shooting at the writing with bulbs bursting like garnet grenades, whose shards we greedily ate when they were hardly out of their sockets—even if the world was coming to an end: this writing kept working when life, thinking, love, and speaking were over and done with; which swelled it up to an inspiring prospect of the future; bleat, paper, bleat. In my writing business I had forbidden Peyer to do any writing in which law and order were perceptible: in order to gain ground against the factors of law and order, instead of doubling them in the texts; which to my surprise suddenly made him, Peyer, incomprehensible. And then I gave him the order that his writing was to be easily understandable and behave like powdered soup in a flapping pouch: what is wanted is direct consumption, drink the thing dry and throw it away. Even the bad conscience about this hesitant act was unenjoyable; the best thing was probably to hammer the report myself onto the compliant paper, guiding it to be read and hence, simultaneously with the reading, to be thrown away . . .

"So far it's working for me! I'm tormenting myself so nicely!" I screamed at Peyer.

"When?" he asked. I became suspicious.

"So where are you with the report?" I asked.

"I'm at 'But to err is nearly human,'" Peyer said.

"Correction: To err WAS nearly human," I screamed. Furious but sympathetic . . .

"About ten pages back. You are faster." Peyer let his jaw drop . . .

Underneath the coat rack . . .

At every touch—before we refrained from any touching at all—the thoughts overflowing the established margins collided with the Grand Old Woman, the dirtily Mercurial One, the incurably Neurospinal One, the primordially Imported One. And yet—secretly I wished her for both of us. A syphilitic final phase still made it possible—as Ann unaffectedly read aloud to me—to think of your own genitals as the emperor and empress of China. Out of misplaced discretion the book said nothing about the addresses where we could dutifully obtain such a final phase, some house or other for both genders, where you came out and from then on you were nothing but genitals. Cutting away the rest of the body, yes, and feeling a hymnodical, droll yearning for this reverse castration . . .

"Did this—what's his name again?—this Peyer get a hold of the keys to your cabin?" I asked.

"He pocketed the case," said Ann.

"Where are you, anyway?" I asked.

"I'm in my room and I'm smoothing out the sheet for your visit," said Ann.

"Are we going to get walked in on while we're at it?" I asked.

With every disrobing those places became visible . . .

Peyer, if he didn't practice for a day, could no longer write by hand. He got back into practice by writing enormous scribblings. (When he was scribbling he thought about fucking, but he hadn't practiced that for a day either. Fucking was urgent, because when he did it he thought about writing again. And because everything was so complexified, he placed stiff beer coasters and mats in front of him, on which the scribbles expanded to the edges; sometimes a coaster burst and at that moment it was as if someone had turned off the lights on him, the day gone past like an express train . . .)

If, once your child reached the age when he could become venereal, you did not have him treated against the effects of love, then he was threatened with a relapse into puberty, a venereal head cold with an unappetizing destruction of the nasal septum, a few rather repulsive little brownish bumps on the palms of the hands and the soles of the feet, nasty loss of hair, simply disgusting weeping papules, deep cracks in the lips, and later severe metasyphilitic symptoms unto the fourth generation, to say nothing of progressive infantile paralysis, aortitis, and aneurysm, which is particularly gruesome in children . . .

All of this ugly vocabulary in Ann's mouth, which seemed to have been made only for that purpose. Instead of songs without words now she sang only lyrics for which she thought up the vocabulary as she went along. Unfortunately, she soon also thought up the hollow sentence molds with which she was able to arrange the vocabulary items in strands of meaning that captivated me. "To be allowed to repeat whatever you say for ten days in a row; Ann, take on the responsibility for my speeches; take me on; take over for me." If that unbearable guy with my downfall on his mind hadn't been breathing down my neck, I would have taken off on vacation, leave, or to my workplace. The work, a hammock that needed to be knotted, which would at the same time be the recompense for the work, was rolledandpackedup in my beach bag . . .

"He takes his pants off and makes a good impression," I said.

"Who?" she asked.

"They were once made of denim, and now they're cracked leather from pissing old age," I said.

"Don't swine like that," said Ann.

"Swine" as a verb. Because her character was not fully developed, she was becoming more prudish before my very eyes. The prudery was shooting up out of the floor next to her, before my very eyes; I watched as in Wonderland, next to the minimized Alice, the prudery virtually shot up out of the floor, or more precisely, out of the rug, for it was out of the rug that the prudery shot, before my very eyes, so that she became more prudish before my very eyes. Already her nice shoulder parts were pure cellophane. And her low-down hits below the belt against my magnificence were a disclosure of her deepest female secret, more than that in fact, out of sheer womanliness she no longer knew what to do; for Ann's sake, without hesitating, I would have sacrificed my beloved profession, which I both embodied and defended; inexplicably, in those churning moments she did not seem to demand any such thing from me, for she was not sleeping with my profession, but with me. How was it—oh! horrors!—that Ann had to move in with that slightly mad M. Hirsch B. and was now settling into his winter villa on the local urban outskirts? . . .

This friction with reality had to lessen or else I would scrape myself raw. I ground the edges off of the stair steps until a slanted surface rose upward that could serve as a slide. A gentle unreality crawled out of its lair and cloaked itself in the mantle of a monstrously dishonest prose in whose wake everything, down to the last word, became a lie, while conversely honesty had no infectiousness for long periods. That's what kind of sludge prose was, contaminated, odorous, pregnant with miasma . . .

Then later . . .

Our circumstances grew more and more uncivilized, while we grew more wretched all the time, more impoverished in our souls, more disturbed in our movements, more opaque in the situations in which we found ourselves together. How it got up there, I didn't know—in any case it was positioned so that it did not fall down again: the seventh desk stood in the tower as if it had grown there. It hemmed us in and with that the space the other six gobbled up also started plaguing us. I sat down and immediately abandoned the other one, in whose typewriter the bread and jam was dripping, and began a treatise, which was actually some kind of summation, on the "Role of Fat in the Diet of Laboratory Rats." Ann shimmied down the rope into the living room; I was not happy with her; she shimmered like a colorblind chameleon that doesn't know which background it should adapt to and ends up gasping for breath from all the color changes. While that was happening: me already maudlin in the introduction on my own initiative. Ann circled below while I placed the court exhibits on the seventh desk as testimony for an insignificant adrenal activity of the "laboratory rat *an sich*" . . .

Some more animosity. It's unfair, because Ann no longer takes part in it: she reveled in my hunger. She aged when I rejuvenated myself and if I rummaged up something young in the evening before the goodnight kiss, the only thing that was still visible was difference, for instance, the difference between the ram and his shepherdess with the eyelid infection. Making myself better; giving myself a shape that I can show everybody without their judging me; fobbing it off on Ann by hardly talking about her, and if I do, then derogatorily; the purpose that these notes fulfill is as good as any other; as long as I end up with someone I imagine to be the better of the two! . . .

"It's a race with time," I sang. And knew that I was singing the race with time to myself as a soap opera, in order to make myself important in this situation of mine. At the same time, no more banal situation had ever been experienced. A race with time was serious, at least; then I had an enemy, time itself. True, no one knew this enemy, but for that very reason it had to be formidable. That's how I justified, with the sheer flow of time, the grinding that I the tormentor staged with reality, my tormentress . . .

No more free field of vision, everything illuminated; the systematician that I was wiped the last fields of darkness away; hopefully it would grow back, the darkness; otherwise, by doing nothing but thinking, I'd still attain clarity! Where was I supposed to look? Maybe where no one has ever looked before? Hardly thinkable; later, at an advanced age, at forty, maybe. Air contaminated by gazing: and then you were supposed to breathe the stuff too? . . .

I felt very unredeemed (no woman came who would get it going with me), scratched my neck and meditated on the miserable state of the soul, while ignoring my own; and then I raised my fist, but I got tired before it was all the way up; I raised my upper lip, baring the inflamed upper gums; I tried to emit a scream that did not materialize, and I pondered this unemitted scream for a very long time, and in the midst of pondering I realized that the redemption, my redemption, had come a little bit closer . . .

"We can never know what is in store for us," I portended. We sang, shortly after New Year's, "Oh Thou Flow of Time," for two voices, with an *oompah* bass that I copied off the Golden Gate Quartet . . .

Through our wide-open gates burglars would stream in and take everything from us; or liberate us from everything; open house for the bulk trash removal of remaining luxury items . . .

More furnishings go missing from luxury hotels than from flophouses. The well-to-do steal more. But not much at a time. They remain within the boundaries of the concept of property, hardly taking anything from anyone, leaving them almost no poorer, and so they themselves hardly get any richer from the appropriation. Getting almost no richer is not yet a violation of the law. Only "becoming a rich man" is punishable; often. They only steal ashtrays, soap dishes, or sugar cubes, things that do not get you ahead or raise you up if they are placed in the home on the trophy shelf over the fireplace. By helping themselves to these small items, the well-to-do, who shell out a multiple of the value of the loot for their hotels, are at least implying how they might like to deal with somewhat larger and much larger items if only people would let them act in peace and not watch them while they're doing it. Only the possibility that they might be observed at their endeavors is the regulative social factor that puts the brakes on them. When they think that eyes are looking their way, these people are inhibited from snatching to a greater extent, and while gritting their teeth (they've stolen the teeth too) they maintain their old—medium-sized—vested rights. Now and again a discreet pinch on the side, in the gray zone, that does not touch the walls of the proprietary palace. And even more secretly, more imperceptibly than they suspect, the prudent hotelier, who can afford it by slapping a certain percentage (the kleptotax) on top of the room rates, is in the practice of placing new ashtrays and new green flat smooth Palmolives or crackling sugar packets in their respective dishes and their respective places. They are able to nip at these acquisitions, no one is watching, but it seems dangerous nonetheless; with every snatch a sum in the millions seems to change owners; an unambiguous sign ". . . will be reported to the police without leniency, plus 150.00 for our incommodity . . . ," stimulates greed in fits and starts until it is exhausted after its gratification.

Some green juice oozes out of the seal of a hand that doesn't usually mess with slimy stuff. It presses down around a bar of soap that it has appropriated at the risk of life and limb, at the risk of its entire well-to-do existence. Soaked in sweat, the guest stashes the thing with its goop in his pants pocket and chokes something down. The most ticklish risk of the past decade of his life! Forty-five steps on a runner fastened down with brass rods, down a curved staircase, past the air-conditioned swimming pool: and he pays for the soap at the reception desk with a traveler's check in the amount of 3,500 francs . . .

Peyer, a man with a reputation who, in the midst of the worms the early bird holds in its beak, opened his eyes and called me up in confusion, informing me over a crackling, presumably wiretapped line that there were differences between me and my great love that no iron could smooth out. She would not have an easy time with her gutter as long as she was with me; I on the other hand suffered increasingly from my short, bigoted moments: cussing, libel, compulsive hollering. After that the caller, Peyer, was banned from entering the tract house, as decreed by me, and I threatened him with the philodendron, which would take him apart neck and crop . . .

Kleptophobia got ahold of me. A cough rattled me. I held a chiffon cloth in front of my mouth and coughed it full. Passed on to Ann, it would infect her with my kleptophobia. The first thing she did was to secure the house key. I scratched the mailbox key out of an old envelope . . .

With all of that we were so overstimulated from squalidness, so teachable from the lack of stimulation, so exemplary out of fussiness, and so offensive in profundity, that we staged one of those body-temperature and rather vaporous invitations—only insinuated here—for a married couple sharing butler duties; weather-sensitive Joseph the Fornicator with sensual Mireille the Chimera softly singing the ardent *réception* songs of unanswered night clerks . . .

In the salon; both of them with shoes and gloves removed; both chained to a cord that originated at the light switch; our two doppelgangers, the butler couple, Joseph the Fornicator with Mireille the Chimera, at the light switch; luckily they scuffled for a long time over who would get to flip it; I succeeded in getting one hand free and I fished out of Ann's hip belt the heavy double-barreled muzzleloader whose barrel was jammed full to bursting with shrapnel and splatter-movie dumdums; I took aim at the butleress, and Joseph screamed "Fornication!" Then he barged out of the room and came back with the roast mother-of-pearl chicken; with goosebumps from wild abandon—the wild abandon extended over the orphaned domains of laughing and crying—Ann unwrapped herself and was suddenly standing right in front of me. One hand pulled my head to her mouth while the other grabbed my member, and she swayed . . .

Quickly tell the two of them a heartfelt good-bye and disappear into the city, never to return to the crooked house and to Ann, who heartrendingly implored me to stay here forever. To the city with me, there to run myself ragged, in order to store up that raggedness, which "came into me for your sake," as a bonus to be produced in a timely manner . . .

Then later . . .

In the laundry room Ann had set up ten little men, in ten little cages, all in a row. The cages stood on a table, and the table stood on a stone floor, which disappeared in the middle, at its lowest point, into a drain . . .

Or else, in case I—run so ragged that I would be anesthetic to pain—had to return to the crooked house and allow myself to be parenthesized in the tempered thighs of her damaged—that is, damaged by me—continued happy existence, then . . . quit, stick, flip . . . no possibility of appending a sequel to the existential series by quickly turning pages, to live on with the illustrated lady and her novel; finis; and to make unfit for marching the body upon which I spurred through life, recklessly trotting; and to stifle any will to keep on trotting after all, later on, with an unscathed body . . .

We had just said good-bye to the butler couple and sent the two of them back to their living room after a merry soiree, when the eighth one was discovered. The eighth desk stood, like all those before it, near the desks that were already in the room. We heard the butler couple giggling—they were the prime suspects in the prank. Satiated to the point of aversion, Ann grew somewhat short of breath; which perked me up so much—I hadn't known that I would be so glad to see her suffer—that all of a sudden I regained all of my respiratory capabilities. Exhaling worked. Inhaling worked. Holding my breath worked. At the eighth desk I felt like I was turned inside-out; at its surface I could put away inside me whatever I had so far suffered only externally. "You're looking sick," said Ann, who had fled to the balcony but came back in because of the cold and sat down in the cramped space on the floor. "My body is just as ill as its surroundings," I said, "and it has to be that way if one is going to feel comfortable." "How is this going to continue?" asked Ann. "Let's wait for the ninth one," I said. Seeming serenity came over my façade. That would continue to proliferate . . .

Previously the following had happened . . .

Ann went back to the vestibule and opened a blue door under the stairs that led to servants' quarters. It had the dimensions of a broom closet. "Our servant couple has the night off," I said. "No, they're looking at their rooms," said Ann. "All I can see is *one* room," I said. Ann closed the blue door and pushed the stairs over next to the coat hook. "Our servant couple are doing a nice job of messing around with the household," I said. "If the butler didn't have the butleress," she said, "he'd be out the door, but quick."

In a state of hyperwakefulness you see things as in a dream, distorted, yellow, and foul . . .

I took a stroll through the quarter where I lived with her. A baker stepped out of his bakery. On his horizontally outstretched arms he was carrying a fresh flan. The winter bees dive-bombed his head, his hands, and his neck. The baker valiantly pedestaled the flan, not letting it fall. The winter bees blustered and he was forced to keep swallowing some of them. He would have swallowed even without winter bees. The retinue of apprentices came out of the bakery and doused the baker with a thin salt solution that drove off the bees. I didn't take any more strolls . . .

Being absolutely accessible to her eyes was the best concealment . . .

Who was I next to her? And how much of me was left over when she was totally present, "fully there," as I sneered in my weakness, which extended to the point of physical immobility and the acceptance of this immobility; tired taunting, attempted again and again as a fourth-class shot in the arm: if possible, a few drops of Benzedrine could be squeezed out of this or that corrosive turn of phrase, if only I squeezed long enough. The baker, his appearance, the expectation that something more would happen with him—this had instantaneously destroyed me; and my taunting, directed at Ann from within this sinking, completely sank that dilapidated coaster ship; all hands away from the cannon, pump up the rubber canoes and abandon ship!; the rats leave the sinking ship by going over to the second sinking ship; and "I sense how your corrosive remarks are getting painful even for you," she who knew everything told me; exhausted taunting, the last stage of loss of consciousness, of nerves, seized marrow and instincts and transmuted their subject back into a gray, hard, prenatal larva . . .

I seemed to be lying in her vicinity. To judge by her desire for contact, I must have felt warm. Unhesitatingly, she grabbed my member, and she pushed . . .

In the laundry room Ann had set up ten little men, in ten little cages, all in a row. The cages stood on a table, and the table stood on a stone floor, which disappeared in the middle, at its lowest point, into a drain. The arrangement of the little men was such that Ann could stand in front of it and put all ten fingers into the cages at the same time . . .

Hatred for sidewalk curbs is followed by rage at the façade across the street, and then by revulsion at the heavens in general . . .

Within me a hatred for sidewalks was forming. I took a few steps across an abandoned one. Then a rage against the façades coalesced, deep within me, but palpable. I no longer recognized myself. The rage in my eyes destroyed at least three façades and immured the presumptive architects alongside the window lintels: "as punishment they should eternally bear weight." Or else, in case the façades remained . . . in case the concentrated power of my telekinetic abilities did not succeed in annihilating them and reducing them to dust, I myself had to be destroyed; which had the advantage that regular kinetics was sufficient for the job. A fantastic idea, that there are so and so many moving parts on this body whose movement can be directed against the same body—even if, according to Geulincx, only with God's consent, who of course always speaks softly and, as a rule, falsely. I stood on the empty sidewalk and looked up the façade. One of us had to be the stronger. And I was the weaker. When I realized that, I lowered my eyes and curiously enough it was then that I saw the sky, and with that my old nausea rose within me. All of a sudden there was no longer any spot that could soothe this nausea, but unfortunately at the same time there was no more possibility to flee from the things that seemed to be boxing me in, because they left only small gaps between themselves and me: that was the nauseating thing about seeing, that it cashed in distances, and liquidated lebensraum, if just a single glance fell across the established border, by suddenly turning everything that was "right nearby" into something "right inside." My optical ability to appropriate was absolute; everything belonged to me, but I didn't want to know anything about anything; imposed possession as hatred for possession, nausea at the façade; I became an impulse to run away on the sidewalk. After I had accepted the futility of these evasive maneuvers, I started to hate myself, simply by making the façade into a reflector that radiated animosity back at me; Husserl would have shrieked for joy if he had seen me in the city, and he would have slapped his phenomenological kneecaps with his perceptive hands out of rapture at this man who let himself be hated by objects. Emanating hate-rays, I felt hate landing on me, my own hate. Finally I had someone who didn't run away from me and who was one with the person who knew him almost perfectly and knew exactly where to strike at his weaknesses in order to hit him where he lived. He immediately struck hard. I cried out. The night fell and I closed my eyes. Since I had kept on walking during this game, I had come to the end of the hated sidewalk and it had come to an end, and my hatred for it was gone. And I fell down. An immense rage at the "come-to-an-end" sidewalk reconstituted itself. But when I got up, all that was beneath me was the "come-to-an-end" thing. I was lying, because everything had now come to an end beneath me, in that which is called the gutter and which was present twice per street; the city provided its residents with twice as many gutters as streets, no doubt so that someone who was throwing away his filth did not need to cross the street, but could drop it right where he stood. The gutter was no longer filthy, but cleaned up: which spoiled the symbolism. It was cleaned up, and it contained some leaves, at most some dry leaves. I was able, when I had calmed down and given Ann my hand and thought everything was fine again, to shake the leaves from my feet without shaking anything else from my feet. Yes, everything had become unproblematical and would remain unproblematical, for the façades were one great big Platonic loveliness and did not mean their promises seriously. With that I felt that I had a future and that I had been admitted to a new space that I could step into with her . . .

Truth at last. Against expectation; more or less like when the eighteenth child is another dead girl . . .

In an exact mirror image, atmospheres of homicide and suicide arose. Even if they were not comforting, they were still familiar; and thus comforting. Since my prose was coming along, I was already taking myself too seriously and liking myself too much to give in to the wish to finally get rid of myself. I also felt, when my hands began to tremble, much too much affection for her to get her out of the way just like that. I felt contempt for myself because of my shabby self-concept, which I called "affection-for-the-cripple," and I also felt contempt for myself because, even though I cut up the onions for the Salisbury steak with a handy kitchen knife, I never attacked her. I should have carved Ann a face, a profile, a name. Whatever prevented the homicide and the suicide magnified my self-contempt at the same time. Whoever stayed alive, I spit at their feet; I had always done it that way. All around me, the spit-at, the spit-at-by-me. It flowed down between my sweater and my shirt; if I was even wearing duds like that at all . . .

Underneath the coat rack . . .

As soon as Berditschewsky woke up (he was sleeping and knew nothing about our knowledge of his sleep: which simultaneously proved that it was he who was asleep and not us: while we could appear in his dreams, for the time being he could not appear in ours) . . . as soon as M. H. Berditschewsky woke up, I would no longer be able to suppress my intimate craving for altruistic soul-plundering . . .

Getting closer to quitting . . .

"Great and manifold happenings would disturb them. A simple life is their lot, and only from stories and writings do they have to become acquainted with the rich contents and the countless phenomena of the world. Only rarely in the course of their lives is an incident allowed to draw them into its rapid eddies in order to instruct them more precisely, by means of a few experiences, about the situations and the characters of the people who take action . . ." (Novalis)

Do you remember, when I harp on it, your deviant relationship with your breasts? You never wanted to stuff them into anything that would constrict them. "They're already suffocating as it is," you said, usually when you were reading one of those awful final dissolutions of Ibsen's—the only one about whom we kept up our contact—and felt deeply moved, "purified, because the system collapses." You wrote off every appearance by Werle with shrill derision. All of my attempts to weave my profound incomprehension of your statements into your reading of Ibsen—you were absorbed as never before—remained futile. And yet I tried for a long time to be an outside influence on you. I only know that in time I no longer took note of your breasts, which—even in the summer—remained white. I was ensnared in a feeling of deviance that even you never succeeded in dissipating within me, even using the most exciting ideas you had for them . . .

In the salon of our Empire . . .

"Being in your company eats me up, you plant," I said.

"That's how I am with every visitor," she said.

"So who else is coming?" I asked.

"Peyer left his right hand here for me," she said.

"And what you have from me is my shirt," I said.

In a corner; besieged by pillows . . .

As long as Berditschewsky was asleep (we were awake and knew for sure that he was sleeping: which may have been evidence for the fact that we were able to make allowances for his waking up and he, as soon as he was awake, could make allowances for our falling asleep) . . . as long as Meyer Hirsch B. was asleep, Ann and I were free to do what we pleased. There was little that pleased; and what did was ugly. If we repeated those few, ugly things they pleased us even less. Repetition as loss of desire. So that we could even keep a mere inkling that it should have been pleasing us, we ... or Ann with me ... had to repeat it unbelievably often. Let me qualify that: very, very often. Let me qualify that: Ann repeated it with me pretty often. Let me qualify that: we often got together and read in each other's faces the benumbed satisfaction about the fact that MHB, demonstrably asleep, could not stir until his nerves tickled him back into the pointless state of being awake ...

That wasn't bad; somewhat worse ...

We would undress the landlord down to his shirt, he would proudly present his naked torso to us, and a cat o' nine tails would undo the last buttons. Just in time I reached for my pink sheet, which she had spread out in her blue silk. The laughter with which Peyer had made Ann happy after reading through the trilogy was a part of his personality like the way he swallowed final syllables; he gobbled up whole halves of sentences until he'd had his fill. She, my love, had her own, unmistakable style. The fleet of my adventures would run aground on the reefs of the flood tide of her tears. The atoll on which we shatter to bits is us. We are the ship as well as the cause of the shipwreck, and on top of that we're the drowned victims too, and I bet we'll drown in our own water, which our hands churn frothy. I threw my shirt over my rickets-ridden shoulders and called through the truncated vestibule

"Damned vermin! Come and take a liking to me! It's enough if you caress my knees, on which I am kneeling before you, pleading to be able to caress your will where it could move you to caress me anywhere, as long as it's not on my knees! You 'filthy varmint!' (Which turned the supplication, if not into a diatribe, then at least into a somewhat aimless supplication.) Do you hear how the vestibule is echoing with my wailing male grievance? Come; only a little pat, and then you let your hand lie there like it was tired ..."

She was lying very close. She was pretty warm. I tried to enter her . . .

All at once . . . I've forgotten where . . . tell me time, situation, place, view . . . something . . . maybe . . . new . . . never before . . . in any case . . . no contradiction . . . no memory, or only a wished-for one . . . unexpected with you . . . on the slanting surface . . . propped up . . . but . . . all of a sudden . . .

Green folding shutters. Thick ash tree. Kept burglars away as well as hopes. Throwing open the shutters. View of the street through the housing complex. Stacked-up horizons, previously magnolias. Yew hedges with gaps, driveways. Puddles in flagstone recesses. Fringy arms of water. A miniature Firth of Forth by miniature Edinburgh. Licked up by the sun. The same hot light made flowerbeds decay. Boiled up tar in sensitive spots. Ignited the street. A stye in my eye. Eyelash rumbles over little bubbles. Not even a milkman. To get to know and to get to know better. In a circle. Nothing. Neat-and-tidiness without an observer. Waxed for inspection, and the sergeant isn't coming. My eye halfway closed. The housing subdivision didn't even get a starting whistle, which would have spurred it on to get even more neat and tidy. Push your nostril wings up to your forehead, tremble nervously with your hands. Severe obsessive neurotics all around me, too bad for me. Each one sprinkles his little pile and eats it up with a bit of salt. The folding shutters made of ash. Slamming them shut. Nothing there anymore. Latching them. Even less is there. "Switzerland," Ann said. "We're rid of it," I said to her. With my back to her. "And still I'm wishing for even less," Ann said. Presumably she meant me again. Thin ash wood. If you mean me, then I mean you too. Ann did then put her hands on my shoulders, warm, I tipped my head, later touched my ear. Touched what? My ear? But now I did still have hands on my shoulders, and they were coming toward me from behind. At this moment a tinny uproar broke out on the street . . .

Her M. H. Berditschewsky fast asleep, snoring and counting his sheep high and dry. In a long Sunday sermon interrupted by acts of gluttony Ann was told: "Do not suffer any shock from this prose, that's just how it is and from now on that's how it will be every Monday." Trembling, she had spent the night with such prospects and heard Tuesday dawning, all of those Tuesday noises in the hallway. In her peachish carnality Ann towered before me like a white, powerful Vaudois. Her velvety-silken dressing gown (moiré, I was informed) whished around her boyish hips so that I was able to forget my symptoms for a few happy minutes; I forgot, when I touched her skin, all of the illnesses of that skin. Noise from a pocket radio, which grew louder, because I touched her raised knee; it gently closed together with the other knee . . .

"Now then, buddy, where are we with that report?" I asked pleasurably.

"Five hundred pages behind," Peyer sobbed.

"*Five* pages behind. You'll catch up," I generously comforted him . . .

Ann's smell. The lamp was hot. The lightbulb was eating the lampshade. A piece of finger skin came loose, violetly. Night light consumed sleeping woman. From desire for her my mouth was dry. Was she not going to ask? She figured me out. And I knew that. She would always figure me out. She put out the burning lamp and covered my forehead with her hair. With her dressing gown hanging open. Sometimes . . .

I seemed to be lying in her vicinity. I probably felt warm to the touch. Gently she grasped my member, and she tore . . .

I believed, in fact I was firmly convinced, that there was a marching band parading down the street outside our tract house. Maybe we were biased, or fixated on a particular kind of music—in any case we saw the musical corps of the Freiburg constabulary moving past. They were playing the "Richthofen Squadron," and I stood next to her at the open window, hanging on her like a heavy tote bag, and spreading my index and middle fingers in a victory sign. Where I put my thumb I did not know, and I knew even less where I got my index finger from. Perhaps my fingers had frozen in the winter, a solitary person and young author couldn't keep track of everything. Or then I spread my thumb and index finger. That didn't make a victory sign, but it promised good intentions, since two fingers were spread, even if they weren't the ones for making the sign. As for my victory, such failings in the sign system did not influence it. For a brief time I, young author at the window of the row house hanging on lady, had something of Churchill about me, just as burned down, just as progressive, just as much a non-smoker as he was. All I would have needed to celebrate a robust victory was another world war, and the substitute that this particular squadron offered me was bitter, puny, and unwelcome. It takes more than a brass band to set up an empire, even if it *rah-rah-rahs* you! even if it *oom-pa-pas* you! . . .

In the laundry room Ann had set up ten little men, in ten little cages, all in a row. The cages stood on a table, and the table stood on a stone floor, which disappeared in the middle, at its lowest point, into a drain. The arrangement of the little men was such that Ann could stand in front of it and put all ten fingers into the cages at the same time. Ann did this, and ten deep but tiny cries echoed through the laundry room, and ten jaws closed on her fingertips . . .

He beats her up. She: "I have a really bad conscience that you got so worked up because of me." He: "I've only been really worked up since I saw you lying there beaten up. Get up, and then I'll knock you down again." She: "Now I'm going to start crying because you have to give up all your tenderness because of me." He: "You're to blame for me, that's for sure." She: "I will improve my behavior. But can I still do it? Have I always treated you right?" He: "The blame for me beating you up and probably killing you someday with knuckle punches to the larynx lies with your inadequate behavior." She: "It's all my fault." He: "If you had defended yourself and been a little feistier in the wrestling match, I would have beaten you up more deliberately and slowly." She: "I remember how I once didn't cook you dinner. Once your bed was unmade when you came home in the evening. And when you called me in, I did not slip under the covers with you." He: "It is your fault that I now feel very uncomfortable, because I'm killing you *slowly* instead of quickly." She: "But do I really have to be murdered right away?" He: "We are not discussing my brutality here, but who is to blame for it." She: "I'm to blame." He: "There's really no need to repeat it so often." (He clutches her neck, making her eyeballs bulge, and with his knees knocks her hands from the chair fabric they had been clenching.) She, choking: "Maybe the burden of my guilt will crush me, and I'll die alone and by my own doing." He: "Getting cynical now too, eh?" She: "Maybe I don't even need you at all to perish slowly. I think I can manage it by myself now." He: "Cynical even now, eh? For you, death is not punishment enough. You're going to stay alive. I'll help you." She: "Dearest!" He: "The fact that now I have to suffer again for years comes down to you. I'll acquaint you with my behavior soon enough." She: "Why's that? I'm going to take the next steamship and settle down in Arizona. Down in the Grand Canyon I'll lie down by myself in a tent and sing to the tent walls." He: "Death is not punishment enough. You will stay bound to me." She: "And what if you feel bad again then?" He: "I will always be worked up when you're lying there, and it's my fault that you're lying there like that." She: "I'm feeling sick to my stomach." He: "I can't stand it when you get sick to your stomach." She: "Will you forgive me for getting sick to my stomach for your sake?" He: "No." . . .

"I assume that most people only realize bit by bit that they are not going to make it." (EV Cunningham, *Alice*)

Now Ann was so withdrawn that she seemed totally possessive, because I, by seeking out this withdrawn woman in her cave—or seeking her out in the cave that she was—sacrificed all of my time, which I had set aside as a comforting pillow and thriftily accumulated hour by hour. It had taken me decades to stash away a few hours in my writing business. Ann gobbled them all up . . .

She and I, we were now ready for anything . . .

Desks, corner desks, records cabinets, replacement bell jars, typing-desk chairs, plan chests, file cabinets, grid shelves, palette frames, wardrobes, chests of drawers, shelf-board frames, workbenches . . .

Getting closer to quitting . . .

All of a sudden, from a certain perspective, looking from the back somewhat from above at a downward angle, Ann looked like a man. Unexpectedly. Kind of weird. Hypothermically challenging. My tongue quickly into her navel before she actually turned out to be a man . . .

In the salon of our Empire . . .

She had a peculiar smell. If I ran my finger over my eyes, I smelled her again. I had no longer expected the lampshade in that form. Did she use it as a hat? Or as a flower vase? But it would be leaky. She could have used it as an umbrella, but it was tattered and ready for the trash. But she couldn't find a wastebasket for throwing the lampshade away, for the only basket-like entity was the lampshade. We could have declared that the lampshade was a wastebasket, but that was a long way from getting it thrown away. No doubt she sweated; that couldn't remain hidden from me; the smell was there . . .

Up to this point everything has been a lie; from here on, everything is true, at least made up significantly worse and therefore more truthful after all . . .

If you're going to do it, then do it right away . . .

You cute little ephebic child, I thought, after I had thrust a tongue into her warm navel. In twice-regenerated deduction I saw Peyer clearly before me; true, the construction of the Tower of Babel had definitively confused the proses, because everyone had to abandon his mother tongue, but the Baby-Lonians had all been infants on whom the Book of Books was not able to foist a language by any stretch of the imagination; the warmth of her heated body brought her influence to bear. "You don't understand no language anymore!" I screamed and slid with my back in a convulsion past the chest of pearwood. The icicle-forming cold poured from above through the bathroom windows, which were damaged from my chin-up. We had neglected to shovel more coal. We finally wanted a finish that deprived the dying of their will. We're going to catch our death, Ann thought, and a crying fit came over her. Death with her, I thought, and spied on the oil-painted narcissus above the antacid pastilles. A white flake melted away on the back of my hand. Scent trails everywhere, whispered my alert nose, which dipped its tip into all of the punch biscuits, to the extent that punch biscuits were being served to me; the punch-biscuit tins were exhausted; we were in a bad way. Peyer, when he was here—he had stayed as a metasyphilitic for too little compensation (an iodine regimen was scheduled)—had presented her with an empty cigarette lighter, to throw away. Without delay, Ann had discovered a LIVER NECROSIS in herself, a severe one, that's how she saw it, LIVER NECROSIS, which could carry us both off if it flared up. That her sensitivity to illness had progressed so far, this Ann could not know. The hand is the man, I thought. "The skin is the woman," she said out loud . . .

"A wild almond bush laden with fruits hung down into the cave, and a nearby trickling led them to find fresh water for quenching their thirst . . ." (Novalis)

Simultaneously with that . . .

The heavy old wooden doors were a peculiarity of the royal edifice that an architect by the name of Walser had erected. The door in whose recessed frame Ann rather unemotionally intimated to me an "I am loved" while lifting her mouth was that sort of wooden door for majesties. In a way that was incomprehensible to me but did not disturb me, the hallway in which this door was located had grown so long that just outside the door a small glassed-in display case had found a spot. It had not been there when we came . . .

Not enough; but also . . .

The role of fat was defined. Now I was coming to the definition of the laboratory rat. There were two chapters devoted to this, which were drafted in gigantic piles of paper that were simply no longer storable. I loved the risks of writing; playing it unsafe, doing it unprotected, was the best way for me to go; and the readers were getting more and more undiscerning, too; so that one way or another only the coldest clarity and the most focused concision were advisable. That called for paper by the kilo for preliminary notes. And actual specimens: eighteen dead and partially torn-apart rats lay scattered on the eight desks. Ann was suffering so much from shortness of breath that she'd had to arrange a place to lie down under the desktops of One and Three. I lifted up four rats by their cold-to-the-touch tails and stood sensitively irritated and helplessly frozen in the living room. There was no surface available to deposit them on. Everything covered with papers, and the papers in part under the feather pillows, wool blankets, and eiderdowns that Ann, if she didn't throw them over herself, at least had to have at the ready nearby. It was the *only one* that was opportune. I stepped out onto the balcony, and Ann kicked the balcony door shut behind me with one foot. I had expected it and laid them on its desktop: four lab rats on the ninth desk. On the white surface they looked more massive; I could possibly have thrown them under the desk, but since Ann was also lying under a desk, I hesitated—both attracted and disgusted by the idea—to throw the rats on a floor where she could also have been lying. With one foot I kicked open the balcony door in front of me and sat at the eighth one for a change and wrote my "On the Nature, Species, Specificities, and Subspecies of Laboratory Rats," which subsequently became notorious (in the bad sense). "We're going to quit," Ann said. Meyer Hirsch Berditschewsky was rustling in the tower. Then he came with something new for me . . .

The snoring specimen of an avuncular landlordship was awakened. I had gone too far with her, and then Meyer Hirsch B. woke up. You little pig, cried the alarm clock, tugging at his ear. He could smell flirts in the deepest sleep; it was not for nothing that in the war the enemy ("the enemy is a personal insult") had never snuck up on him; he had survived by swimming, swimming exclusively in deep water, along the underbrush. Meyer H. Berditschewsky had a wound, for he had been deprived of his apprenticeship as an apparatus glassblower, because in his youth his father had died suddenly and he, as the oldest of seven siblings, had to provide for nine families. My youthful sitting around, a mute, not very active occupation, had a provocative effect at a moment that at any moment could cost us our jobs, at the latest at the moment at which our employers in the city had the letters sent to us . . .

From the university to the observatory, from the observatory to the art academy, from the art academy to the cathedral, from the cathedral to the south portal, from the south portal to the palace, from the palace to the museum, from the museum to the university, from the university to the art academy, from the art academy to the south portal, from the south portal to the museum, from the museum to the observatory, from the observatory to the cathedral, from the cathedral to the palace, from the palace to the university, matriculate, study at the art academy for eight semesters and enter the museum for good . . .

Hirsch's Swiss National Day rug; his oaken marriage bed that sleeps three; his touching photo of approximately forty Swiss men, suffering from severe South-Alemannic infirmities, at the municipal bowling alley . . .

Life strange and sorrowless. From early childhood on this life has been subject to unremitting atrophy, mentally and especially gesturally. Laughter is the first thing to fade away. The pensive boring at one's temple with one's index finger fades away later. The sour droning mealy-mouthery fades away last. They are quiet and threatening like oaken cupboards when they roll their bowling balls in the pubs. They also rip talking, swearing, cussing, and even slander out of themselves root and branch, and their petrifications rattle: like empty marrowbones lined up on a string. Fossils with abstract feelings of angst. Essentially, not much more can happen to someone who has become so hardened that there is no longer anything harder than he is; but his angst without cause or object is diabolically abstract. And so these massive moraines ultimately split apart on some psychological theory or other, which catches up with them, outmans and unmans them . . .

If the chronic problem of holding back and damming up the flow of time toward death is not solved without outside help, when someone, e.g., ME, stiffens and produces in himself the feeling of his own static tectonics, then every major project is a wretched one: because I know it will deprive me of much of the little time that remains to me; too much . . .

"After so many years I still dream off the mark . . ."

"Or that's why you dream off the mark . . ."

"How do you know that I dream? . . ."

"I only talk to you when I'm sure that you are absent . . ."

That was bad; now a pain . . .

The male condensate of totemized protective instincts approached my kitchen chair, formless pajamas, in his hand the shyly ticking alarm clock, which was being subjected to malignant suspicions. That mass stood before the bathroom mirror and asked:

"Has day broken out?"

Refuse an answer.

Shaken, her Meyer H. B. ran his hand over his forehead when

I made it clear to him that he had slept away months, almost a whole season. Honor to age, our one-way goal; this introit sounded cynical coming from the mouth of the sitting man. Hirsch cawed five mouthfuls, thickly, quarter-hour-quickly, and expellantly . . .

An open mouth; the throat not illuminated; a clenched fist; then someone, in accordance with conventional signaling, would pound on the table while summoning his maximum energy, so that no more grass would grow there. The mouth was assigned the task of letting go the cry expelled during the controlled pounding, a battle cry, into the Swiss air; the nationality of the air was of secondary importance . . .

M. Hirsch B. unscrewed the bulb from my lamp, stuck it in his mouth, chewed on it, tried to swallow, choked on it, and coughed up blood and slivers with shreds of skin hanging on them.

"He's injured!"

I took him by the arm, put my hand like a plank under his armpit, saw that I had not taken him by the arm hard enough, grabbed him by the upper arm until he moaned contentedly, dragged him to the sink, even though he crumpled halfway there, dragged him, let go of his upper arm and his armpit, shoved myself under his chin, choked his head upward, and threw him with a helpful push over the edge of the sink, down into the sink . . .

"The poor pilgrim was remembering the old times and their inexpressible raptures. —But how dully these delectable memories passed by . . ." (Novalis)

"I'm not a member of anything," I said.

"If you're any good at all, then you'll write the story of your continued survival," said MHB.

"I don't write anymore, I have OTHERS write for me," I said.

"Who?" he asked.

"Peyer and guys like that." I turned away, but was confronted with rock.

"I'm coming up, and you're not coming," said Hirsch.

"You're not coming either." It was a desperate blow that I landed.

Before that the following had occurred . . .

Ann walked slowly out of our writing room, leaving me behind with the perspective of her getting smaller. This perspective was linked in me with that departure and the continual abatement of her affection. I made no movement, nor did I act as if I would ever make one again. I did a convincing job of such passive states; I even convinced Ann with them. An Ann Age was passing, and I spent it by myself in the writing room. One day—I had gotten a couple of chapters farther, which for me always happened to be the "most vital ones"—Ann pushed past the desk and swept up small pencils and a hooked-up tangle of paper clips from the drawer that hung open. The sky outside was green. Ann pulled out a handkerchief and held it to her mouth. She was wearing a fairly small amount of clothes, having taken off a good part of the many clothes she usually wore and left them in the bedroom and in one of the hallways where she was in the habit of scattering a portion of her many clothes. I no longer undressed her, and hadn't done so for months. The yellow sun exerted strong pressure on the windowpanes. The tower trembled. Ann gasped through the handkerchief. She had gotten this whole gasping thing from me and because she did not declare it to be my means of expression, she had stolen and usurped it from me. I asked what was with her, whether she wanted to talk to me or once again talk past me. Ann left the door behind her a tiny escape crack open and answered, "I had to get out of that writing room. It's too full of you." I took a drink from the glass that stood in front of me. Someone was waiting for her outside the door. Her running away. Again . . .

"I'm a young author and will stay one till I'm sixty," I said.

"You are not a member of anything," Berditschewsky stated.

"Of what?" I asked evasively. Hopefully I would make the curve with him.

"The authors' association that you refuse to join has become an industrial trade union," B. said, daubing paint on something.

A short time later he issued the screw threads of the lightbulb; I looked for a pencil for him for a purpose that he did not want to reveal to me. I told him how he looked; I wasn't telling him anything new. At that time I put myself in the other person's position. I even put myself in the position of people who lost their position. It was not sufficient for more than sympathy; I made sure I didn't change all that much when a position was lost. Suddenly I was MHB, and an MHB was an author; which could not be expected of him. To suddenly be an author and have to acknowledge that, from the point of view of the foreman he had been, he had undergone a drop in social status—I wouldn't wish that on anybody. As characters we, Meyer H. B. and I, remained neatly separated; I gingerly protected the outlines drawn with thin India ink so that the figures in the comic strip didn't blend into each other and their speech balloons didn't pop . . .

Out from the locked bathroom . . .

"I'm allowed to do anything, I'm just a beginner." My statement.

"No one's going to protect you." His quotation of a *conditio inhumana* as a quasi-threat.

"Protect me from what?" I naïved farmer's-almaniacally.

"The industry is going to take you all over," Hirsch snorted, rustling like a leaf on a sukkah.

"And so according to that I would not be protected," I said.

"Itinerant Talmudist!" screamed Meyer H. B.

"Every goliard carries his knapsack disdainfully past the minnesong," I philosophemed.

"It's only that I talmudiate better than you," was his (closure-assuring) statement . . .

Object loss with frustration aggression that is directed at my own person. Was I, the attackee, the same one as he, the attacker?

His voice sounded monotonous, like it did previously in Ann's bedroom, as if he were repeating a complaint with which he had often injured himself in his mind and which thus had become a part of him, so that without *that* pain he would have felt himself only half as much . . .

Everything up to this point is a lie; the promise issued twice already: from here on, everything's true; or this promise issued: from here on an attempt at a new lie; not to issue any more promises; a new variation, please; but he's issuing another promise after all; but he has promised that this time there'll be a deviation; it, my report, no longer tears me away from my desk; that's how I put it; the way things continue would be less inconsequential if I attached more importance to myself; no more promises; everything up to this point is a lie; from here on everything will be different, that is, *everything* will be a lie . . .

Slowly crushing some brain with capers between the tongue and the palate . . .

Then later . . .

Halfway to the bathroom . . .

*MHB's discussion model* "Index 1111. and 1112. correct":
1111. What does a person do who is working and is afraid for his job? He reads prose, doesn't he?
1112. What does a person do who has been working and loses his job? He reads prose, doesn't he?
112. In his sharply increased volume of leisure time, the unemployed person reads a piece of prose whose subject is the unemployed person.
12. I have written about that person, and now I'm writing about the author.
1211. What does an author do who writes, and reads his prose? He loses his job, doesn't he?
1212. What does an author do who has finished his prose and has read all of it? He loses his job, doesn't he?
2. The connection is clear.
211. While a person, when his livelihood is taken from him, turns to prose so that it can distract and console him, the author whose livelihood is taken from him intensifies his prose production so that it will rescue him and put him back in business.
212. Jobless people read more because they have more leisure time and need advice. Jobless authors produce more because they are in need and would like to reintegrate themselves.
2121. Thus the jobless author's need for overproduction of prose and the jobless person's need for overconsumption of prose accommodate each other.
213. The jobless person invests his entire unemployment compensation in prose.
2131. The jobless author, thanks to the hoarding purchases of jobless people, who only think of prose as a means of bridging

their increased volume of leisure time, is employed again.
21311. Qualification: if the person, when he becomes jobless, would just as soon never even hear about prose again, then the lovely discussion model guaranteeing the author full employment on the basis of the correctness of 1111. and 1112. collapses . . .

There followed the discussion model index "1111. and 1112. incorrect." Hirsch was familiar with 1000s. All of them fatal . . .

Then she had told me that's how it was, and then I said it can't go on like this, but when it did not stop and finally made an impression on me, I felt that it really could go on like that, and then when she told me: "You see, it really can go on like this," she was only telling me what I had figured out myself in the meantime, namely that it really could go on like that, and when she yelled time after time that it could go on like that, then I stopped objecting . . .

*1st Round:* I immediately come out swinging. I land a left hook and then drop back to the side. For twenty days Ann slugs away at me, the title defender, but without hitting more than my gloves. I start dancing and land a few jabs. —The round goes to me.
*2nd Round:* I start out with dancing and short straights, but I have no impact on Ann. After about 1 month I go back to my corner and let her hit my guard again. She stays on her man and toward the end of the round she hits my body multiple times. But she doesn't get through to my head. —Round to Ann.
*3rd Round:* I try going with jabs again and am forced to absorb a good hook from Ann. But then I hit her with a left-right combination and add a few good hooks before going back to the ropes and yielding the initiative to her. However, she can't take advantage of the situation for about twenty days. —Round to Ann.
*4th Round:* Ann hits me with two lefts while I go back to the

ropes. I gradually get free of the pressure and am able to land a combination. I still have time to clown around. At the end of the month Ann has to go to the ropes, and I hit her multiple times with a left-right. —Round to me.

*5th Round:* A counterpunch hits Ann, who is wandering, full in the face and stops her attack somewhat. Now I'm faster on my feet, but I am forced to absorb a sharp left hook from Ann. My jabs aren't hitting their target as often as they were. The round ends with both fighters tangled up in the ropes. —Round to Ann.

*6th Round:* I stay in my room again, and Ann punches away almost in a rage, always looking for an opening. Toward the middle of the month I get through a few times by jabbing with my leading hand, but I have to go back to my room. Then I free myself from the desk and hit Ann with two good rights and just before the end of the month I succeed with a few jabs. —Round goes to no one.

*7th Round:* After small advantages for me at the beginning, Ann hits home with a good combination that drives me back onto the ropes, that is: into the tower room. Ann "mimics" me and gives the champ a slap on the butt. I'm given a warning for forced hermitting and Ann stays on the offensive even though I stiffly hold out my left fist in her direction. —Round goes to Ann, of course.

*8th Round:* A good left hook, guarded by arguments, hits Ann in the jaw. After a brief rearing up, she's forced to keep at a distance: she's in the lower rooms, and the tower room now belongs to me. She lets a warning not to hit below the belt pass over her without comment. I am quicker and land another good left hook. —Round to me.

*9th Round:* I "explode" with four or five hits to the title challenger's head. I follow with a few good jabs and noticeably force the tempo. Ann is nailed to the ropes and has to absorb two-fisted

hits. My straight jab is getting more and more accurate. —Oddly enough, the round again goes to no one.
*10th Round:* Ann seems tired. She has for months. She has never lived with anyone longer than ten months before and it's starting to show. I hit her with a well-placed left and knock her off balance. She answers with a sharp right to the chin that hits me too. I stay more active and by the 10th of the following month I manage to land two more hits. —Round to me.
*11th Round:* It seems like I'm fresher, but now Ann is already defending herself desperately. She has me on the ropes again and smacks a couple of ineffective lefts into the champ's face. Our mutual acquaintances start to divide up into two blocs whose cold war accompanies our fight. I hit her on the ear with a right, but Ann blocks with a high right over her head. Just before the bell. Summer vacation. —Round to Ann.
*12th Round:* Ann has her "second wind." She immediately gets a right through to my chin. After a few of my jabs she's back with a combination. Now I'm tired and have to absorb a left toward the end of the month. The tower room is taken from me. —Round to Ann.
*13th Round:* Fired up by cries of "Give it to her!" from my acquaintances I move forward once again. Because of her longer reach, Ann no longer has any difficulty prevailing over my jabs. At half-distance she gets in a couple of heavy hits. As soon as I settle back, she moves in tight. For months it gets close. My eyes are swollen. In the final spurt, Ann has definite advantages. —Clearly, the round goes to her; even I realize that.
*14th Round:* Ann's fans have caught wind of her chances. True, I start the month off furiously, but Ann keeps up with the increased pace like it's child's play. She has learned from me, not I from her. In the presence of acquaintances of these colors or those, the couple now deliver each other an unguarded exchange of blows in which Ann makes the stronger impression. While suffering from

pain I admire her and feel sorry for her, when I hit her; which doesn't happen very often anymore. Even though she's almost falling over from exhaustion (I'm already lying there, practically comfortable from being beaten), in the last forty-five days Ann has been bringing the better arguments into play. —The match is decided without a final round 145:127 in Ann's favor . . .

I fought like a harpooned grizzly against a drunken oil prospector in southern Canada . . .

We woke up in the morning. Not a rooster crowed. They had recalled all the roosters and sent them to the country. There the manure piles were destroyed. No sooner were we awake than it became clear to us: we had a roof over our heads. We were lying under the tenth desk, or it had pushed itself over us. This situation was terrible for Ann, who was doubly covered up; not only had I climbed onto her in the night, but in a muscle cramp that pursued me into my dreams I had not let go of her again. No sooner was she awake than she threw me off. Then she saw the desktop of the tenth one above her. And she closed herself off entirely; I kept urging her to go ahead and keep sleeping until I had pushed the tenth one away a little. "Where are you going to push it, on top of the sixth one?" Ann asked. "A bit to the side," I said. "In fifty years this is going to seem like a wine joke to us." "You're aggressive," said Ann. "I am not aggressive," I said. "That's part of your aggressiveness," Ann said. "In ten minutes I'll be at that point," I said. "That's part of your aggressiveness, that you deny it," said Ann. "Nine minutes to go," I said . . .

"Honestly, I have no idea what you guys at the agency are writing about me."

"Right now we're writing something about your penis," Peyer remarked.

"You're twenty pages ahead of me," I warned.

"Twenty years ahead," Peyer smiled, pretty non-subordinately . . .

To calm down I took a stroll through the city, during which I forgot the streets, parks, and squares I was traversing even faster than I could read their names on the signs. The city had a lot of resting spots, but seemed to me very dense with impressions. In the worst case it was simply over-stimulating. Its rhythm, which it imposed upon me, between great density and gigantic density, could not be toughed out for long; anyway, it filled my head with city and emptied it of Ann and consequences. Either I perceived the replacement parts of the city with an absolute lack of awareness, even though they assailed my consciousness and had something like desecration of the dead in mind for me, or I tied fine, invisible thought-ropes around several adjacent objects and attempted to establish a primitive bundle-order based on this model: "This sidewalk belongs to this house, but does this tree belong to that house?" My attempt at order, with its difficulties, in which the category "questions" grew much more rapidly than the category "answers," pointed toward the fantastic disorder that prevailed; may God grant that it is a simple case of anarchy! It was actually more a question of non-simultaneity pursuant to imaginary network diagrams of the morphological conditions of being built—existing—being torn down: when the house was built, the sidewalk was presumably not there yet, and when the sidewalk was laid down, the house was presumably already torn down. And the tree in front of it had its own existential music, fading in and fading out, a different music than the house had: the house probably lasted longer, which is why various trees belonged to it which I could not see because they had temporally shifted relative to me; a few of them had slipped in before my time, and others limped along behind my time. Within one narrowly limited space over 100 years, 3 houses, 8 sidewalks, and 27 trees may have stood. Because with this in mind no order could be established, I quickly grew tired and once again I put a scrap of Ann into my head, for she was contemporaneous; then I gave up ordering things and retreated to one of the prepared municipal resting spots. Of course, I incurred some unwelcome effort with the margins, the cessation of these so-called parks. I slid on an icy path into a case of claustrophobia: I knew: *I can't stretch out*, there's no more way out for me, I am more tied to a leash than a tame, lame pointer dog; in order to attain a picture puzzle, I had to venture so far into the center of the green space that the trees blocked the whole city from me. Then all I had left were green crowns and a hissing that sounded like the scratchy sounds of a worn-out record with traffic noise on it. Then my mood was renewed. Then I was granted the impression that I was in the countryside. Thus the city was telling me some kind of lie, and it contained at least four centers where there were comparable conditions. I know that Ann, because she didn't let herself get illusioned, also never got dis-illusioned by going outside and by continuing the stroll through the city . . .

Peyer met me by the front door; I did not want to ask him into the architecture. He had made it to the tract house with his remaining strength and on the threshold his knees had buckled. He had gotten off two stops too early; he did not know the address of that profaned woman for whom I would soon play the pimp, with my twisted strategy that made the cripple into a king. Peyer came from the writing business and was enjoying an enviable state of good health. By way of a test I procured him as a customer for my love, in fact, I did not procure her any other customer besides Peyer, who was healthy and would write my prose under my name.

For the first time I knew that Ann would die. All of us would be permitted to die. There wasn't much you could say about that. It would either drag us along or make malicious demands on us . . .

"At headquarters they're making lists," Peyer said, looking around in agitation.

"The lists contain names?" I asked.

Ann's teakettle was boiling and Peyer was standing in front of me as if he didn't see me.

"Whoever goes to a pro is on the list," he said, looking past me.

"Right now you're with *two* pros," I said.

It made me angry that he wasn't looking at me, because I understood him so well that I could empathize with him. All of a sudden: hatred for my house, which did not belong to me.

"Are there police around here?" he asked.

"All the time," I said.

"What's he asking?" asked Ann, who, with the smoke from the kettle in her hands, was walking over to the table with the oilcloth cover. I started to say something but kept silent and sat down . . .

That wasn't so bad; somewhat worse . . .

The day before I had seen a man who I knew was going to die. I knew neither what his illness was nor did I know when he would go away and leave us. I only knew that I did not know him and that somebody, maybe Berditschewsky, had told me he would no longer exist. The day before stayed in my memory because it hadn't even moved me very much. For a short time I became quite natural because things were so self-evident. Then the stranger's death again seemed to me like something complicated and I inquired about the man's profession and thought about how his sudden dropping out of his occupation had to have some difficult consequences for him . . .

Then later . . .

Zeppo was in the vestibule, getting some exercise on a mental stroll. Groucho stormed out of the latrine and acted out the same walking movements as Zeppo, right behind Zeppo, as if Zeppo were happening one more time behind Zeppo, with a painted-on mustache. That didn't go well for long. Zeppo turned around and discovered Groucho, who also turned around (instead of taking refuge behind Zeppo and rescuing himself by forgoing symmetry!). But now Groucho was highly indignant and cried: "Man, did you scare me. How did you get into the vestibule . . . ?"

Not enough; but also . . .

"The master forester, while uneasily getting up again from his seat, said that if the marquise was thinking at all of the possibility of delighting him at some time with her hand, then it would be necessary right now for a step in that direction to happen in order to prevent the consequences of an impetuous deed: thus wrote Heinrich in an undisclosed passage of his marquise prose," said Peyer, who had finally tracked me down . . .

Simultaneously with this . . .

Incidentally . . .

"How far along are you with the report?" I asked Peyer.

"I'm thinking over MHB's discussion model," he said.

"I think we're writing the same thing," I said.

"You, the boss, and little old me, my unveiled humble self,

we're writing the same thing!" Peyer purred like Oblomov's Sasha and brought me a pair of shoes that he hadn't polished.

"The same thing!" I gave the shoes a kick that made Peyer fall over.

"I'm approximately three pages behind you!" Without being instructed to, he picked up the shoes again. I was glad to see that.

"The boss is better." With this statement I was entirely in line with the ways of the world . . .

"I am totally talentless," Peyer said.

"That's why I have you; that makes your appointment provisional; which I am very glad to see," I said, snapping my fingers in Ann's direction . . .

It was time that she got to know me as the strong man that I was for Peyer . . .

If you're going to do it, well then, do it coolly and calmly . . .

The eleventh desk hardly was hardly a nuisance. It was in the hallway. Thus we took note of the hallway. You had to squeeze past it; its desktop stuck out almost to the opposite wall. If Ann wanted to get from the living room to the bedroom and I wanted to get from the bedroom to the kitchen, we couldn't meet on the way or else we'd get jammed up and fall panting onto the desktop until one of us had pried him- or herself loose. Nonetheless, late in the evening and early in the morning I was sitting over a small matter at the tenth one. The piece was called "On Changes in the Oral Cavity in Cases of Leukemia." I broke off working on it and resolved to pass it on to my writing business to work on it . . .

To that the businessmen said: "Of course, we've never concerned ourselves with the secrets of the poets, even if we do get enjoyment from listening to their song: It may well be true that a special alignment of the stars is necessary for a poet to come into the world; for art is certainly quite a wondrous thing . . ." (Novalis)

*Ann's Diary*
*"I'm writing this diary so that you will find it. If I know you, you'll publish it. Nobody will ever read it, that's been taken care of. It is an intimate confession that you are free to reveal to anybody. In fact, publish the diary only fragment by fragment, not in a way that it makes any sense. People could assume we had a relationship with each other, whereas it is precisely our wonderful little secret that we didn't have any relationship with each other. If you publish it so that it gets psychological, then that's your fault and you deserve the consequences. From now on I'm going to leave the diary lying around. Please find it quickly."*

For the first time I knew that I would die. We would all have to die. There wasn't much to it, that's what we were facing . . .

*"With Peyer, whom I neither let in on it nor wanted to spoil in any way (I am sure he would have been appalled at me in a good-natured, subaltern, but persistent way)—with Peyer I spent a day on which he told me about your writing and your relentless dictation. At midnight I dismissed him and went to my room. He shuffled across the courtyard and grew smaller. No sooner was I in my room than I started thinking over how I could find someone who could be bought, and I had heard that our city was the first one in Europe to set up a bordello for women. Everything, so I heard, proceeded very symmetrically. I went down to the ground floor, made sure that Peyer had caught his streetcar, and took a taxi to the train station. In the vicinity."*

"Are there patrols here, and lists of johns?" asked Peyer. Agitatedly.

"Oh, you and your reality; make me a nice piece of prose," I said. Condescendingly.

"I'll make it," he confirmed. Compliantly, submissive as a dog.

"I've just written 'In the Salon of our Empire . . .'" I said. Impetuously.

"Is that right?" He was silent. Taken aback.

"We're writing the same thing, it's just that you're two pages behind," I said. Calculatedly.

"Right; I'm at the 'master forester interspersion,'" Peyer said. Simplemindedly and proudly.

"Kleist," I said. Seeing through both of us.

"Kleist is right," he said. Dismissed and dismissive.

*"Practically at a parade step, I went about my task. Basel had to be combed through, for I was determined to cheat. For half an hour I ran through totally deserted streets from which all of the Protestants had withdrawn in disgust. Maybe a mass exodus of Baslers to Zurich or South Baden had occurred. I pulled my senses together in the face of every stray dog until I got to the Mela Bank, that dubious bank that, when it opens its windows, looks out on so and so many bordellos. Of course on the women's bordello too, which the Baslers, who have always been the spearheads of Europe, have set up for their women. A sparse gathering of women instructed me that there was nothing going on yet at this hour. It turned out to be a house in red light that was integrated into a large block of houses. You could walk around it, which always interrupted the observations somewhat. The block had entrances everywhere like a piece of cheese, and over the entrances were illuminated red strawberries. Hôtel, tout confort: like the Parisians, the Baslers provide for their homeless and well-bred women."*

Placeless, aimless, massless, and standpointless is how I seemed to her when she wondered about it, and she never grew tired of repeating "I wonder, I wonder" . . .

*"But to continue, I walked toward the house with the windows, each individual one of which looked like a palace. I took a turn around it. I was very intimidated, since I didn't know how to and didn't dare to talk to it, to ask it about its price. After my first turn around the house with the palace windows, behind which the red light burned behind some kind of Christmas paper, there were still two guys who came into consideration. An intellectually built man of medium height whose man was showing through his pants, shirt unbuttoned, thick fur on his chest. And a second man, somewhat broader; a brawny pageboy. He was tanned and rushed out onto the street to link arms with me. But to continue."*

On the desktops, to set ourselves up in a makeshift fashion, we had put up a geodesic dome. Ann had made me aware of Buckminster Fuller. We had extracted building material from smashed-up furniture by crushing and floating the wood fragments on faucet floods throughout the tract house. Ann was nearly stupefied from the cold and I was dissolving in sympathy, but sympathy wasn't going to heat the house. So I slapped her on the back, boyishly, euphorically, and unleashed every possible worn-out joke on her. A Meyer Hirsch was in every one of them, committing a miserable faux pas at a banker's soiree. The banker was talking about fishing, and Berditschewsky didn't know how a fishing reel worked. Ha . . . and ha. The fourteenth desk. Door from the hallway to the dining room. Please don't! . . .

*"And the desire remains alive for hours, I talk to you, the desire is there, I walk beside you, the desire is there, I eat a chicken with you, the desire is there, I look at you, the desire is there. By the way, you've developed a hard expression around your mouth, I'll show it to you in the mirror sometime. You'll claim that there's someone behind the mirror who is fooling you into thinking he's you. If I lose my mind I love someone, and with you I'm constantly losing my mind. I even get into quarrels*

*with you and it's going to end fatally. But it's a shame to enter the fray for less."*

Before the time of the twelfth desk . . . in a time that, when it was, was called unhappy by both of us, and which, when the subsequent time came, was retrospectively actually quite lovely . . .

*"I sped it up when that was within my modest powers. It stretched out a little, got tempered, around 98.6 degrees, which mean to me what they mean. Even my sleeping head was shaken. It was so palpable that right after that he threw me off with great tenderness and rolled out from under me, and when I saw a large whitish drop fall onto the bedspread, he was already in front of the sink, half visible behind a synthetic curtain. Behind that everything was out of focus. He was washing up and getting ready. The next woman. Since the men's bordello in the city has been open, the world is ugly. When I got up, very crumpled, he was sitting on the chair at the foot of the bed, smiling at me without a word."*

Inadequately, out of wariness toward me, she scratched the corners of her mouth with her nails . . .

*"And that's why a certain robustness is necessary. Physical robustness and energy behind which I surmise there is mental strength. Thus a thoroughly primitive selection process that has bestowed upon me, among other things, the intern. You should have pressed him against you, then he was wonderful, a gentle, soft, will-less and pleasantly childlike orgasm. Mentally he was a tough nut to crack. As a professor he probably sleeps differently. Here, sensuality went to his brain. He even accepted marriage proposals from female students of both laws!"*

The corner of her mouth rose up mockingly for the message . . .

*"You can't do that. You don't have anyone. Then it gets more intellectual right away. Besides, he is not that thing. Then it gets lonesome. No, I prefer average. Just like I preferred you fifteen years ago. Then you would have had me. They have to be there, that's all. Besides I have this ridiculous fear that really big ones, when you lift them up, are destroyed. At their root they have something like a wasp. Dead wasps. Big ones are hotbeds for insects, they're teeming. In their gnawing even starving grasshoppers retreat under big ones."*

With just a little imagination you could draw a picture of that, and with lots of imagination it would still not be a very precise one . . .

*"Just don't revive your horror at matted genitals again! Maybe I'm telling this because I believe that you can't let yourself be put on the defensive for ever after by the activity of these friendly organs. In this regard you're still a little bit immature, and you also like to play with your sonny-boy-shamefacedness, which your age and your deflowering have long put out of date. That fits you like your bib when you eat ravioli. Where was I? Oh, yes—I grew up and was back in the room again. In front of the window there hung some kind of Christmas paper. I had gotten into one of the rooms that were located up high in a sort of tower and radiated red light. I felt no reactions to nothing anymore, and the fatigue had increased again. Everything had grown visibly more matted within me."*

Now I too was suffering, without relief, from a constant whistling sound in my ear, like Smetana just before his incurable nervous breakdown . . .

*"I had acquitted myself valiantly, that is, less than well, but the house still exists. All in all, it wasn't too bad for so late and so tired. The last big drop also planted the fear of consequences. I felt that before my*

*memory closed down and, the next morning when you knocked on the door of my room, stayed closed down."*

Inaccessibly, due to wariness with me, she scratched the corners of her mouth with her pointed fingernails until I made her aware of her pain, which had no effect on me . . .

*"Four weeks after that, suddenly this little story. Do you understand that I feared the worst? It should have shown then, but I didn't know that. What else? Oh, yes—my visit to the pros is of course only really complete now that you've read this diary carefully. You'll flip and flip. I assure you you can do it. And on top of that, everything will turn out to be your fault."*

*"The best thing would have been for me to take a little boyfriend while I continued to pursue the affair with you. He would have relieved my tensions during the day and in the evenings. I would have taken him on very quickly, while thinking of you. Old, eternally serviceable methods of impossible love. Any scullery boy can substitute for Emperor Franz Joseph when a woman is desperate, but I didn't even see a scullery boy. Peyer, whom you distrusted, was taken care of. Besides, he was subordinate and even more subordinate than you, but of course he always had something like unfolding on his lips. Then he was endowed with a peepy penis that was sticking up in the air somehow and seemed to be crying in a falsetto voice: Wait a minute, I'm here too, don't forget me! Impossible to get Peyer to stand in and up. In the artists' bistro, the wine hall, a few aggressive fatsos, very bare, willing, but unappetizing, then a few left-wingers in whose laps the free-ride streetcar grew. For one evening, yes, one didn't have to pay for the tram for once and they talked about how people were going to leave their cars at home to ride into the outer districts. But over several evenings I couldn't stand the free-ride streetcar. A pricey mode of transportation and as a Swiss citizen I get an hourly rate of thirty francs per man and hour of discus-*

*sion, and so we collectively frittered away nearly half a million on the discussion about the free ride. This half a million will be missing from the Swiss GNP at the end of the year, and the streetcar will get more expensive. A three-stop ride will cost five billion."*

He doesn't know how to help. Except for himself . . .

*"For a hundred he'd lick me twice as good, he said; as if I weren't used to that! In the bordellos, oral eroticism is considered something out of the ordinary; I can't figure out why. 'Mais tu es riche, chérie!' and opened my wallet and saw my hundred-franc bill. And now I'll show you the photos, he said. I haggled like a market woman over not having to look at the photos; naked, but good at haggling."*

*"I see you reading my diary, the only writing that I'll ever do, assuming a hedgehog posture and bristling. Don't forget to sit down on the chair and cry."*

Every time I have the feeling you're criticizing me, I grant you that authority without hesitating—I'm sure I must have *some* fault or other—but I can't come up with any ideas at all about what I should improve about my blueprint. But go ahead, criticize, just do it, go right ahead . . .

*"My escort walked over to the chair in the alcove and started undressing. He was covered with just the minimum, a refinement of wearing clothes that I was privileged to admire. Under miniature pants he wore nylon stockings that went way up, and then strange old gentlemen's garters, shunted upward, that no doubt were for a certain type of fétichiste that frequented the establishment. I stood there with my eyes half closed, and my fatigue was almost causing me to collapse. The bed high, protruding and provocative, no doubt still warm from my predecessor, but unfortunately when it comes to such considerations*

*I'm pretty insensitive. But sleep: that I could do in this bed. My escort had taken off his shirt. I looked at him distraughtly without knowing why. No doubt unaccustomed procedures were necessary to wake me up at this stage. The room, which was located at the top of a tower, was not conducive to transforming me. I was dreaming on two feet, that is, I did not sit down and did not comply with the invitation. Then the second, more pleasant, side of fatigue showed itself. I was not enervated by his not standing, and thus by his not delivering the quite usual service, and this had a positive effect on that service. I think, without exaggerating, that it is not quintessential whether he stands or not; but I had paid, and as a Swiss citizen I am accustomed, as soon as money changes hands, to a trade-off on either my part or the recipient's part."*

The pathogenic shoddiness of South Alemannic everyday life . . .

*"What followed was the worst, after I had only shyly stroked him on the shoulders. Stroking a pro's shoulders! I don't know whether I noticed the sarcasm of this caress in this place. Then came the payment. Once again: 'Tu me donnes cent, n'est-ce pas.' Sixty was the agreement downstairs, I said. 'But listen, I'm sure you've got a lot of dough, let's have a look.' I didn't show it to him, my wallet. On this point, extreme prudence was called for."*

I read in Ann's eyes how much pain her loathing of me caused her . . .

*"It wasn't that it wasn't meant to be any fun, on the contrary. If it wasn't done with zest, then the deception was not complete. My escort wore an undershirt with a high collar that might have been cut out of a boat's tarpaulin; trains of thought that were enough to make me laugh when I was so tired that it was going to pull my legs out from under me."*

I stood in the doorway, extended both index fingers away from my hands, bent my knees a little, moved my thus configured hands to face level, turned them around 180 degrees, jabbed with my index fingers, and experienced both eyes popping out of their sockets; and at this moment I stiffly extruded my knees backward. The blood that was now tangible on my shirt mixed with my howls of pain, in which no surprise resonated. And while slowly pulling my hands with their pointily pointing index fingers out of my two eye sockets, I entered the tower room and howled: "Now you . . ."

*"It must have been about two-thirty in the morning. Beyond the window, gray clouds combine to form little men, a circle of clouds talking about women. Was it any wonder that rain was pouring from the little men? Physically I had involved myself in this deception; intellectually I had remained faithful to the man I had left at home. 'Are you getting on top of me?" he asked before I rolled on top of him, clumsily like a pastry that was being pushed into the oven by the baker at about this time of morning. Disappointment at first; I did not feel his thick fur under me. I had become completely insensitive. 'Hey, what you got there?' 'An old love bite on the tip,' he said, 'that won't hurt a thing.' True enough, it didn't."*

Peyer was led in by the butler and introduced to her. Ann seemed to like him, but right after the stabbing pain in his lower abdomen he careened toward the city, taking three sandwiches and onion rings along in case he got off ten stops too early again. As he departed, softly singing and reciting, I had the melancholy feeling that I would no longer achieve dominance of prose production in this country. I wasn't even the King of Prose yet, and already proceedings for high treason were coming at me. Spitting in annoyance, I stamped the snow on the forecourt down flat, bent over, and saw, as far as my bent-over eyes could see, the tread on the sole of my own winter boot. I was going to die. We would all have to die. That was no big deal, it was what we were expecting. The fact that it didn't happen right away afforded us the pleasure that such a postponement could grant us; we lived somewhat more intensively. Before we died (perhaps euthanasia would be accorded us) our prose would regress to the stage where barracks commands made poor suckers stumble. We wouldn't die today, we would die tomorrow, tomorrow was another day, how come everything had to happen today, impatience was a symptom of immaturity. Certainly the time until then, because we still had a lot of time, would not be so enjoyable as back when we didn't know anything about time, but I could not care less about this end, replete with loss of language, after considering it unimportant for so long. Contradicting this lack of importance were fear and shame; but what did they mean? Certainly not much for the death of prose.

A person can be far away while their smell is close by. I penetrated her smell, and things looked pretty destroyed . . .

Later I went on my outing to the city; I was the first and the last Real Person. I was already familiar with everything; the "occupied" areas lay close to each other. I had to calculate every step in advance: whether it wouldn't lead me to pieces of memory cement that would drive me back to her, the woman who stayed home. A café called Odeon, with a neon tube over every table. Waiters serving sunglasses on watermelon halves. A symbol of writing that's bitten the dust. I wept briefly . . .

In the tower room . . .

Unbearable; he was letting the spatial conditions turn into one big insufferableness. The twelfth desk was located in the tower again, but in such a way that it halfway covered the hatch. I was just letting myself down by the rope, the rope clamped between my legs, my legs scraped up from the endless shimmying, when above me the brightness went out. A glance at my watch. In order to do that, one of my hands let go of the rope. I found myself on top of the eleventh desk, so banged up that I could not even scream. In spite of having fallen down, I tugged myself back up. No sooner was I hanging on the rope again than Ann sashayed discreetly and weightlessly through the bottleneck below. She seemed to sense the projecting desktop, for without looking down, she glided past the protrusion. Of course downstairs it was already dark anyway. She wouldn't have seen anything even if she'd looked at the projection. But I, hyper-awake and in shock, was at the point where I was brain-burstingly aware of it when somebody wasn't looking at a spot that would be pointless to look at; the fact that Ann had realized the pointlessness of her looking at this moment presented me with puzzles that were all the more unsolvable because I had *not* realized it. On the contrary, I looked very intensely through the blackness up toward the desktop of the twelfth one . . .

It was probably thanks to Ann's insistence, which was not equal to my growing compliance: the remodeling and expansion of my writing business. I would like to say up front that I finally pushed through the monastic atmosphere that had been my wish for a long time; hermitism, absolute celibacy during the writing process, not even slight physical contact, complete control of the digestive system thanks to disciplined portions of food intake, lots of dried meat, a little fish, cold spinach, now and then a soft-boiled egg, yogurt, rolled oats; the last mixed up into a semisweet health food. The expanded writing business looked something like this: the three structures were seamlessly connected by foot-walls, but separate above these thresholds. The longest seamless ceiling measured thirty-five meters, and in order to prevent cracks from forming due to the contraction of the concrete, construction seams to be left unfilled were arranged at appropriate intervals. The influence of temperature remained a delicate problem, as did the influence of relative warmth. For some time now I had been realizing quietly and privately that every one of my architectural projects had something to do with the exchange of affection, or with the lack of it. There was probably also a connection between expressions of affection and the digestive system; it wasn't becoming entirely clear to me; it seemed to have become more obvious to Ann, since she was the one who turned "my hand is your belly" into a fixed phrase that could be used pretty much anywhere, whether in the evening in the tower room when we rolled from the first desk onto the next ones, or while inspecting my construction site, which permitted my writing business to expand into a mid-size giant, until every pointed feather key—even the recent sight of the feathers sticking out of the dead birds that had flown into the windows—suggested to me the abstraction of potency. Because of the façade insulation, the daily fluctuations of the unheated buildings were less problematical than the annual fluctuations. Peyer and his team were now writing fine, classical, very compliant texts that seemed as streamlined as an ostrich egg, and presenting me with the aerodynamics; and Ann's commentary was: "Do you regret the remodeling, the expansion?" to which I referred when talking to Peyer, like Aquinas referring to Averroes. Ann's insistence could be bloodcurdling: she did not curdle Peyer's blood; instead he who always waited for my signature in the kitchen at the table with the ubiquitous blue-and-white checkered tablecloth seemed to find a relentless pleasure in her more frequent incursions; in the kitchen—as I suspected while skimming over the streamlined sentences produced in my business operation, with its head office at the fourth desk—my compliance was a topic of conversation, and it seemed to me as though I had often taken part in this conversation by defiantly remaining absent for far too long . . .

Underneath the coat rack . . .

"The industry is taking all of us over?" I said.

"That's right." Hirsch was certain.

"What do you mean to say by that?" I had to know more precisely.

MHB leaned back as if he were sitting in a Barcelona chair by Mies van der Rohe. On the shelf at his head level there lay, from left to right: a gingerbread heart, an immersion boiler, a cufflink, a small clay bowl. On the shelf against which I, as his audience, was leaning, there lay, from right to left: a flashlight, a police whistle, a drop counter, and a metalized siphon bottle.

"Only if . . ." M. Hirsch Berditschewsky began.

"Careful, the washed sepia drawing of Franz Schubert!" I threw myself on top of it. "Saved!" Hirsch breathed a sigh of relief.

"I love Schubert," I said without prompting.

"Composing instead of writing," Hirsch confirmed.

"What is that supposed to mean, that the industry is taking all of us over?" I asked.

Hirsch took a bite out of the gingerbread heart.

"Now that the big oil companies are starting up publishing companies. That new book of poetry with BP, the new novel with Texaco, and all essays are perfectly placed with Esso. There's so much to do, and they get right down to work. And then there's that anthology of oil-shale stories published by Shell, with the fantastic title story 'We Are All the Tank.' The person behind whom the author, as the cognoscenti suspect, is not difficult to discern comes from northern Canada with a 53-ton truck that has a load of 52.7 tons of oil shale and drives into New York State. Suddenly he has no more oil in the engine and everything is terribly overloaded. The truck, which weighs fifty-five tons, has a load of 52.7 tons and the remaining 0.22 tons are the weight of the driver! I tell you, Shell has a nose for business and takes first place. And the driver gets out and stands on top of the ten-foot-high X-Minus tires (the author was going to write 'Michelin tires'—the Frenchmen offered 5,000 in cash if he managed to work Michelin into the story, but Firestone put Shell under pressure via Ford until the author, by the skin of his teeth, was able to make up a tire brand, the X-Minus, whose grooves, by the way, are more Firestonelike than Michelinesque, but the French pocketed the cash anyway—you know that there was a danger that Firestone would pull the basis for the next anthology about oil sands out from under Shell), and as the driver stands there thinking '52.7 tons of shale in the load and not a drop of lube under the hood,' a grizzly comes hitchhiking from Buffalo and mashes him into a pulp of tissue. He looks down at himself and sees. 'Ha ha, I'm dying,' and sees that the splintering he just heard was his foot bones in the grizzly's jaws . . ."

"Kafka," I interrupted.

"Kafka with British Petroleum, for a long time now," snorted Hirsch.

"Go on," I egged him on . . .

". . . and that's how the industry is taking us over! I tell you, Atkins from Shell, you know, the guy from Newfoundland who also came up with the idea for the title 'We Are All the Tank,' that VP who will always be only a VP because his region doesn't possess enough gas stations, so that he finds time and space to fool around with prose, that Atkins guy whinnied when he read it and roared: 'Bring me this crazy writer, a true madman! I have a job for him as a gas-station attendant in the North Woods!' . . . What he writes about shale, and the way he connects us all with the tank, so that we'll simply die from all that identification . . . I'm not going to give anything away ahead of time . . . read it for yourself, Hecht, and you'll turn into a tank . . . since the big oil companies have started up publishing companies, things are on the move again, and the gas-station attendants are writing again for us, the public. We have once again become, in the most imperial sense, an audience, an audience. We grant and refuse, all according to the haulage quota and sulfur content."

"Sounds like a blessing," I said.

"The industry," Meyer H. B. bared his teeth as if he was going to gnaw at a barrel.

"Have *those* publishers started up?" I asked.

Hirsch once again made a very tired impression. On the shelf at his head level he had shifted the objects. The gingerbread heart was eaten up; even Peyer, the trencherman, couldn't have added anything to that.

"Oil companies and writing work together like well-lubricated parts," I said.

"That's enough to make you laugh yourself sick and stay that way," Hirsch opined his opinion.

"I can't choke that one down." This commentary was my last utterance.

"Canada is slippery." This statement was his last commentary.

We quickly got up off the chairs and placed our shoes next to the metalized siphon bottle . . .

The tree was a tall, wide, rustling, matted one. Its green flirted with whitishness, it was shaking fish bellies. A lot of branches, for one single tree an unbelievable amount of branches. And somebody had been busy at its roots. The felled and chopped-up tree was probably a felled and chopped-up grove of trees. The area was sloshing with water. One big sponge. If I got up from my kitchen chair, which I was noticeably doing less often, the tract house lurched on its subsoil, leaned at an angle, made a smacking sound. Like Chaplin as an emigrant I slid onto the next-lower piece of furniture and still I was a young author. On the next-lower piece of furniture, cacti were writhing and sweating water from their quills. A damp area with the withered, wizened one. The reddish one with a knobby trunk . . .

No doubt I left the tract house at least one more time. It goes without saying that I sank through the crusted surface of the snow that had broken off more or less all of the branches of the tree or the grove. Modest twigs could have waved in a melancholy fashion; I would have wandered destroyed among them. I preserved in my memory—which was luckily not running off on its own anymore—a shop sign and an endearing idea, a business-minded idea, but still, compared to the forms that business-mindedness could assume, also an endearing idea, namely: "When was the last time you brought flowers home?"

On the balcony of the tract house pipes opened up and put the balcony under water. In the ice cold, Ann was very close to me and felt so warm that a slice of bread laid on her would have gotten toasted. The central heating emptied out and I tried to enter her, and she slid . . .

Simultaneously with this . . .

In the salon of our Empire . . .

The continuous-motion machine TIME was ticking. At the end of its ticking, a piece of wrapping paper, hastily wrapped around the explosive device that half the city was mobilizing to fight against. Plumes of a collective moved past the tract house. In the desire to survive even only a possible ticking, many discovered the meaning of a life, which, if it was not running under the title of "Getting Away from Something or Other" or the title "Live

Down with Force Someone Who Wants Death," was subject to a teleological drainage: the good people were bleeding the meaning of life from every wound and scarcely knew that little more was left to them. In my decisive thinking, hardly well-disposed to them, I denied them any meaning at all; they were to have no advantage over me as long as the continuous motion accompanied us and, in the absence of serious cases and for the purpose of creating such cases by suggestion, made them wallow around in brownish wrapping paper . . .

"They" don't know what a simple light switch is, which is to say, *I* don't know much anymore. This guy here had two trip switches that glowed in the dark. Two screws as if forgotten high up on the trigger circuit. Anyone who tripped them stabbed himself, and rightly so; one round synthetic shell enclosed the switch, and another shell encased the outlet. It was impossible to get into its narrow openings, within which murderous current raged ready to strike, unless "you stuck something in there." This happened by looking for and selecting an object that was so thin that it could be plunged into the narrow opening and given an extra push, furtively, hopefully without being caught in the act; that would be bad. The light switch ran on two tracks that stuck out from it at the top and bottom; thus it could be pushed across several bright, sparking contacts, a pure technicity become an end in itself, true to the era. But it was a switch for multiple lights; which light lit up when the trip switch was thrown depended on which contact the switch was on; it was freely adjustable from top to bottom, as could be read from the length of the tracks; I took readings from morning till evening. The negative parts together with the threaded part lay within a perfect square; that was the outlet outside our bathroom door; it, the door, became more and more complex in my descriptions and—with a number of pages' delay—in Peyer's "Images of a New Plasticity" as well (later suppressed by me!); there arose during the description of the door an infinity of extension and of purpose that only approximately corresponded to its actual dooristic infinity; that was only natural. Never before in my life had I seen anything bigger and more terrifying than this bathroom door: it snapped shut, it snapped, it snapped open, it created suction, and it never lost any part of itself or anything from within itself. I could not get close to Ann. Not even by writing. Even though I had thought early on about getting close to her by the writing route. She denied herself to me, and in time I fell into a respect for this former task of mine, sliding into a state of anxiety and into a weltschmerzy-for-evermore withdrawal; Ann denied herself to me; and my nocturnal marital duty, the description of a woman, writing above and beyond a woman or beneath and through a woman, disintegrated and made me hollow-cheeked. So that I, if I want to describe her, do not talk from the start about Ann anymore, but about the light switch next to her. "Next to her"! "Next to it," I'd have to say, for she has become a thing for me, a household object. Again and again I treat her like a human being; a writer must never do that, for he isn't one either, even less so than his mate. It may be that Ann now deserves better treatment. And behind her? Nothing more than our bathroom? Really nothing more? Because I acknowledge that I no longer know much, I often start from the beginning and say my stupid sentence: "They don't even know what a simple light switch is." Of course they KNOW what a light switch is. Nor is it a matter of the switch and the trigger circuits. It's a matter of it, the door, and when it is no longer a matter of the door, it will be a matter of the next everyday object that has attached myths to itself. Am I still on the right track!? Isn't it me above all who wants to know that? Is it Ann's fault that I don't? After all, by this time it's basically assumed that I'm not on the right track anymore. And I probably shouldn't be anymore. I probably don't even want to be anymore. Once while studying higher mathematics I caught sight of and recalculated the equation of a curve whose curve mostly wasn't even there and simply didn't appear within the axes of the coordinates; that's how I know how enormously profoundly and unimaginably complex it remains to ascertain simple temporary lack of presence. I want to be lost *in that way* and no other. But why do I want that? So that some man or some woman will help me? Does it do me any good that someone is doing me any good? A man who has become distrustful no longer dares to go into the bathroom, through the door. The man outside the door says: "I dunno what a light switch is, but please, please flip it like you were plannin' to; then I don't have to see everything anymore, including you and me."—Stupid sentences; but is there anything about the guy who's saying them that's any smarter? . . .

Incidentally . . .

"But even without these stories, if you only had a dream in your lives, then wouldn't you be amazed and not let yourselves be denied the miraculousness of this event that has simply become a daily one for us! The dream seems to me a protective bulwark against the routine and normality of life, a free recovery of the bound-up imagination, where it jumbles up all the images of life and interrupts the constant earnestness of the adult with a merry child's game . . ." (Novalis)

Generate constant insecurity by means of constant talking. Lines draw themselves and so he has to wipe them away again. The fox he's riding leaves behind tracks in the snow, and its rider operates the fox's tail like a snow eraser, obliterating the little paw hollows on the tablet of snow; thus the only memory—that of the plain or plane that has not been traversed, of the wreath of hills that were not broken through, of the shafts that one did not fall into and in which one did not suffocate—is lost. Who recalls the walks he took, his brusque stops, his heavy nodding, who recalls his untenably full glasses; who ultimately gloats over having been a scaffolding for this existence, a corset for this body? . . .

No doubt bringing home a gift would make Ann very happy; it didn't have to be flowers; after all, I had good taste. Four promptly delivered pieces of short prose yielded a slimline flash camera; I was investing my honorarium in the photo industry . . .

"There's even operating instructions included at no additional cost," I said as Ann ripped open the film wrapper with her teeth.

"Is the operation already regulated?" asked Ann, who seemed amazed, uncertain, and who wanted me to be amazed that the regulations had already ventured inside a ridiculous little film package that is churned out by the billions.

"Read the instructions, then you'll know everything," I urged her and monetized the amazement she wanted from me as a timely reimbursement for her efforts at reading.

"PAN F Perceptol min 68 Fahrenheit 10 ASA 25 DIN 15," she read.

"Come again?" I asked.

"Microphen min 20 Celsius 4 ASA 64 DIN 19," she read.

"HP 4?" I asked.

"FP 4, rookie," she said.

I tore the directions out of her hands.

"Then it would be Microphen 68 F 5 650 ASA DIN 29, but it goes down to 125 or else 22 with ID-11 from FP 4," I said, as nimble as a weasel.

"ID-11 from PAN F," said Ann, who refused to place the film into the housing and plucked it out of the case with a pointy nail inserted into the feed track.

"PAN F ID-11." Ann stuck to her guns and repeated it like the cue for a robot in a second rate science-fiction play.

"That's the kind of prose we can expect in the future," I said.

No sooner had I said that than I felt that I had forgotten something. I turned my head away from Ann and screamed at the wall:

"PAN F Perceptol min 68 F 10 ASA 25 DIN 15 Microphen min 20 C 4 ASA 64 DIN 19 or 68 F 5 650 ASA DIN 29 with reduction to 125 or 22 with ID-11 of FP 4! Do you understand *that* prose?"

"The industry is taking all of us over." MHB's bed stood behind the thin wall and I heard a snarl of satisfaction when he heard how the objects behaved faithful to his theory, and how the goblins toiled away so that it would be correct.

"The sun is standing in the middle of a cool spherical sky whose blueness would outdo a garden border of domesticated cornflowers," said Ann.

"Yep, f/16," I confirmed; with which I had concisely said the same thing . . .

She took the camera out of the cardboard box, looked through the lens, laughed, and dropped the piece of junk. The delicate housing covered half the kitchen floor. The next four short prose pieces were due in a year. Or never. For the time being she still had me, because there were no more honoraria left, even as a present. The present was capable of distributing friendliness. I supposed that I was determining the beneficial influence of the weather on my sexual prowess. It was waning rapidly; briefly; good deeds, as far as I could feel . . .

Then later . . .

Tears before smiles, like Robert (Walser), just not tears that are so inaccessible to the world . . .

Stomping in from the forecourt, I took off my coat and hung it by the other coats . . .

She was lying very close. She felt good. She felt the way she would assume I would assure her that she felt. Her body, I tried to . . .

The period furniture of the room we were occupying had a quality that certificates of authenticity spoke of, and they spoke over several whole pages for each piece of furniture. I tranquilized myself quickly within the torment that the small high buffet with its two doors and two drawers caused my even more excessively style-sensitive eyes. One drawer could not be pushed back in, and the left rear corner was covering up a milled-out recess in which a cabinetmaker had spread a bag of loose wood shavings with a gluey paste. Why tranquilization? If at first the torment at that sight was such that I absolutely wanted to end either the torment or the sight, in order not to suffer aesthetically any longer, then when I no longer looked at it, the torment diminished so much that I quickly discovered and perfected the technique of ending the torment of the sight of the period furniture by a constant closing of the eyes. While I was doing so the heavy white wall of the wooden door interrupted my walking, and the pain of the impact would probably have forced my eyes open if there hadn't been a similarly damnable entity behind the wooden door: the dinnerware-display cabinet, which was infamous to me and which I had recently chopped to bits. Its doors had carved garlands glued to them . . . the gritting of the teeth and the stammering of soft pertinent curses did not remove the doors, and even less did they de-joist one of the plate rails that could so slickly have let one of the stockpiled Montmorency plates fall through onto the chili-pepper-colored tile floor. No tranquilization? If I was calm, then Ann seemed to be possessed by a slight fickleness, which was understandable to me to the extent that here two different styles came together that could be adjusted to one another only in a simultaneous destruction of all items of furniture down to the same degree of destructive style. Who would deliver the first blow? After the "Dynamics of Small Groups Concentrated In a Small Space with No Exit," which was known to both of us and thoroughly discussed by both of us in the evenings, the prospects were good that the end would take place in the room we were occupying and the beginning of the end would take place in the hallway to the room we were occupying. "We're going to bust up the plate rails," I said calmly, inhaling and pulling my lower lip back over my teeth. "We're going to get right down to smashing the plates," said Ann, after she had let a quarter hour pass in which she had been looking at my hair whorl and at my temples and at the tip of her cigarette, which I wrested away from her . . .

As soon as I closed my eyes—I now consisted entirely of an aficionado of the expectation of closing the slits of my eyes, and of a doppelganger of the condition of hearing myself (leaning back with closed eyes) groping about, thanks to my inner man on the move—as soon as I closed these eyes in this way, I fell down as if anemic and cooled off by a few more arctic degrees . . .

The burden of my long arms and short legs lay on the author's torso. I lay there thrown on my side. Ann was lying above me, more hovering than heavy. No contact took place; it may be that there were intermittently perforated cellophane membranes between us. Tight, non-distorting glass in the porthole. Skin lay upon skin. The contact was pushed apart again every few inches. And so the ship started moving. And dead on target, I launched my torpedoes, shoving them into the water like the surviving local baker pushed his bread into the oven. Spastically trotting snail feet; my nose locations; their washed-up cartilage insteps; only they made the reptile capable of crawling; it crawled away from Berditschewsky, who was inspecting us, consuming us with his eyes. His black shape. Half in the doorway. Our reptile with two backs capable of crawling. The intersection of two crawler lanes, that's what it was . . .

She was lying very close. She was pretty warm and grasped my member. I didn't try anything, but withdrew . . .

The worst thing with Peyer was that both of his eyes had different vision defects. One was deformed cylindrically, while the other was deformed elliptically. He would be blind at forty-five because the two retinas, in a dialectical process that was going on between them, were negating each other . . .

The synthesis attained, from which no further thesis would emerge, would be lifelong black . . .

In search of the city that promised me more tangible experiences than the ones I had, I covered myself with a constantly growing number of coats. The weight of my arms and legs lay on my torso. If I was lying on my side, the upper organs weighed down on the lower ones, and a certain pressure was at fault for the moaning contentment of the man lying quietly. *Down with your own person.* A synthetic coat for my feet, a fur coat for my chin and belly area, a cotton head bandage for my splitting ears and if needed for my staring eyes. My nose got pushed between thumb and index finger, and the backs of my hands, thanks to great insensitivity, were left in the open air. At all critical points, with the aid of burdensome and covering organs, there formed bundles, warm, thermostatic body spheres, so that on toward springtime my burdened breast could finally quit breathing . . .

In a dirty corner, under a mountain of sheets . . .

Turning my head meant setting my head hair-first on my collar, having my chin where my forehead should have been, and thinking in my lower maxillary sinus. To the extent that I was able to lick myself on the uppermost vertebra, I was also capable of a soft gurgling, unless I turned my head again and slid up the esophagus to my palate . . .

True, that didn't do any good, but figuring that out didn't do any good either . . .

Everything up to this point: wrong. From here on in: everything suddenly wrong. Only at the end, at the very end: do everything wrong one more time. Then, all of a sudden, a ray of hope: all is wrong . . .

Every act of fleeing from a person is a an act of moving toward him . . .

I recall that M. H. Berditschewsky favored a form of Delaware kitchen English that tended to introduce his darkest passages; presumably he was doing it to damp down a fear that would have overwhelmed him while he was still talking, for he was actually a member of the class that spoke felicitously and, with the attitude that "the talk is the walk," measured circumstances most felicitously to fit one's skin even more snugly . . .

"Let's put it *nüchternly*," Hirsch intoned psalmodically.

"Put it as you say," I ping-ponged, with great expectations.

"I seh it perfectly anders than thou." Hirsch as horse trader, precisely helping himself.

"But how do I see it?" I asked.

"Different than me Jew." Hirsch was starting to sing softly.

"Stop that, it does vey," I pled.

"Shall it too, shall it too." And he struck hard on the level of the highest abstraction . . .

"Abstracly sprechend, it's still in my mind, see. Das Ghetto 1 in Ghetto 2 in Ghetto 3. Surrounding that, Warsaw. Surrounding Warsaw, Poland. Surrounding Poland, the Nazis. What then could have to do Ghetto 1 with the Nazis? They are so far away, still so far away, long way to their Tipperary . . . and doch . . . Some way . . . they come one day together, the Nazis and the Ghetto 1 in Ghetto 2 in Ghetto 3 . . . at once is there no Ghetto 1 more, but teem the Nazis in Ghetto 1 in Ghetto 2 in Ghetto 3 in Warsaw in Poland . . . it's the right Ende and definitiv . . . Change der Nomenklatur, namely . . . Nazisturmstaffel 1 in the Nazisturmstaffel 2 in the Nazisturmstaffel 3 inside the Warsaw Naziarmee inside the Polish Naziarmee . . . pretty many . . . overall the Nazis . . . the places where one can still put up a ghetto have gotten fatally few . . . one will have to concentrate oneself on Non-Nazi-Ground in small Lagers, but on this same ground are they also already and close everything off . . . Hirsch had to go, away from there, East-USA, wide away . . ."

"Talk about trees, please," I did not say, but suppressed it . . .

"Fed up mit that, nicht wahr . . . maybe to forget, the whole thing . . . yes Sir, we forget, are forgetting born . . . it gets repeated, later sometime . . . due to urgent demand reopening the performance . . . one will report again . . . this time are the prospects for Hirsch hardly better . . . whither shall he, when thou him throwest out from the tract house?"

"But I'm not throwing you out," I said.

"Me have these thoughts," Hirsch said, blinking.

"Speak correctly again," I requested.

"You see, when I, in my very long sleep . . ." he began.

"You have been sleeping for practically the whole story," I confirmed.

". . . sleep I get excited by these dreams of my getting thrown out . . ." Hirsch looked at me.

"Berdy, just shut your trap and ratchet up a schnapps for yourself," I yelled.

"Whenever I think 'thrown out,' I think of the Nazis," he said.

"The simplified version," I ventured.

"I can only do very complicated or very simple; there's nothing in between," Hirsch said softly.

"Didja sleep well?" I asked, convulsively jumping away from there.

"There's nothing in between," Hirsch insisted . . .

There was nothing left for me to do but reprise the joke . . .

"Look once," I said.

"Stop with that already, I'm not feelin' like it anymore." Hirsch, in a foul mood.

"We still cultivate the Art of Racism, we goyim here." He had to hear that from me.

"Who since years is so tired as me will hardly want to listen to you." Hirsch, many thousands of years old.

"You shouldn't, dear Hirsch, even be in this story of mine at all, for it is now customary that for each Jew that the Non-Jewish-Writer has appear in his story, a caution is exercised vis-à-vis that 'hot-potato character' that is roughly twice as big as the Torah and often nearly as incomprehensible."

"Aha, and how do I appear in your story?" he inquired.

"Well, just the way you are," I said.

"Aha, so that's how." Hirsch seemed relieved.

"I think you'd rather not appear, because I like to document," I said.

"I would like me comical to see," he growled.

"Nu, it depends on how you look at it," I mellowed.

"Comical, very very in this way something very good," he insisted.

"It can only turn out badly, Hirsch, let's leave it out." My error became clear to me . . .

Hirsch wept silently. Weeping made him tired. He would fall asleep right away and disappear, so to speak, from the report . . .

"You're deleting me just because I got onto the Nazis again," he whispered.

"Never." I was trembling with semi-sacred wrath.

"Just go ahead and delete, I'm always getting deleted, we're always getting . . ."

"Hirsch! Quiet and sleep!" I yelled . . .

And decided TO LEAVE HIM IN . . .

The suitor for the hand of the lady with the blue rose, when the pink sheet tore, had by way of precaution pressed himself into the cracks between the rust-red bricks. They seemed thin; cement crunched and powdered under his clawing grasp. Never again would the sunset, into which his broad, white collar was dipped, disappear from his memory, unless the next three days expunged it without resistance. From the tiled men's lavatory, after the unemployed foreman had rinsed himself onto the pearwood chest, emanated the rustling of the forest. The breeze that had swept through the Common Spruce trees did not stop at the weather-sensitive Norway spruce. The young suitor was spared a further collision with the monster that spoke annoying prose. The massive Hirsch pressed the alarm clock onto the lamp, emptied the alarm clock into the toothbrush holder and slurped little toothed wheels and then, breaking through the hardwood floor and coming back up, retreated to his recess, and during the preparations for finding a shallow sleep toward morning he lovingly crumbled the round-bodied nightstand to bits . . .

Then later . . .

Attempt at a definitive indictment, according to which the High Court would have to convict Ann. "She becomes infantile when he goes out into society without her, which he regards as his right. Then she takes revenge and invites people to her place. Her home is his home, and so she is in no way permitted, legally speaking, to make free use of it, but she must consult with him: but he is out in society, and therefore she must wait patiently with her invitation, which—occurring against the law, indeed against the laws of nature—also includes the artists hated by him, all of them horribly bad authors, incompetent painters, and utterly addled musicians. Now, judges of the High Court, the instinctive happens. If he comes back and hears people in the tract house that he himself has not invited, and if he then perceives this entire terrible troupe of artists sitting on his pillows, then he behaves publicly—the public sphere would now have been established—and also index-fingerly as if she had no right to extend any invitations herself. But she is already in the infantile stage and screams "You same-old-same-old man," followed by pejoratives like "sod" or "journeyman baker," depending on the state of her infantilism. All of which does not fail to annihilate him and he is sitting quietly, screamed-at and belittled in his natural dignity, in the roaring-toasting-festive circle of guests. Judges of the High Court, he revokes a right from her that she never had to begin with; and for that he is now forced to sit among artists! I can only demand the punishment of eternal life for the accused woman . . ."

Then later . . .

"With that I believe my torment has reached its pinnacle," I said.

"What torment?" asked Peyer.

"Where are you anyway?" I asked.

"MHB wants to something say," Peyer simpered.

"Let him be. That's enough," I ordered.

"Only two pages behind! We're moving, writing the same way!" Peyer enthused . . .

Then later . . .

"You're so cruel," she said.

"A harmless game," I said.

"I'm so happy," said Ann.

"Our doings full of curlicues," I said . . .

Incidentally . . .

She bit herself on the fingers as if she wanted to hold fast to them with her teeth and pull them out of her hands . . .

Some mother-of-pearl chicken in the masticating mouth . . .

Yes, you were just about to blackmail me with your stupor. I should have kept quiet from that point on, but I didn't let you do it. I wasn't listening to you; my inner audience ratings were 5%, not a single bit more, everything slumped. For you I would have had just as much commitment left over as for the Federal Police, that didn't bother him. He came. I don't think that we—if I may speak for both of us, since you as a woman have no mouth and are not permitted to have one—I don't think that we were thinking of expectations at all in this series. He stood outside the front door and showed us that we were locked in. Still, he hardly took any space away. Its desktop smashed up the door panel, but we were able to push the left one a little to the side and lift it up. This caused my reworking of the topic "The Introduction of Constitutional and Communal Self-Government in the Grand Duchy of Baden" to slide onto the threshold of the front door. We had no more door, just a ripped-open entryway. And it came flowing inside, the following . . .

I had gotten too close to her. She had already grasped my poor member, and I tried in vain to . . .

Down with your own person! His shoulders were shaken by dry, intermittent sobbing, and a choking rose in his throat, which caused him nauseousness; pain and disappointment deprived him of consciousness, almost . . .

Ann inclined her head as if she were interested in my claptrap, busy unraveling the red thread. There was no red thread besides me. She could have done some unraveling on herself in order to get to that dispiriting consciousness of guilt that would have thrown some light for her onto her absolute guilt and onto my absolute innocence, both of which were being slowly turned through the mill of an illness. This illness—and this was the most definite thing about it—would come to an end . . .

The feeling of an impending loss of personality. I was losing my-self and looking for what I had lost in all the old haunts that had somehow imprinted themselves on me. Stood around for two hours in Peyer's office not knowing what to say. Didn't even talk to him at all; at best it could have been a babbling monologue. Yeah, it could have been. But it wasn't. There was nothing to talk about, we had enjoyed each other, and one had drawn out of the other what there was to be drawn out of the other: if anything that was meant for the other had remained in one of the two, then it was because one or the other had not asked his way deeply enough into himself; and heaven knows—yes, it does—that one can do a fine job of asking one's way into others. There was no more to pull out of Peyer than what I had put into him, but that was not allowed to come out in conversation because basically no more conversation was planned. I tried, after my expectations for my own monologue had been disappointed, to get one going and keep it up with my co-author: he broke down over and over again and tried to get me involved in his downfall. I had hardly ever wallowed before so helplessly in the characters I knew by sight; I no longer even knew whether it was me who knew them; all because I didn't really know myself anymore. Even if I didn't exaggerate the idea of the boons that sufficient self-knowledge would cause to shower upon me, still I did try to convince myself that it would be very agreeable to me to be familiar with so many of his characters as well, because only this would make a conversation with him, Peyer, possible. "You don't want to go on with me," he said. "But that's the only reason I came," I said. "Go now," he said calmly. "Tell me about it," I said, resigned. His office was messy, cramped, lightless, shabby. "MHB will be a father someday, then he will be more lenient, oh, much more lenient. Or else he'll increase in acidity," I cynicked. The two hours that I had allotted myself for Peyer were over. I left without knowing any more than I had ever known, and I wished him a good . . .

Then later . . .

Not far from my place of work I saw a rust-red tomcat. He was scampering around in the rear courtyards. Pretty quick, too quick for short legs. If he saw me from a distance, he seemed deathly frightened. There were people who wanted to slaughter him. They slaughtered cats, nothing else. I, for example, was safe from them. I tasted worse than the tomcat. Maybe it was because of them that he was so quick. The tomcat did not work. He let others wait on him. Mice, pieces of tire, and sewer rats. He sent his females into the underground. They even found brown fish and sturgeon roe. Presumably in the sewer networks. In any case not on me. I didn't carry any sturgeon eggs around with me. If anybody gave me caviar I spooned it up right away. However, I had to use my break time for that. Every break got used up for caviar. Every day. And there weren't many breaks. While I was spooning, I saw the cat scampering. "He's afraid," a coworker said. The coworker was eating bread with raw meat on it, steak tartare. A Pythagorean who liked to tell about cosmic pain. This is how it went: if a person is being tortured anywhere in the hemisphere, then everyone else automatically suffers too. Without compulsion. That is to say they are connected to him with their nervous systems. The neurospinal realm is being collectivized. Then they will no longer allow anyone to drill through even one person's surface anywhere in the world. Because it will hurt all of them. "It'll get better," I said, spooning. The tomcat sent a female down the storm drain, a rust-red one with a plum-sized caste mark on her forehead. She was acting Indian, the assistant, and for that she was being humiliated. "She's afraid," said my coworker, who could only think up things that made him feel ill at ease. Other people made you familiar with what seemed certain to them. Then they forced the world on you once again, which had to be round. I fought for the dinner plate, in which I believed. "You're going to catch him," said the Pythagorean, who made Beethoven rumble, evenings with his wife, fourhanded on two grand pianos. "Piece of cake," I said, "the tomcat is in the midst of an existential struggle." "You did a good job of misunderstanding that," he said. "I hardly saw him," I said. "If you slaughter *him*, then it'll be *you* who bleeds to death," he said. Stuffed a second open-face steak tartare in his mouth. Me and caviar: the same procedure . . .

Underneath the coat rack, where he was snoring, hollow-cheeked and painfully . . .

"And Ann, who is she, in the final analysis?" I asked.

"Ann will remain hidden to you." Hirsch woke up and, reaching from his bed, laid his cool hand in mine.

"Strindberg?" I asked.

"Always," said Hirsch.

"Tell me what you think of Ann!" I was trying to yoke him in as the High Court that was to convict me because I was of course absolutely in the right.

"Ann is an enigma," he said.

"If no one knows who or what she is, then at least tell me the unguessed secret of how it presents itself on the surface," I implored. Hirsch reached for the gingerbread heart that he had eaten. When he couldn't find it, he started nibbling at the washed sepia of Franz Schubert. Composing instead of writing: I no longer rushed to the aid of the sepia.

Schubert's face lay under M. Hirsch-Berditschewsky's teeth. The impression of his jaw directly over Franz's chin. Franz composed op.100 D.929 Andante con moto, the song of the tenorist Isaac Albert Berg, which he had performed in Ann's salon. Franz made the cello float upward—and Meyer H.B. took the bait:

"Ann talks like the fairy in a fairy tale: if you wish for the unconditional, you shall have your wish, but not in recognizable form. The truth of your discursive knowledge is unconcealed, whereas Ann has the better knowledge: the knowledge which Ann is has the truth, but as something incommensurate with her. That's how ironically she be's. Ann, through the freedom of the subject within her, is less subjective than the discursive knowledge that you have of her. Now, little author, is Hirsch teaching you that or isn't he? Ultimately, in the enigmatic character by means of which Ann opposes herself to the unquestioned existence of the affected subjects, your own enigma lives on. I would say, with borrowed tongue, that Ann became an enigma because she appeared to you as if she had solved what is enigmatic about your existence, while in you, dull-witted author in the tract house, the enigma was forgotten through its own overwhelming hardening."

"How's that?" And I withdrew my hand, which was now somewhat warmer. "That's what I think of you two." Hirsch laid his hands, with the leftovers of Schubert's head, in his lap and slumbered like a tea kettle waiting for its Englishman . . .

MHB felt cubicles, halls, rooms, and chambers around him like a bell cape. Everything that surrounded him was "pretty far away: it is not adjacent," but everything had its "ad nauseam" point, i.e., a geographically precisely defined place that H. did not want to occupy. This particular place did not take him in; even cities had such places, and they could move around, e.g., at the beginning they could be a favorite place where he was once turned down or lost love by his own risky behavior: this place assumed its outlines without delay; it burned itself into his mind, it became repulsive, and it disappeared from Hirsch's habitual activities . . .

Truly, it would be impossible for me to draw on paper what was between us two bloodhounds at that time. I met her at a fair and laid my flattened-out hand, extended slightly coolly, ready to carry, beneath her thigh in order to seesaw her up infernally quickly to the little swinging boats; suddenly her closed hand is lying in my flattened-out hand, this is getting nice . . .

On a rope a set of teeth was hanging down from the kitchen ceiling. I put it in my mouth, drew up my legs, and kept hanging there by the mouth for hours . . .

In the salon; both of them bound to a chair by the butler couple; each was able to touch the erogenous zones of the other with the tip of the one, non-tied-up, foot.

My writing that moved in parallel with all experiences was coming along, page by page, and on paper I was the prize-winning whirlwind of old. The pages were thrown by the bundle on the paternoster principle into the circulating dumbwaiter, which never stopped running. It received the bundles that were brought to it on conveyer rollers or on a bundle-delivery system. At the elevator compartment, with the aid of a pusher and a shuffler, I set the receiving destination, and my destination setting was verified before every push of the actuator by sensing brushes, while I laid out the next page; no, it laid me out. And so it ran without a pause: the page bundles, which could attain a maximum of 25 lbs., after passing through the ripped-open tower room door, automatically entered a small elevator that changed their level by several stories. With a shattered bottle of Clicquot I had christened the elevator with the name "Peyer"; it was on its way down. While moving down, at the destination floor—determined by the sensing device—the page bundles rolled through an exit door opened by selenium cells and arrived on the roller conveyer and from there onto the bundle-conveyor system, which transported them directly to the big typesetting department in Peyer's basement. Of course, I was familiar with the entire procedure from the egg to the finished chicken; the sobering effect of that familiarity was discouraging because I realized that I had become an industrialist, which did not prevent me from talking about "inspiration" or the "kiss of the muse" from one visit to the tower room to the next visit to the tower room; it was also well known that Marx—Karl for once, as Groucho's scriptwriter—had compared inspiration with a bellows; but Marx did not know the sensing brush, or else he would have joined inspiration and the paternoster principle in his spirit level. No matter how I twisted it and Ann turned it (Ann, who considered me uncharitable, decrepit, and dulled by fine technicity), it was still nothing but a circulating dumbwaiter, a conveyor-belt system, at best a hoisting bucket that responded to the push of a button. In among the epiphanies, the eloquent prosaist inserts his own erogenous zones, and the roller conveyors moved the page bundles with élan toward the final curve. At most I defended myself from time to time with "fine electric contacts are the epitome of sensitivity; a sensorium without voltage doesn't come close"; but—admittedly—even this belief was, no matter how low-ohm the inflow lines were, dehumanized; which gave Ann the indisputable advantage of remaining a human, or else a huwoman, among nothing but bellows, paternosters, switches, and destination floors, which were all subsumed under the term "I." I; the chaos was born as a system and functioned brilliantly when the irrelevant fleshandblood was abandoned . . .

Now the post-operative vomiting . . .

I scooted my tongue through my lips, drew my brows together into a hairy lump, and extended my right hand with the palm facing forward into the green-wallpapered room, where every gesture froze at once and I was doing business as a statue with innumerable extremities . . .

The worst thing with Peyer was that both of his eyes had different vision defects. One was deformed cylindrically, while the other was deformed elliptically. At forty-five he would be blind because the two retinas, in a dialectical process that was going on between them, were negating each other. The synthesis attained, from which no further thesis would emerge, would be lifelong black. Luckily Peyer's life expectancy was nothing like forty-five years. He ate a lot, being oral to the core, and it was mainly his stomach that noticed this, because it was an oral attitude that he directed at himself as sole beneficiary. What came to mind for me when I thought about him were many good old acquaintances, namely tropical fish in an aquarium. Whenever they were looking for something to bite or simply wanted to pointlessly gnash their teeth, they always found a little green stalk under water or, in the worst case, the glass wall of the aquarium to attach themselves to by their mouths. By that I mean to say that Peyer's mouth did not gratify anyone else but Peyer's mouth, and it could do that best by gorging. I'm groping in the dark about whether the gratification, Peyer's sudden exhaustion of all of the plaguing desires, which was introduced by an orgiastic cry and a motionless collapse in a cup chair, stemmed from the fact that something soft and semi-sweet (his mouth couldn't even distinguish between sugary and salty!) had slipped inward past his lips, as a goody he'd started to suck on, or whether his stomach—in any case a whale-sized, wet, unfathomable enclosure—sent a signal upward to Peyer when digestion started, always assuming that Peyer's orgiastic cries were agreed upon in his brain. In Peyer's case it might have been that his stomach, whenever anything made its way into it and pushed apart its incredibly strong, blood-supplied walls and poured in contents, somehow sent an opposite signal upward . . . in any case, Peyer, when he wasn't writing what I wanted from him, was a hearty eater. He still saw most of what he ate except when he was eating in his sleep because he had fallen asleep while eating and automatically kept on eating and made his fork describe a fixed path so that anybody could set the (semisweet!) sausage at a particular spot on the table for him in order to watch how the sleeping Peyer speared it and popped it in. In a short time Peyer weighed about ninety pounds more than before, and eating was a captivating stimulant for smoking. So he consoled himself over his imminent blindness by eating whatever he could while his eyeballs boxed each other to death and his retinas seemed ready to obliterate all rainbows. Smoking took its toll on Peyer and if his death did not happen from obesity or heart failure, then he would die from lung cancer. He told himself, as a consumable principle: if only you bet on enough numbers at the same time, then in time one of the numbers is certain to come up a winner . . .

Getting closer to stopping . . .

Everybody I locked up, I was rid of. If I relinquished even our small rooms and by free choice retreated to the dining room in order to take up, on the basis of the utmost voluntariness, only a fraction of the space granted to us—which was tiny enough to begin with—then she would have to acknowledge that as a peacemaking sacrifice, for with me she was getting rid of the one person who was standing in the way of her getting rid of me; in a word: I would draw conclusions, given in evidence but not evident, from that which perhaps I had perpetrated; as far as I'm concerned, I might have deserved the accusation. Hence she would still talk to me through the door after all, for I hung on her true words, which I no longer wanted to believe . . .

I believe she summoned me to be executed because she would summon me again and again for that purpose . . . but she did not carry it out—presumably some kind of formal error. I was so lethargic that I waited for her again and again . . .

With her weight Ann pressed the young author's bed sheet onto the window ledge in order to make it easier for him to climb when he was in love. Carefree, he tramped on the threatening snow overhangs, approached the vanishing point, slipped, while climbing down the outside staircase, on a banana peel, and when he tried to stay on his feet (hands and feet were knitting away at the counter-rotation) he smashed a six-foot-tall pane of glass. Behind the window the disqualified man was breathing and emitting short, extinguished cigar coughs. The suitor's bed sheet warmed the glow of the white lamp at the front door of the white lamp of the glow of the warm bed sheet . . .

Of course I was very afraid; sometimes I was even slightly grumpy; but I could not expect the executrix to worry about that. If she ever stayed away, then all paradise broke loose with me . . .

Some utopian lines had crept into my study of laboratory rats. As I read through them, they told me a lot about myself; I was grateful to myself; the only possibility for getting to know the man that I did not want to know came from such sorties, which were not afraid to break the sense of happiness that integral forms imparted, in favor of something more genuine:

"On hot days the city is full of water faucets. From all apertures come dribbles, and sometimes a mouth sticks itself under the drips. The days can also be cold, and night can fall too, darkening everything, and then the sound of dripping is even more acute; often the water faucets are missing as well, and then when I pass by the dripping I am unsure where the dripping is coming from: but where there are walls, there is also dripping. What are the properties of the faucets? They have: 1) a small aperture; 2) no handle with which they could be turned on or off—the dripping is regular, the amount of discharge (of whatever it might be) is consistent; 3) no shaft by means of which they could, for example, stick out of a wall. On point 3 it should be added—and I will add it as soon as the ponderous dripping noise fades as I ponderously walk away—that each of these apertures, because there is no shaft, is located in a horizontal-vertical plane. The drops: hardly drip down, but the discharged wet mass distributes itself evenly over the plane, to the extent that it is horizontal. It distributes itself less evenly, spreading more in a downward direction, to the extent that the plane is vertical. The more summery the city, the damper the plane. There are apertures that have run dry. At these apertures I stop and suck on the wall, on the plane. Often they come back to life again, but not when the days are cold; then they stay empty, dry, dead. And in the night? At night I sleep, I don't walk past the dripping, I don't know the city, I get lost, in fact I've lost my way so often now that I've cut off all of my dreams that the manure spreaders hoick away from the retained wetness. In the tract house itself it is dripping too; how could it not? Where exactly? Sometimes my mouth sticks itself under the dripping, but my eyes stay closed. It happens in the connector between the front door and the room door closest to the front door. And Ann? I forgot to mention Ann. She behaves similar to me, but not exactly the same way. I think she has access to larger quantities of discharge. Without further ado. That's due to her perceptiveness and the greater resorptive capability of her pore system. I make a spongier impression than she does, she is spongier than I am, and both of us believe the opposite! The sound of the dribbling, similar to a clock with a fitful spring rebounding soft as butter, really is expanding now by the hour and making me realize Ann's nearness as hardly anything else could. Is she walking with me; is she near me? To be honest: absolutely not; she is walking far apart from me, somehow parallel, but in no way in the connector reserved for me; she prefers the bathroom to my hallway, and within the bathroom she prefers a narrow strip of floor between the washbasin and the bathtub. In the bathtub I had committed suicide in order to let my blood flow out painlessly: this was now my second life. To the extent that the plane around the foot of the tub, which I consider a disgusting one, is horizontal, none of the dripped-out liquid spreads out there, but if there are drops there at all, they coagulate into gleaming tongues that lie there still, with tremendous surface tension which, under the influence of a detergent, should Ann pour one out, would dissolve and turn into a puddle. An even distribution of moisture is just as impossible by the vertical planes of the white washbasin. Right next to it, the electric toothbrush dangles on its far-too-weak cord. I know that Ann, in search of apertures that dribble, has used it to file her teeth down to the gums, simply by plugging in the brush and turning it on HIGH and letting it clean her. Without teeth she looks more attractive. If only she were closer to me! But I complain and let her partake in my yammering without returning to my initial insight: IT IS THIS DAMP ALL OVER THE CITY! If it were otherwise elsewhere, then I could firmly count on being able to move in there and set myself up for good. And no sooner would I be there than it would be there just like it is here and now. "Come along," I would say to her and leave no room for doubt that I meant it affectionately. But as it is I'm here, she's not far, and it's always dripping. What are the properties of her faucets? Are her days cold? I'm doing whatever I can. The city gives the best it can. All of the bread is softened up. I often just go along through this and that, and all the way through this and that. Does she too? Her too? But of course . . .

That seemed authentic to me. It broke the form of my study of laboratory rats. In that case I could also let Ann stand in for me. She didn't play with rats, but with tiny, finger-sized men who all looked like me . . .

In the laundry room Ann had set up ten little men, in ten little cages, all in a row. The cages stood on a table, and the table stood on a stone floor, which disappeared in the middle, at its lowest point, into a drain. The arrangement of the little men was such that Ann could stand in front of it and put all ten fingers into the cages at the same time. Ann did this, and ten deep but tiny cries echoed through the laundry room, and ten jaws closed on her fingertips. Then Ann abandoned herself to various malicious games, pulling her fingers toward her, pushing them away, always with the little men on them. They could no longer emit their tiny cries, they couldn't even bite anymore, and now, with their teeth sunk into the fingertips, they had muzzles on. When the fingers moved, sometimes they fell on their backs, rarely all ten at once, usually only about six or seven, in any case more than half, in general. After about ten days, one day for each finger, Ann started the next chapter. If a little man fell on his back, the finger shot forward in a flash and pressed in his stomach wall, maybe his diaphragm too, and made his entrails stick out in a finely veined bundle. Most of the little men did not stop biting even then, proof of the fact that they simply could no longer quit, or would perish of their own accord if they were not biting, whereas if they were biting they still stood a chance of getting out of the laundry room again (even if it was in a cage). But there were always little men who wouldn't let themselves be put on their backs. As nimbly as sonny boys they ran back and forth, after the finger, always on guard against Ann's forward shots and backward pulls. Only once did it happen that a very fat, lazy one and an even fatter and lazier one appeared unimpressed by Ann. These Ann set free. They were allowed to enter the big cage. Then—this round was conducted in deep silence, Ann was overheated, perspiration vapors filled the laundry room, and the fur on the little men grew sticky with zeal—the third chapter began. With a jerk, Ann pulled her hands back, much farther than usual, beyond the edge of the laundry room table; the little men's snouts were pressed against the bars of the cage, there were little knives there, and the little men's snouts got cut up, more and more deeply; but at each step that Ann took backward, the cages moved a short distance along with her too; they jolted across the rough wood of the table, but only until the little knives encountered the nose bones of the little men. From then on the cages rolled, bumping along as swiftly as the wind, until they glided off the table and fell into the void. Their weight caused them to plunge irresistibly downward, and the little men still did not let go of Ann's fingers, but stuck to the knives, their eyes now wide open with certainty. With a jerk, the knives ran through the little men, and ten times the impact with the stone floor made a thud, wood on stone. On Ann's ten fingers there hung ten little man-slices, one on each finger, each one still with at least one tooth. And Ann held her hands out away from herself, calm and collected. Some of the man-slices fell off, but the majority remained tenaciously hanging on her fingertips, no matter how much she shook her fingers. Eventually Ann spun around in a circle, both arms stiffly angled outward, turning faster and faster, and in whirls the remains of the little men came loose and settled in a circle around her. She kept spinning, now also shuddering with revulsion at her own supremacy and with the *dégoût* of the endless rotation. Now Ann was spinning like mad and could no longer pull in her arms in order to reduce her own centrifugal force. She felt her head go off its axis. Hardly was her pivoting interrupted when her own momentum hurled her into the midst of the remains of the little men. Blood, fur, and stench covered her, all sticking to her clothes, to her face, to her soles. Then she lay down in the big cage with the liberated little men and let herself be cared for. For the whole week that followed this day, she talked to me about the tenderness with which the free little men had cleaned the remains of the deceased little men from her skin. She said she had never had more charming men around her, but she had also never had tougher ones. —Whereupon I retired to the tower room, suddenly climbed down a rope to the balcony, whipped out my machine pistol behind the geraniums and shot a puny little weep hole into the eaves trough across the street . . .

Then I again wanted to hit very hard; we were both standing half dressed in the bathroom; I was wearing somewhat less than she was; the screw-on lid of a jar had gone missing; she bent over; at this moment the long fluorescent tube over the mirror went out; I didn't know whether she could still make out me, who could make her out; that was no longer the method that provided me with information; information, more information about me and about her; there was only one thing left: to hit hard from behind. Darkly I decided to make her do something good for my head; I believed I could suddenly get out of this darkness happy and imagine a future with Ann, but I only believed; she turned up next to the laundry hamper, holding the screw top in her hands. "Give me a head massage," I said. Unresponsive in my own unwashed condition. "Right away, just sit down, I'll turn on the heat, not here, don't catch cold, did you bring any warm clothes, always tell me right away if you need anything," Ann reacted. Out of indifference toward me (and I could see the indifference and was not able to become indifferent myself, but I had to bring it to a close slowly, in my own way) . . . out of indifference she had become—just like she used to be—quite sociable again. I had hit hard. On the desk we finished getting dressed. Before she could get the jar closed tight with the screw top, what should have happened (nothing will be said about that) happened to her: the jar slipped from her hands and shattered shortly before a step that I took onto the shards; I gave a soft cry, and she started doing something to me that I recognized only much later as the punishment for this cry . . . Ann turned on the fluorescent tube above the mirror and . . .

When Peyer leaves me, he rips the piece that he is right out of me, and I am left behind with a serious injury. No sooner have I gotten used to the open wound than he presses himself against me again. The loss of pain at his reappearance is such a relief and sweetness for me—as a transition from absolute suffering to absolute contentment—that when his new departure rips a new wound in me I howl aloud. In general, I like to cry. It saves on tranquilizers and ambiguities: everybody knows what they're dealing with when a man cries; and from the way they make known what they think they're dealing with when they deal with me, I can tell in turn what I'm dealing with when I deal with them. A man's weeping is still an unmasking of those who are watching—assuming you want to force tears, the last means of expression before physical wounding, into a function. I do not want to remain abstract, and I will go so far as to say that Peyer has gained a constitutional elemental force over my psychophysical makeup that he never would have gained if I had not conceded it to him willingly. This absolute ruler comes and closes up the edges of my wounds and dams my pyorrhea back into me—or he leaves me and, as a consolation, leaves the illnesses here, which he has the power to take from me. And so I live. "Live" is an absurd term for that which is still possible for me in my degenerating dependence on Peyer. To make the thing more understandable: My name is Peyer. I am the one who . . . and I do not believe that I will ever be able to leave it alone, namely that . . . and that's how everything is, or maybe even worse. He is stronger. Stronger than me. And while developing great inhuman warmth, he will annihilate, extinguish, and grate me down on both sides, down to a no longer perceptible stub. My wound is open; bring him on; I want it, don't I?; this glass, which is broken to bits on my skin and massaged into it: the shards, massaged in . . .

Up to this point everything is true; from here on, an attempt at a final lie; the lack of interest in truth is distinguishable by the quantity of language used; how could this conglomeration of nearly arbitrary half-images have approached any truth; even back then, years ago, years that have ground me down, Ann indulged me in being pregnant with the intention of transforming arbitrariness into a lie, to insert a life behind it, producing the lie of a lifetime, a grand illusion; to insert a credibility behind this constructedness; so that I would have to believe of myself that I am a liar; but is that so? But can I put the previous question that way? But is the question of the permissibility of that question acceptable? From here on in, the attempt; I played an etude, and all at once I saw the name Czerny, and the keys became a squishy pulp; Ann tore the first page away; that's what I expected of her . . .

Previously the following had occurred . . .

In the dining room . . .

Was she Ann? Was she Ann's predecessor? Any similarity is like a shadowing of element X by element Y. X is tiny, Y is huge, and so X is black, and whoever shouts "Y!" is right . . .

"What is he doing at this moment?" Ann wondered between a puff pastry and a tartlet.

"He's thinking of me as I am of him."

From my observation chamber I intensely watched the supper that was coming to an end. Ann was trying to calm herself down by reciting to herself in a low voice the worries that made her tremble.

"He can't know anything; he loves me, he trusts me . . ."

She had just eaten an apricot; on the tray there remained only the deadly fruit. She took it between two fingers.

"And yet, if he knew . . ." she said under her breath, in a throaty voice. Then she took a bite . . .

The effect was immediate. She got up to close the window to the courtyard, then reared up as if under hands that were tightening around her throat, pivoted around several times and batted the air with her arms. She fell down dead on the rug, as violently as if she wanted to fall through the floor into the level beneath us. The rug kept her from doing that.

Slowly I came out of the observation chamber. Then all of a sudden I ran after all and snuffed out all the candles that stood in the two silver candelabras on the fifth desk; with spit-moistened fingers. Immediately after that it was pitch dark in the tower room; all that remained was a moonbeam that came through the open window and laid a pretty white collar around her neck that almost warmed me.

On the bed I saw my coat, my black collared coat, unfolded it, and spread it over Ann's phosphene. At first I thought that I couldn't do it, but then I got the idea that I could pull it off, and ultimately I did it: I dropped down on my knees and was silent and considered whether I would repeat it with this woman or whether I might have failed to do it with another woman. My belief grew stronger and stronger that I would have failed to do it if Ann were not Ann. But I didn't know for sure. All I knew was that I would know for sure someday . . .

Ann, no longer very mobile or tormented by temperament, looked like marble, the marble of the contents of an icebox. Covering almost all of her lay the black coat, and by chance I was not in it. Of course her head was peeking out from under the coat; of course her head was no longer young, just as mine was not; the black hair shone clearly, as if there were a small lightbulb under the crown of her head; the crown of Ann's head was starting to irritate me. Touching her, I mussed up her hair.

She lay all pallid in the cone of pale illumination that came from the window.

The effect was a tragic one. I cried. Pretty loudly, loud on purpose. That lured her over to me. In the doorway she stood and asked what was wrong.

"It's because of you," I said.

"What's he doing at this moment?" she asked.

"He's cleaning up the traces," I said, feeling worth fifty pennies that one streetcar is running over and right after that a second one . . .

From the dining room, which I no longer dared to enter . . .

She brought the clothes of the weary dancer, who had sunk down dripping with sweat, and was recovering from the unaccustomed effort for a few moments. With great adroitness she undressed the lean and handsome man, who did not neglect to heap abuse on the petite servant. She put the new clothes on him, which were made very cutely and an excellent fit. During this transaction she praised the charms and the lovable character of her master, and the boy seemed duly pleased with the flattery and the daintiness of the suit . . .

BUT I YEARN TO BEHOLD THE BLUE FLOWER . . .

"I have to say that the fact that I made her my wife rests largely on her sexual willingness. She never says no, she hardly ever hesitates, not even when she has her period or two or three lovers. She likes stew, and I don't like stew. (reflecting) But the willingness that I'm talking about, this relaxed openness that takes everything you slip her, whitewashes our deeper differences in the matter of stew. We quarrel when we're standing, or lying, on the rug, but we reconcile easily in bed. Over and over again. And the bed that someone else shares with her or with me never pushes us apart. It will always be that way, as long as that guy (I indicate my penis) cooperates. Someday, of course, it will be over, which means that in due time you have to establish a basis that doesn't have to do so directly with sexuality. For example, send her to a hospital and develop unanimity with her in pitying the poor, the old, the weak, and the underprivileged. Then she'll feel understood and bonded without that guy (I indicate my penis) having to do anything. As soon as he can't do anything anymore, the hospital visit is elevated to a main principle . . ."

Suddenly I was very contrite, and ruefully I hung my head until I smelled the smell of my sweater. I folded my hands into a pious position, crossed my legs under the table, and allowed an expression of inner contemplation to appear on my face. Now all that my mouth and cheeks were saying was: "Do something to me, I beg of you." My heart was beating audibly, and my conscience had grown black and small like a sow bug, and even my perky forelock drooped guiltily. This would not be tolerable for much longer. As soon as I lifted my head again, I felt that the contemplation thing was pretty much over, and I would have been happy to see it if my vis-à-vis was crushed by a falling chandelier. Her head ran toward the tabletop on which the tines of a dessert fork were sticking up. She paused, I dashed my head onto the tines, she hit me on the back of the neck with the palm of her hand, and I lay down on the tabletop. I smelled blood on my sweater, stood back up, stuffed little corks into my piercing wounds and, standing still and tidying my hair with my hand, pondered my behavior. Edifying contrition was gaining the upper hand within me, until I . . .

Not enough; but also . . .

Hirsch What can I do for you?

Me I have nothing to laugh about. Validate me! It will give me strength.

Hirsch Validate you, that's all?

Me That's all.

Hirsch I . . . validate . . . you.

Me Question: Are the things I'm practiced at and can do professionally important for me as well as for the general public that I serve?

Hirsch The window was open. Now there's peace and quiet. Please repeat what you said.

Me Am I indispensible? Or will I be replaced within a short time?

Hirsch I validate you.

Me I know that. But now we're getting down to the details. Is what I'm doing right?

Hirsch That it is. Right, that's what it is.

Me You seem to be of the opinion that I'm putting the question correctly. But that cannot claim to have the status of an answer to that question. Once again: Is what I'm doing and the way I'm living right?

Hirsch For nothing.

Me Is what I'm doing and how I'm living for nothing?

Hirsch You mean: Am I happening for nothing? That is an ontological question, to which God has an answer. But only sometimes. Do you believe?

Me I have no idea of the thing.

Hirsch None at all?

Me Validate me.

Hirsch For nothing.

Me Not for nothing. I have assured you that it will help me if I am validated.

Hirsch I meant to say that I cannot validate you for nothing.

| | |
|---|---|
| Me | That's what was agreed upon. |
| Hirsch | No. There's something I'm having lots of trouble with. Advise me against it. |
| Me | I beg your pardon? |
| Hirsch | "Advising against" in abstracto. Like "validating" in your case. |
| Me | Advising you against the thing that you're having trouble with? And this as a quid pro quo for being validated by you? |
| Hirsch | *Absolutio contra dissuasionem.* |
| Me | Satisfactory. Getting to the point: I generally advise you against it. You hear: I urgently advise you against it. When something is up to you yourself, you generally do not do it. |
| Hirsch | What? |
| Me | Abstractly.<br>My quo, I see now, was given before your quid. Now I would like to ask you kindly to validate me. |
| Hirsch | I just advised myself against that. |
| Me | I'd have . . . ? |

"It's different with those serene, unknown people whose world is their mind, whose activity is contemplation, and whose life is a gentle development of their inner powers. No restlessness drives them outward. A quiet possession is sufficient for them, and the immense spectacle outside of them does not stimulate them to take a role in it themselves, but it seems to them significant and wonderful enough to devote their leisure to its contemplation . . ." (Novalis)

From the dining room, which I was strictly prohibited from entering . . .

Was she Ann? Was she the one that succeeded Ann? Every mistaken identity is the failure of a desperate attempt at drawing distinctions. If I meet her again, she will also mistake me for someone else. It is impossible to figure out why one of us should ever have gotten an inkling of the other. Unfixed, as we were: no imprint, no profile, nothing but blurriness. Everything has probably always been uncannily precisely blurry . . .

Then later . . .

Incessant talking approximates silence; asymptotically toward the mute person that one is becoming . . .

Then later . . .

Then later . . .

Ann was locked up in the crowded dining room. How was it going for her? It had to go somehow. I had heard her outcry. It seemed to me only distantly related to a cry of pleasure. The dining room was emptier than the living room. In addition, above the living room was the tower, which could cave in on top of me at any moment. The fifteenth and final one had blocked the door from the dining room to the living room. If I had initially been able to undertake assistance efforts, sweating till I was blue and exposed to myself and sad and satisfied at their fruitlessness, now I myself was walled in. I ran a few times against the top of the fifteenth one, but soon gave up. The living room was more space-deprived than the dining room. I would hardly have taken any comfort if the less dangerous part had fallen to me. Danger bought me off, at least for the short period that I wanted to spend in the same situation as her. The fifteenth one was not particularly heavy, since I and only I succeeded in breaking through its top with a windup, a run at it, and a leap on through. Ann somehow remained closed up in the room, where for the first time the food had been located. After I again had the living room and hallway for myself, I was able to prepare myself for the pickup. I wasn't picking anybody up, but someone was picking me up. That was a good thing. I wouldn't have gotten away from the tract house by myself; I would probably have lain down at the threshold of the dining room and in time, with a spontaneity that would have lasted three weeks, let myself be carried away to liberate Ann. They were picking me up; I wasn't letting myself be carried away to do anything. What was happening with Ann escaped me. All of that had to be opened up again, because it had hinges and joints. But when it opened up . . . don't try to imagine it, I told myself. I gave myself a good pep talk as if to someone in a fever, and I felt like it was an almost undeserved benefaction to listen to myself as I calmed myself down. True, I didn't calm down, but it was the intention that counted; and if I took the intention, then all in all I had almost achieved what I had undertaken to do on desks one through fifteen. Ann was at fault for everything; I was simply the more cold-blooded one. And insane with trust, physical closeness, warmth, and affection, I had acted, gone for it, got things moving and completed. I knew that about myself, I knew everything. I feel fervently domestic every time I remember it. I don't like to do it, but as far as I'm concerned . . .

"Love is a bliss for those who are extra heavy in a horse harness," he quoted, and mentally pictured the fords; she struck a match, and asked for an apple and a mineral water. When he reported to her that the Count had fallen asleep again, she gave him the crooked hook to the chin that people of his fabric did not like . . .

Mostly she came punctually. So I knew it right down to the minute if she didn't come. I could have rebelled. I never had done so . . .

Encouraged by similar blows to fetch her what she demanded, he went into the kitchen; the tiles had become vitreous, covered with a wafer-thin layer of ice, and quickly the crystals formed of which he, before freezing solid, let a tip melt in his scotch; in the clearly contouring light of the winter night the set of teeth hung from the kitchen ceiling, and the kitchen was not to be found, even though he had found the scotch in the kitchen . . .

I heard steps and practiced closing my mouth and the monologues that went with it. She would find me at the edge of town, pick me up from the tract house, and lay into me . . .

After their death from hypothermia, the two of them were found covered with the three thousand hearts that they had extracted from their venereal partners, need times three. On warm days he or she sometimes managed to climb up the outside staircase to the latrine towers . . .

I was already so subordinated to her that shutting my mouth seemed too bold to me. I was poorly trained, and yawned tensely in the direction of the set of teeth . . .

She came pretty quickly and was right on time . . .

In the tower room . . .

"You're calling me up."

"I'd like to talk to you."

"I thought we were fighting."

"And I dreamed about you."

"You're doing things to me again."

"We were married . . ."

"You're free to get a divorce."

"That's what I mean. All of sudden, still in Paris, we were married. And for me it was the shock of my life. I didn't know much about you in this condition. Of course I immediately started trying to get a divorce. That even got me running, I ran from Tom to Dick to Harry, all of them uniformed, and luckily I found out that a divorce cost thirty French francs. This amount made me nervous, and the fact that I found out about it so exactly somehow outraged me. We were already on the ship. Don't ask where to, I didn't know. Then we ran like crazy . . ."

"We 'persecuted' each other; we're after each other!"

"Across every deck, and again and again there were crossroads that ended up in a point. You came from the right, I from the left, and we ran inside of each other. Instead of colliding, only the cloth of our sleeves brushed crisply past each other."

"Then you woke up."

"Then I . . . how do you know that?"

"A surmise awoke."

"Then I woke up. And called you up. We were married."

"Now I lay me down and dream of a divorce that costs even less."

"How much?"

"It only costs me you."

Does my wife belong to me? / Can one ask this question? / Can one ask the two preceding questions one after the other? / Is this third question, the object of the fourth one, which has to do with the sequence of the first two questions, even a question anymore? / Should one, after all of the attendant difficulties, once again ask the question "Does my wife belong to me"? / And is this sentence a truth function of the sentence "Something has grown together with me, so does it belong to me"? / Is this sentence about growing together even correct? / But can the question even still be put this way? Is the question about whether something is correct always correct? / The impulsive person will say: In the absence of other solutions, my wife belongs to me. Except: as soon as I state that or else ask about it in language, everything becomes so uncertain that I can easily lose my wife. / Does she know these correlations? / But is "she knows" the case? Can such a thing be the case? . . .

I am very unimportant. I would like to write about that just briefly. I don't know what to write about. I have said all of this already, only better. I love concision when writing except when I can't manage it. That's how my concentration is. I can also read along with someone else only for a much shorter time than with myself. So then, if you please. With this I would like to have said my piece. I would consider myself more important than I am if I now ignored the fact that my concentration on this (on what, anyway? Hopefully that will still come to light with my assistance) on this is now almost at an end. If I therefore did not know what I was just talking about, then I would keep on talking without concentrating, at the lowest possible level of concentration and not even notice it myself. I would probably also talk longer. And much more clearly. What about? Hardly even important. I have almost nothing to say on this point. Ann once said that lives run parallel. She was right about that. If the frequency with which a topic comes up is small, then you can do something with that topic. My topic occurs with a frequency that drives its value down like coalmine stock just before Black Friday. All of this can make me sad. Sadness is the worst thing about me. From sadness I feel dull and leathery over my whole body. Like I was made of animal hide; no matter. I would like to put that down for a short time. I am now losing what was left of my concentration and of my good will. Now comes the stage of the great efforts. That is, now keeping my thoughts together is causing me tremendous pain, and it's too bad that I did not know Russell, who said to Wittgenstein: "Logic is hell." That's my consciousness. It is wide open. I am seriously wounded and deeply uninterested in it. One really can't be that way. That's why I'm so unstable. I am always seriously wounded. Surely, when a certain heaviness has been reached, that will win me over to myself. It can go that far if I don't watch out. It is certain that I'm going to die. Music, music. But I almost can't figure out why that has to be. But soon, nonetheless, unfortunately, *paulo post*. I do not feel sorry for myself or ashamed of the truthfulness of this obituary. Ashamed before whom? Immaterial. I just wanted to write this down briefly. I'm suffering. That's all it's supposed to be. That's all it was supposed to be. The rest is arabesque . . .

There are still, dear Ann, kitchens in which things heat up. It doesn't even have to be Sunday for that. It's been a long time now since Sunday painters became Tuesday roasters. The oven is turned on, nicely turned. Take a look, this is a mother-of-pearl chicken de Bresse. Unbeatably superior to all chickens in the flesh. You can tell that as soon as it's skinless. Its skin is easier to get off, too. That's because of the brand name. De Bresse. Between Lyon and something else, north of, always north of. All these chickens are north of. I believe, the more northerly, the easier the skin comes off. The meat is produced in a different way. That is our kitchen. Not the kitchen that raises these chickens. That one is in Bresse and nurtures poulets. All at once they're alive. Have to grow bigger. And develop all that meat that becomes so visible after removing the skin. No fattening. No force-feeding with the food injector in the mealtime throat. Instead, they're nourished purely in the kitchen. As long as they live, from kitchen to kitchen. The poulets de Bresse are liberated from fear. Their fear of death is fed out of them, they have this elastic muffling ring, only muffled products. That is the work of the kitchen in Bresse. There they are waited on hand and foot. These poulets in Bresse eat the tenderest meat as long as they live. And anything besides meat they turn down and step on it with their claws. Only tender white meat. Without skin. Skinless meat. Naked meat is set before them to peck at. And they do peck it right away. Oh, metaphor, limping, your goose will be cooked anyway. That's why they're so good at repressing. Repressing what comes after the pecking. After the pecking comes nothing, mostly. They repress that too. The more northerly, the fewer ideas they have. Especially Bresse . . . there's something about that place. The chickens don't think about anything, much less about themselves. Nor do they think about what is nourishing them to death. They eat only white, tender meat. Meat like their own. Flesh of their flesh. That's why they're called poulets de Bresse and are suited for Tuesdays. How does one become a poulet de Bresse, I ask you. That is a pseudo-question. I know the answer. I probably only recounted the biography of the Bresses because I know the answer. What an answer! How does one become a poulet de Bresse? Can anyone become one? Is it easy, or does it require an accredited execution, I mean education? Now, it requires. Yes, it is required, one has to go through it, the education. Every poulet de Bresse, its whole life long, since it crawled out of the round egg, has been in the kitchen. And eaten flesh of its flesh. Never on Tuesday. You become a poulet de Bresse, I tell you with my current level of information, by never again eating, as soon as you are out of the egg and have slammed the shell behind you, anything besides other poulets de Bresse. These chickens feed on chickens, they eat fellow members of their species, devour their own, freeload off their dismembered family anatomy, throw their own clan in the stew pot out of which they spend their lives picking vitamins. Every cackle of a chicken de Bresse is the soul of another chicken that travels through his throat into the hunting grounds, into the burial grounds patrolled by the Big Rooster. There. In front of you. That's it. That's one of them. From Bresse. Must have come early this morning, I picked it up myself at the train station. But it did not come on its own. It was loaded on board. It tried to speak with the conductor of the transport. To no avail, fortunately; the man had a thing about chickens. It wanted to be let off the train somewhere. The fellow must have laughed and ridden on by. A clever one to boot. A clever chicken from Bresse. Bresse . . . there's something about that place, so that even clever chickens turn up, now and then. This one here is one of that kind. It caught wind of something. While still in the basket it must have caught wind of it. The right thing. The thing that befell it then, out of a clear blue sky; but the sky was made of white meat. But it caught wind of that. A clever chicken. Always on Tuesday. It is also unbeatably superior to all other chickens in its meat. Even while melting in your mouth it pushes the tempo of melting sky high. You can measure its melting time with a stopwatch, its melting in your mouth will knock you off your seat. You can tell as soon as it's skinless. And now I'm going to take the skin off of it. The danger that, if we don't eat it, it will eat us, us white ones, us tender ones, quasi as fellow citizens of Bresse, was considerable, but it has been averted. It can be taken off quite easily. That's because of the brand, Button-in-Ear. Bresse. In the north between Lyon and someplace else. Not all of them are always, but this chicken is definitely north of. I would have to be way off the mark, and you would bear the consequences. But that is de Bresse. Unbeatably superior. It comes from the finest kitchen. Therefore, this exclamation is allowed: Back to the kitchen with it! Now the chickens are in the mood for it! Heat up the kitchen and oven the bake spot for the hot and fresh, beg pardon, for the pot of flesh. Stew à la française, to each his chicken and a Bresse in every pot. Chewsday Pot, pot away!

Then later.

I, or rather he whom I am listening to, or rather he of whom I assume that he plays a role in Ann's conversations; if I can ever prove that she carries on conversations with me, I will also be more certain about him. Or I don't know what "to be certain" means. It might not mean anything. But that's not so certain. Unfortunately it cannot be said definitely whether "to be certain" means anything. Let's believe half of everything, the way we were taught. Stay in the middle, nicely in the middle. I presume it means something indefinite, and emphatically so. Perhaps it means that it has crossed someone's mind, without one's knowing him or ever having heard of him, a mind that he himself does not know. How do you suppose he does it? It's all the same, I, or rather he, or rather he whom I mean when I am meant by him, asserts that he has once again written something down. The trilogy is finished; "My Bob" is what it started on; and now "on" is what it ends on

Jürg Laederach was born in 1945 in Basel, where he still lives and works as a freelance writer and translator. He studied mathematics in Zurich, as well as Romance studies, English, and musicology in Basel. He has received a number of prizes and distinctions and is a corresponding member of the German Academy for Language and Literature. He was awarded the Austrian State Prize for European Literature in 1997 and the Italo Svevo Award in 2005.

Geoffrey C. Howes is a Professor at Bowling Green State University. He has translated texts by Peter Rosei, Doron Rabinovici, Lilian Faschinger, and others. Swiss Literature Series

## Swiss Litrerature Series

In 2008, Pro Helvetia, the Swiss Arts Council, began working with Dalkey Archive Press to identify some of the greatest and most innovative authors in twentieth and twenty-first century Swiss letters, in the tradition of such world renowned writers as Max Frisch, Robert Walser, and Robert Pinget. Dalkey Archive editors met with critics and scholars in Zürich, Geneva, Basel, and Bern, and went on to prepare reports on numerous important Swiss authors whose work was deemed underrepresented in English. Developing from this ongoing collaboration, the Swiss Literature Series, launched in 2011 with Gerhard Meier's *Isle of the Dead* and Aglaja Veteranyi's *Why the Child Is Cooking in the Polenta*, has been working to remedy this dearth of Swiss writing in the Anglophone world with a bold initiative to publish four titles a year, each supplemented with marketing efforts far exceeding what publishers can normally provide for works in translation.

With writing originating from German, French, Italian, and Rhaeto- Romanic, the Swiss Literature Series will stand as a testimony to Switzerland's contribution to world literature.

## SELECTED DALKEY ARCHIVE TITLES

Michal Ajvaz, *The Golden Age.*
*The Other City.*
Pierre Albert-Birot, *Grabinoulor.*
Yuz Aleshkovsky, *Kangaroo.*
Felipe Alfau, *Chromos.*
*Locos.*
Ivan Ângelo, *The Celebration.*
*The Tower of Glass.*
António Lobo Antunes, *Knowledge of Hell.*
*The Splendor of Portugal.*
Alain Arias-Misson, *Theatre of Incest.*
John Ashbery and James Schuyler, *A Nest of Ninnies.*
Robert Ashley, *Perfect Lives.*
Gabriela Avigur-Rotem, *Heatwave and Crazy Birds.*
Djuna Barnes, *Ladies Almanack.*
*Ryder.*
John Barth, *LETTERS.*
*Sabbatical.*
Donald Barthelme, *The King.*
*Paradise.*
Svetislav Basara, *Chinese Letter.*
Miquel Bauçà, *The Siege in the Room.*
René Belletto, *Dying.*
Marek Bieńczyk, *Transparency.*
Andrei Bitov, *Pushkin House.*
Andrej Blatnik, *You Do Understand.*
Louis Paul Boon, *Chapel Road.*
*My Little War.*
*Summer in Termuren.*
Roger Boylan, *Killoyle.*
Ignácio de Loyola Brandão, *Anonymous Celebrity.*
*Zero.*
Bonnie Bremser, *Troia: Mexican Memoirs.*
Christine Brooke-Rose, *Amalgamemnon.*
Brigid Brophy, *In Transit.*
Gerald L. Bruns, *Modern Poetry and the Idea of Language.*
Gabrielle Burton, *Heartbreak Hotel.*
Michel Butor, *Degrees.*
*Mobile.*
G. Cabrera Infante, *Infante's Inferno.*
*Three Trapped Tigers.*
Julieta Campos, *The Fear of Losing Eurydice.*
Anne Carson, *Eros the Bittersweet.*
Orly Castel-Bloom, *Dolly City.*
Louis-Ferdinand Céline, *Castle to Castle.*
*Conversations with Professor Y.*
*London Bridge.*
*Normance.*
*North.*
*Rigadoon.*
Marie Chaix, *The Laurels of Lake Constance.*
Hugo Charteris, *The Tide Is Right.*
Eric Chevillard, *Demolishing Nisard.*
Marc Cholodenko, *Mordechai Schamz.*
Joshua Cohen, *Witz.*
Emily Holmes Coleman, *The Shutter of Snow.*
Robert Coover, *A Night at the Movies.*
Stanley Crawford, *Log of the S.S. The Mrs Unguentine.*
*Some Instructions to My Wife.*
René Crevel, *Putting My Foot in It.*
Ralph Cusack, *Cadenza.*
Nicholas Delbanco, *The Count of Concord.*
*Sherbrookes.*
Nigel Dennis, *Cards of Identity.*
Peter Dimock, *A Short Rhetoric for Leaving the Family.*
Ariel Dorfman, *Konfidenz.*
Coleman Dowell,
*Island People.*
*Too Much Flesh and Jabez.*
Arkadii Dragomoshchenko, *Dust.*
Rikki Ducornet, *The Complete Butcher's Tales.*
*The Fountains of Neptune.*
*The Jade Cabinet.*
*Phosphor in Dreamland.*
William Eastlake, *The Bamboo Bed.*
*Castle Keep.*
*Lyric of the Circle Heart.*
Jean Echenoz, *Chopin's Move.*
Stanley Elkin, *A Bad Man.*
*Criers and Kibitzers, Kibitzers and Criers.*
*The Dick Gibson Show.*
*The Franchiser.*
*The Living End.*
*Mrs. Ted Bliss.*
François Emmanuel, *Invitation to a Voyage.*
Salvador Espriu, *Ariadne in the Grotesque Labyrinth.*
Leslie A. Fiedler, *Love and Death in the American Novel.*
Juan Filloy, *Op Oloop.*
Andy Fitch, *Pop Poetics.*
Gustave Flaubert, *Bouvard and Pécuchet.*
Kass Fleisher, *Talking out of School.*
Ford Madox Ford,
*The March of Literature.*
Jon Fosse, *Aliss at the Fire.*
*Melancholy.*
Max Frisch, *I'm Not Stiller.*
*Man in the Holocene.*
Carlos Fuentes, *Christopher Unborn.*
*Distant Relations.*
*Terra Nostra.*
*Where the Air Is Clear.*
Takehiko Fukunaga, *Flowers of Grass.*
William Gaddis, *J R.*
*The Recognitions.*

FOR A FULL LIST OF PUBLICATIONS, VISIT:
www.dalkeyarchive.com

Janice Galloway, *Foreign Parts.*
*The Trick Is to Keep Breathing.*
William H. Gass, *Cartesian Sonata and Other Novellas.*
*Finding a Form.*
*A Temple of Texts.*
*The Tunnel.*
*Willie Masters' Lonesome Wife.*
Gérard Gavarry, *Hoppla! 1 2 3.*
Etienne Gilson,
*The Arts of the Beautiful.*
*Forms and Substances in the Arts.*
C. S. Giscombe, *Giscome Road.*
*Here.*
Douglas Glover, *Bad News of the Heart.*
Witold Gombrowicz,
*A Kind of Testament.*
Paulo Emílio Sales Gomes, *P's Three Women.*
Georgi Gospodinov, *Natural Novel.*
Juan Goytisolo, *Count Julian.*
*Juan the Landless.*
*Makbara.*
*Marks of Identity.*
Henry Green, *Back.*
*Blindness.*
*Concluding.*
*Doting.*
*Nothing.*
Jack Green, *Fire the Bastards!*
Jiří Gruša, *The Questionnaire.*
Mela Hartwig, *Am I a Redundant Human Being?*
John Hawkes, *The Passion Artist.*
*Whistlejacket.*
Elizabeth Heighway, ed., *Contemporary Georgian Fiction.*
Aleksandar Hemon, ed.,
*Best European Fiction.*
Aidan Higgins, *Balcony of Europe.*
*Blind Man's Bluff*
*Bornholm Night-Ferry.*
*Flotsam and Jetsam.*
*Langrishe, Go Down.*
*Scenes from a Receding Past.*
Keizo Hino, *Isle of Dreams.*
Kazushi Hosaka, *Plainsong.*
Aldous Huxley, *Antic Hay.*
*Crome Yellow.*
*Point Counter Point.*
*Those Barren Leaves.*
*Time Must Have a Stop.*
Naoyuki Ii, *The Shadow of a Blue Cat.*
Gert Jonke, *The Distant Sound.*
*Geometric Regional Novel.*
*Homage to Czerny.*
*The System of Vienna.*
Jacques Jouet, *Mountain R.*
*Savage.*
*Upstaged.*
Mieko Kanai, *The Word Book.*
Yoram Kaniuk, *Life on Sandpaper.*
Hugh Kenner, *Flaubert.*
*Joyce and Beckett: The Stoic Comedians.*
*Joyce's Voices.*
Danilo Kiš, *The Attic.*
*Garden, Ashes.*
*The Lute and the Scars*
*Psalm 44.*
*A Tomb for Boris Davidovich.*
Anita Konkka, *A Fool's Paradise.*
George Konrád, *The City Builder.*
Tadeusz Konwicki, *A Minor Apocalypse.*
*The Polish Complex.*
Menis Koumandareas, *Koula.*
Elaine Kraf, *The Princess of 72nd Street.*
Jim Krusoe, *Iceland.*
Ayşe Kulin, *Farewell: A Mansion in Occupied Istanbul.*
Emilio Lascano Tegui, *On Elegance While Sleeping.*
Eric Laurrent, *Do Not Touch.*
Violette Leduc, *La Bâtarde.*
Edouard Levé, *Autoportrait.*
*Suicide.*
Mario Levi, *Istanbul Was a Fairy Tale.*
Deborah Levy, *Billy and Girl.*
José Lezama Lima, *Paradiso.*
Rosa Liksom, *Dark Paradise.*
Osman Lins, *Avalovara.*
*The Queen of the Prisons of Greece.*
Alf Mac Lochlainn,
*The Corpus in the Library.*
*Out of Focus.*
Ron Loewinsohn, *Magnetic Field(s).*
Mina Loy, *Stories and Essays of Mina Loy.*
D. Keith Mano, *Take Five.*
Micheline Aharonian Marcom,
*The Mirror in the Well.*
Ben Marcus,
*The Age of Wire and String.*
Wallace Markfield,
*Teitlebaum's Window.*
*To an Early Grave.*
David Markson, *Reader's Block.*
*Wittgenstein's Mistress.*
Carole Maso, *AVA.*
Ladislav Matejka and Krystyna Pomorska, eds.,
*Readings in Russian Poetics: Formalist and Structuralist Views.*
Harry Mathews, *Cigarettes.*
*The Conversions.*
*The Human Country: New and Collected Stories.*
*The Journalist.*
*My Life in CIA.*
*Singular Pleasures.*
*The Sinking of the Odradek Stadium.*
*Tlooth.*

## SELECTED DALKEY ARCHIVE TITLES

Arno Schmidt, *Collected Novellas.*
*Collected Stories.*
*Nobodaddy's Children.*
*Two Novels.*
Asaf Schurr, *Motti.*
Gail Scott, *My Paris.*
Damion Searls, *What We Were Doing and Where We Were Going.*
June Akers Seese,
*Is This What Other Women Feel Too?*
*What Waiting Really Means.*
Bernard Share, *Inish.*
*Transit.*
Viktor Shklovsky, *Bowstring.*
*Knight's Move.*
*A Sentimental Journey: Memoirs 1917–1922.*
*Energy of Delusion: A Book on Plot.*
*Literature and Cinematography.*
*Theory of Prose.*
*Third Factory.*
*Zoo, or Letters Not about Love.*
Pierre Siniac, *The Collaborators.*
Kjersti A. Skomsvold, *The Faster I Walk, the Smaller I Am.*
Josef Škvorecký, *The Engineer of Human Souls.*
Gilbert Sorrentino,
*Aberration of Starlight.*
*Blue Pastoral.*
*Crystal Vision.*
*Imaginative Qualities of Actual Things.*
*Mulligan Stew.*
*Pack of Lies.*
*Red the Fiend.*
*The Sky Changes.*
*Something Said.*
*Splendide-Hôtel.*
*Steelwork.*
*Under the Shadow.*
W. M. Spackman, *The Complete Fiction.*
Andrzej Stasiuk, *Dukla.*
*Fado.*
Gertrude Stein, *The Making of Americans.*
*A Novel of Thank You.*
Lars Svendsen, *A Philosophy of Evil.*
Piotr Szewc, *Annihilation.*
Gonçalo M. Tavares, *Jerusalem.*
*Joseph Walser's Machine.*
*Learning to Pray in the Age of Technique.*
Lucian Dan Teodorovici,
*Our Circus Presents . . .*
Nikanor Teratologen, *Assisted Living.*
Stefan Themerson, *Hobson's Island.*
*The Mystery of the Sardine.*
*Tom Harris.*
Taeko Tomioka, *Building Waves.*
John Toomey, *Sleepwalker.*
Jean-Philippe Toussaint, *The Bathroom.*
*Camera.*
*Monsieur.*
*Reticence.*
*Running Away.*
*Self-Portrait Abroad.*
*Television.*
*The Truth about Marie.*
Dumitru Tsepeneag, *Hotel Europa.*
*The Necessary Marriage.*
*Pigeon Post.*
*Vain Art of the Fugue.*
Esther Tusquets, *Stranded.*
Dubravka Ugresic, *Lend Me Your Character.*
*Thank You for Not Reading.*
Tor Ulven, *Replacement.*
Mati Unt, *Brecht at Night.*
*Diary of a Blood Donor.*
*Things in the Night.*
Álvaro Uribe and Olivia Sears, eds.,
*Best of Contemporary Mexican Fiction.*
Eloy Urroz, *Friction.*
*The Obstacles.*
Luisa Valenzuela, *Dark Desires and the Others.*
*He Who Searches.*
Paul Verhaeghen, *Omega Minor.*
Aglaja Veteranyi, *Why the Child Is Cooking in the Polenta.*
Boris Vian, *Heartsnatcher.*
Llorenç Villalonga, *The Dolls' Room.*
Toomas Vint, *An Unending Landscape.*
Ornela Vorpsi, *The Country Where No One Ever Dies.*
Austryn Wainhouse, *Hedyphagetica.*
Curtis White, *America's Magic Mountain.*
*The Idea of Home.*
*Memories of My Father Watching TV.*
*Requiem.*
Diane Williams, *Excitability: Selected Stories.*
*Romancer Erector.*
Douglas Woolf, *Wall to Wall.*
*Ya! & John-Juan.*
Jay Wright, *Polynomials and Pollen.*
*The Presentable Art of Reading Absence.*
Philip Wylie, *Generation of Vipers.*
Marguerite Young, *Angel in the Forest.*
*Miss MacIntosh, My Darling.*
Reyoung, *Unbabbling.*
Vlado Žabot, *The Succubus.*
Zoran Živković, *Hidden Camera.*
Louis Zukofsky, *Collected Fiction.*
Vitomil Zupan, *Minuet for Guitar.*
Scott Zwiren, *God Head.*